PEACEMAKER

THE ARCANE WEST TRILOGY
VOLUME ONE

K.A. STEWART

Also From K.A. Stewart

The Jesse James Dawson Series
A Devil in the Details
A Shot in the Dark
A Wolf at the Door
A Snake in the Grass
A Line in the Sand

Second Olympus

The Music Box Girl

For you, Dad

Acknowledgements

The list of people I have to thank on this one is long and illustrious. Anne Sowards, editor extraordinaire and Ginger Clark, my own personal superhero. Scott and Aislynn, always. My plethora of amazing beta-slaves, in no particular order: Alice Loweecey, Ramsey Hootman, Jenn Wolfe, Will Sisco, Alex Harrow, Janet Yantes, Caleb Malcom and Dr. Gita Bransteitter. And a big thanks to Stacia Kane, who insisted that yes, fantasy and western did indeed go perfectly together.

1

The bead of sweat rolled down Caleb's nose to hang there, quivering, before it fell to join its brothers in the fabric of his denim shirt. It was a testament to the length of his journey that he hadn't even bothered to mop his face in the last hour. Beneath the low brim of his hat, he squinted toward the horizon, his gaze following the seemingly endless chain of telegraph poles as they disappeared against the haze of the distant mountains.

"Are we lost?"

Caleb sighed, leaning on the pommel of his saddle. "They said follow the telegraph wires. So we are."

"This isn't a road, you know. This is barely a path. Maybe the poles are a mirage, leading us to our doom."

Caleb turned to look at his companion, pillowed on Caleb's own coat on the rear of the transport. "We're optimistic today, aren't we?"

The odd creature sniffed, its quivering nose a clear expression of irritation. "You try riding back here while this thing goes to pieces. See how optimistic you are." The rabbit-like animal gave a toss of its head, nearly gouging the man with its spiny antlers.

"Hey, watch where you swing those things." The jackalope just rolled its deep brown eyes and sulked. "And it's not really a comfortable ride up here either."

Somewhere in the last fifty miles, the transport had developed some kind of hitch in its hindquarters, resulting in a nasty grinding noise and lurching stride. Caleb wasn't an arcanosmith, but if he had to guess, he'd say the bearings had frozen up. No surprise, with the constant dust and heat they'd been suffering for the last two months.

"Hopefully, they'll have a smith at the next stop, and we'll get it repaired." If the next town didn't have an arcanosmith, they'd be stuck for at least a month until one could be sent on the stage from Kansas City. That was going to put Caleb seriously behind on his circuit.

The jackalope grumbled under its breath as Caleb kicked the transport back into a trot. The normal wheeze and sigh of the mechanical construct was ruined by the grinding in the back end, and every other step was enough to painfully jar his teeth together. If they couldn't get it fixed, he was going to shoot it himself.

They'd ridden for another twenty minutes before the furry passenger remarked casually, "I think I see a crack in the casing."

"What?!" Caleb nearly knocked the jackalope off its perch, turning in the saddle to examine the glowing blue casing at the transport's flank.

The animal scrabbled frantically with its claws to remain aboard. "Damn, Caleb!"

The casing was pristine, not a single flaw marring the transparent surface. Beneath it, the blue arcane energy whirled serenely with no sign of having found an escape route. Caleb's heart pounded in his ears as he fought to calm himself. "That wasn't funny, Ernst!"

"Well, it was before you tried to knock me off the transport." Ernst smoothed his brown fur, twitching his long ears to express his displeasure.

"You do that again, and I'll skin you for a hat."

"You have no sense of humor, you know that?"

"So I've been told." The man turned to face forward again. The dusty track stretched out before them, barely visible in the tall prairie grass. Only the never-ending line of telegraph poles marked where the road might be. "It can't be much farther. We ride any more west, we'll wind up in Indian territory." The Rocky Mountain range had been claimed as the land of final retreat by many tribes in recent years, leaving a nearly impassable wall across the budding U.S. frontier. Only the desperate and the foolhardy ventured close to that wilderness these days. *Which one are you, Caleb?*

"You know, it's possible that they gave you bad directions." Ernst settled himself in his little coat nest again. "They didn't seem to warm up to you."

Caleb didn't respond, only kicking the transport into motion yet again. The last town had seemed rather cold, welcome-wise. As had the one before it. If this was how the entire circuit was going to be… He was sorely tempted to turn and ride back east, if it wouldn't mean career suicide. *What little career I have left.*

His "career" currently consisted of a lonely, miserable circuit in the wilds of the frontier. Over the course of the next year, he'd range from the souther-most reach of the U.S., skirting the still-contested Texas-Mexico border, all the way to the north and Canada. He would mark a trail straight down the eastern slope of the Rocky Mountains, the very edges of what was considered the borderlands, and cover everything between there and Kansas City. Such was the life of an itinerate lawman.

The mountains to the west never seemed to get any closer no matter how long they rode. The behemoths merely sat there, watching over the grassland from a bank of purple mist. Small clouds played ring-the-rosie around the peaks, teasing with a promise of rain that never came. The lack of moisture showed in the prairie grass, which had long ago gone brown and brittle in the summer heat.

Caleb finally broke down and wiped at his face and neck with a bandana, fanning himself with the wide brim of his hat. It brought middling relief at best.

"Can't you just put the heat elsewhere? I'm turning

into stew back here."

The man eyed the dry prairie and shuddered. Yes, he could have taken the heat around them, shifted it elsewhere. But anywhere he put it would spark a fire, and in a dry environment like this… "Better stew than turned to charcoal."

"Says you. You're not wearing fur." The antlers jabbed Caleb in the back again, and he grimaced.

"Enough! I've got four days of stubble on my face, five gallons of sweat in my shirt and not an ounce of water in my body, and my ass feels like someone's been at it with a carpet rod. If you don't like fur, shift form. Not another word out of you until we hit town." Immediately, Caleb felt bad for snapping, and his shoulders sagged. They were both hot and increasingly miserable, but that was no reason to bite the poor creature's head off. "Sorry, Ernst."

The jackalope gave a peculiar little purr, indicating that there were no hard feelings. "Wake me when we get there."

About an hour later, "there" appeared suddenly out of the tall grass like a jack-in-the-box. It was a decent-sized town, bigger than the last two they'd visited, and Caleb stopped the transport long enough to evict Ernst and inspect the transport one last time.

Built to resemble the horses they had replaced, they had four metal legs that moved with arcane-powered gears and pistons. Though some inventors back east were experimenting with arcane powered wagons on four wheels, the transport design made them better at irregular terrain and simply had more power. Transports were capable of great speed and strength, and only rarely had to be recharged with arcane energy, as opposed to a horse, which had a limited range it could travel in a day and had to be fed and watered often.

This particular model had been one of the newest available when he'd left St. Louis, a gift from his director.

A banishment present. It was fast, to be sure, but it had been designed for paved city streets and short country strolls. The extreme conditions of the west were taking their toll on it, and quickly. The ball joints in the knees were still moving freely, but the gears in the rear workings were grinding audibly, and it was only a matter of time before it wheezed its last. Caleb simply didn't have the knowledge to repair it himself, and once it quit, they'd be on foot. In this heat, it'd be a death sentence.

Mindful of protocol, Caleb shrugged into his heavy duster and adjusted the star badge pinned over his heart with a sigh. *Wonder if they wouldn't be happier to see me without it.*

As if his familiar knew his thoughts, the jackalope mused, "We could just say no one was home and go on to the next one." The plucky creature hopped around the dusty trail a few times, stretching his furry legs.

"You know as well as I do, this thing won't make it to the next town." In spite of his misgivings, Caleb squared his shoulders and tugged his hat down over his eyes. "Come on, one last short ride, and then we can turn this heap of scrap over to someone else." He scooped Ernst up, depositing him on top of the battered trunk attached to the back of the transport, and swung himself into the saddle.

As they rattled and clanked their way into the town, Ernst peered at the high sign spanning the width of the road. "And what's the name of this place? Dusty Hollow? Dry Gulch? The Backside of Hell?"

Caleb smiled a bit to himself as they rode under the sign. "Hope."

The townsfolk stopped to watch the stranger ride into their midst, as Caleb had known they would. He tipped his hat to those who would make eye contact, but most kept their gazes down, daring to stare only once he'd passed them.

They rode past a small barber shop, what appeared

to be a dressmaker's shop, and several nondescript structures that might have been personal dwellings. A church with a modest steeple dominated the north side of town, and a half-constructed something sat just beyond that. There was no sign of a hotel or boardinghouse until Caleb spied a card in the window of the tavern that said "ROOMS TO LET".

"Looks like this is our best bet, Ernst." He dismounted, stretching muscles that were cramped and complaining from the long hours in the saddle. Even after three months, he was still green enough that the long rides hurt. "Watch the transport. I'll be right back." If the jackalope grumbled about being reduced to guard duty, Caleb missed it as he stepped up on the wooden walk.

The inside of the tavern was just as hot as the outside, but the dimness was a startling change after hours under the ruthless sun. Caleb pulled his hat off, surveying the room to allow his eyes time to adjust. The tables were empty but clean, and a piano stood in one corner, carefully covered with a linen cloth against the dust. On the far side, the staircase presumably led to the promised rooms for rent, and the bar stood to the right of the swinging doors, backed by mirrors and a wall of glass bottles of varying alcoholic content. There was even a cold box, hissing softly as the arcane power in its tubes cooled the air within. All in all, it was one of the nicer places they'd been lately.

"Hello? Anyone here?"

An answering yell came from a doorway on the right, and the door soon swung outward to admit one slender fellow with dark black hair and shockingly blue eyes. He grinned through his beard, drying his hands on a towel. "How kin I help ye?" The brogue was unmistakably Scottish.

"Looking about a room to rent. I saw the sign in the window."

"Oh, yessir! Rate's two dollars a week, meals not

included." The dark-haired Scot came out from behind the bar, offering his hand, but his smile slipped a bit when he saw the star pinned to Caleb's coat, the six-gun on his belt. "The last Peacemaker used ta take rooms out at the Warner ranch, about ten miles south of here."

Caleb took the offered hand for a firm shake, feeling a faint tingle against his skin. If he had to guess, he'd rate the barkeep on the low end of the power scale. Nothing someone like Caleb couldn't handle. "My transport's not going to make it another ten miles, so I think I'll just stay here if that's all right. Name is Caleb Marcus." Digging his wallet out of his coat, he presented five dollars to the tavern owner. "For meals, too."

The Scot's eyes lit up at the sight of the money in advance, but there was still a caution there, a wariness that Caleb had seen in the other towns he'd visited. "Teddy MacGregor. Owner of this establishment."

"Well, tell me, Mr. MacGregor. Do you happen to have an arcanosmith in this lovely town?"

The man snorted, retreating behind the bar to put the money safely away in his cash box. "That'll be just Teddy, thank ye. And we got a smith on the west end of town that can do for most things. Otherwise, you'd have to ride out to the Warner place. Abel keeps his own arcanosmith out there."

"I'd rather shoot the thing myself than ride another mile." Caleb grinned and was relieved to see the tavern keeper return the expression, though the man's gaze kept drifting to the right side of Caleb's face. Inwardly, the Peacemaker sighed, but if the Scot wasn't going to ask, he wasn't going to bring it up.

Finally, Teddy shook himself and tossed Caleb a key attached to a large chunk of wood. "Up the stairs, last door on the left. We serve food from five to nine, and whatever you'd like to drink until midnight."

"Thank you, sir." Tipping his hat as he put it back

on, Caleb stepped back out into the searing summer sun. He glanced to the west and paused to look at the mountains suddenly looming large over the plain. When did they get so close, and why did it feel like they were watching him just as much as he watched them?

A clamor of childish voices drew his attention, and he smirked when he saw Ernst atop a convenient barrel, surrounded by curious youngsters. He could hear the jackalope purring over the din, and the children oohed and aahed obligingly.

"Enjoying yourself?" Caleb leaned against a pole, grinning at his companion. Anytime he lost Ernst, he could be certain to find him in the arms of the nearest child. The furry creature just rolled his eyes in absolute ecstasy, carefully holding still to avoid jabbing anyone with his antlers, which, Caleb noted, he had blunted for safety's sake.

One of the older boys, all of seven maybe, looked over at Caleb. "Is he yours, mister?"

"Well, we travel together. So, in a way, yes."

"He's so cute!" The children seemed to understand not to pick the small animal up, contenting themselves with stroking his downy-soft fur, exclaiming over his long, supple ears.

"That's a helluva scar, mister," said another boy, sandy-haired and freckled, and he got swatted by what had to be his sister for his language.

Caleb idly fingered the smooth scar that cut down his right cheek. "It looks worse than it is."

One of the girls, braver than the others, went on tiptoe to examine the man's face. "Can you see out of that eye?"

Caleb chuckled and nodded. "Perfectly." Children were so innocent in their curiosity. Very few adults would have asked him about the scar, which began at his jawline and extended upward right into the iris of his eye, leaving a stark white line across the hazel.

"Abigail!" The alarm in the woman's voice was enough to make Caleb alert, scanning for any danger as the woman hurried across the street to snatch one of the little girls from the throng. "Don't you be bothering the Peacemaker now, you hear? None of you all! Git home!" The youngsters scattered like a flock of startled crows.

"They weren't bothering me, ma'am, really…" She didn't seem to hear him as she shooed the children quickly away, darting worried glances back over her shoulder. She and her daughter disappeared into the dress shop.

"Well, you're a sure conversation stopper, aren't you?" Ernst leapt to the transport's saddle in one graceful bound, his ears drooping in disappointment.

"Seems like it." The curtains twitched on the dress shop when his gaze passed over them. They were watching. "There's a smith just down the street. Let's see if we can get this contraption fixed."

Tripping the appropriate lever, he urged the transport into motion, cringing at the grind and clank in the hindquarters. It was a wonder it had made it this far.

The smithy, once discovered, was labeled simply "SMITHY", and the heat rolling off the forge made the oppressive summer day seem positively spring-like. The smith himself seemed oblivious to it, wearing a thick leather apron over his shirt as he labored over the glowing coals. Orange coals, Caleb noted, not blue. Unusual.

"Hello there!" The smith kept working with no response to Caleb's hail. "I was told you might be able to repair a transport."

That at least earned a grunt in answer, and after a few more moments, the smith laid his long tongs aside and stepped away from the forge. He was older than Caleb expected, his hair already gone white, and there was no warmth in his pale eyes. "Ja. I can do, yes."

Ah, not white hair, but very pale blond then. The

Swedish accent gave everything away. Caleb nodded toward his malfunctioning machinery. "It's got some kind of hitch in the back end."

Wiping his sooty hands on a rag, the smith came out to inspect the transport, paying no mind whatsoever to Ernst perched on its back. He made thoughtful noises as he circled the construct, bending to look along the belly workings, poking at the transparent casings in a few places.

Caleb finally broke the silence. "Can you fix it?"

"Hmm. Ja. Maybe. Bearings seized up here." He poked with a grimy finger. "Gear stripped here. No parts. Need to make new."

"And how long will that take?"

The Swede pursed his lips thoughtfully. "Week? You come back, one week."

Caleb's heart sank. That was going to put him behind schedule. "You don't happen to have another transport I could rent in the meantime, do you?"

"Ja, maybe. Dollar. Tally up price for repairs when done." There was humor glinting in the smith's eyes, but Caleb was too tired to even guess at the joke. He forked over the dollar, eyeing the few remaining bills in his wallet dubiously. If the repairs took the last of his cash, he was out of luck until he reached a town with a bank.

"I'm Caleb, by the way. Caleb Marcus." He stuck his hand out to shake, and for a moment, the smith eyed it like a striking snake. Finally, the Swede gripped his hand, pumping it once.

"Sven Isby."

The Peacemaker fought to keep the surprise off his face. There was no tingle in Sven's skin, not even the faint hum of a low-level power. There was only the warm calloused hand, and the sense of... nothing. The man had been scoured. The smith raised his chin in challenge, almost daring Caleb to say something. Caleb forced a smile. "I'll check back with you in a couple days to see how it's going."

"Ja. Do that. Rented transport stored around back." That seemed to end their dealings, as Sven went back to his forge and began working the huge bellows.

Caleb retrieved his saddlebags, throwing them over one shoulder, and his trunk, which he propped on the other. Ernst hopped up, his slight weight barely noticeable, and Caleb took his staff out of the scabbard on his saddle. He waited until they were around the back of the building before he asked, "Ernst, did you notice—"

"Yes." Caleb could feel the creature shudder, even though he was perched on the trunk.

"Could you tell—"

"Looks accidental. Trauma as a child."

Some of the tension in Caleb's chest eased. Accidental scourings were tragic but did happen, most often before a child learned true control of his own power. But better that than someone who had been scoured deliberately. That was reserved only for the most dangerous of criminals.

The fact that the town had accepted the blacksmith as a contributing member and business owner, despite his disability, only served to highlight the differences between the borderlands and the urban sprawl back east. In the city—any city, really—it was nothing to see packs of scoured or barren men living rough in alleys or slums, making do with society's scraps, the occasional odd job, and the few charities that catered to such. No one wanted them. No one wanted to see them. They were a reminder of what could so easily go wrong.

For all that he didn't have a lick of power about him, Sven Isby was a lucky man.

The humor in the smith's eyes made sense as Caleb surveyed the "transport" he'd been rented. Ernst snickered from his place atop the trunk. "You paid a dollar for this?"

Well, it was at least a construct. It was also tall

enough that Caleb couldn't see over its withers. With the broad back and extra pinion hooks, it had obviously been designed for hauling, not riding. It was also at least four generations out of date—it had actual reins instead of levers—and some of the metal pieces gleamed brightly where they'd been replaced with newer parts over the years. Still, the soothing blue glow of the arcane power swirled within the casing as Caleb inspected it. "Better than nothing, I guess. It could have been a horse."

Ernst traded his trunk seat for the back of the hauler. "Comfy up here! Lots of room to spread out." And he proceeded to do just that.

Muttering to himself, Caleb took the reins and led the lumbering monstrosity back toward the tavern. Each steel hoof was as large as a dinner plate, and Caleb grimaced, just thinking about getting a foot caught under one.

The streets were largely deserted, an oddity for this late in the afternoon, but Caleb could feel the eyes on him as he walked the length of the town. And not all of the gazes were friendly. He fought the urge to funnel a trickle of power into his staff. Lighting the runes was impressive-looking, but showing off would be beneath him. "What the hell is wrong with this place, Ernst?"

"Must be your innate charm."

Somehow, Caleb didn't think so.

With the rented transport left at the tavern and his things stored safely in his room—he kept his staff out of sheer paranoia—Caleb went in search of the one thing he'd been missing for the last month, without much hope of locating it. Through some miracle, he found it at the general store.

"Ernst, I may have died and gone to heaven." He could see at least two tins of his favorite cigarillos on the shelf, and if there were more in the back, he might be tempted to buy those, too, before he left town. He hadn't had a decent smoke in longer than he liked to contemplate.

The jackalope, now without a convenient place to roost, hopped his way around the store, idly sniffing at things on the lower shelves. "And how much are the repairs going to cost you?"

Caleb sighed, examining his wallet again. No, no more bills had materialized into it. Reluctantly, he plucked only one tin from the shelf.

The storekeeper had eyed them from the moment they walked in. His eyes looked like two black beetles under his bushy salt-and-pepper brows and followed them as they perused his wares. Ernst got barely a glance, unusual in most places, but the Peacemaker badge had earned a wary scowl. The general feeling of hostility was starting to weigh on Caleb, and he scowled right back as he set the tin on the counter. "Just this, please."

There was no mistaking the surprise on the storekeeper's face, his prominent eyebrows rising almost to his hairline. He stood up from his stool, proving that he towered a good four inches over Caleb and weighed a good deal less. Good Lord, the man was gangly. "Um…er…six bits." Caleb counted out the seventy-five cents from his wallet, pushing them across the countertop. The storekeeper bit one, then dropped them into his till and took his seat again.

Caleb leaned his elbows on the counter. "Can I ask you something, sir?"

"You can always ask." There was caution in his voice, but Caleb read curiosity in the set of his lanky shoulders.

"Why is everyone in this town treating me like I'm about to eat their children?"

At least the tall man had the good grace to blush. "Well, sir… To be perfectly frank, you're new, and no one really knows you yet. But the last Peacemaker…he made it real clear that he wasn't required to pay for anything.

Which was fine, really! 'Cause this close to Indian territory, we surely appreciate all you do for us. But…sometimes maybe he took a bit more than folks was really comfortable with, you understand?"

"Yeah, I understand." Caleb gritted his teeth. It explained a lot about the reception he'd received all over the circuit. "Maybe you could do me a favor and let folks know that I'm the new Peacemaker, and I pay my own way."

The old storekeeper's face broke into a slow smile, like he could scarcely believe his good fortune. Good gossip was better than a bag of gold dust, if everyone came to see what the storekeeper knew. "Yessir. I could do that." He offered his hand. "Hector Pratt."

"Caleb Marcus." There it was, the tingle of faint power just beneath the skin. More than Teddy at the tavern, but still relatively average. Caleb often wondered what people felt when they shook his hand.

"Well, Agent Marcus." The storekeeper offered him a jar of lemon drops. "Welcome to Hope."

2

Caleb had never met Donovan Hazard, but he already knew he didn't like the man. He sat at the bar, sipped his coffee, smoked a cigarillo, and listened to Teddy MacGregor expound on the life and times of the previous Peacemaker for the borderlands region, and he developed a quiet seething hatred.

"So whatever happened ta the mon? We just got word a few weeks ago that a new agent would be takin' his place." Teddy, like most good bartenders, seemed content to spread whatever knowledge he'd gleaned.

"He was at the Little Bighorn." Caleb took a swig of his coffee. The urge to grimace had passed finally, but the coffee was nearly mud it was so dark. "Scoured."

Teddy winced. "I cannae say I liked the mon, but I wouldnae wish that on anyone."

The Peacemaker nodded his agreement, and whispered the word *vonk* to himself, channeling a small bit of power into his fingertips. The tingles were pleasant on his skin and discharged in a static spark when he touched the metal bar rail. "But for the grace of God, and all that."

"That's the truth of it there." Teddy raised his glass of water in respect. "So what brings you out here? I cannae imagine this is a route you'd pick, given the choice."

"Even the frontier needs law. I swore an oath to uphold that law." That was the polite answer to that question, but as Caleb finished his coffee and pondered the twists of fate that had put him here, he couldn't help but feel the glimmer of bitterness deep in his chest. "I was an artillery captain in the war. Got injured." He gestured to the vicious scar down his face. "By the time I was on my feet again, the war was over and the president was forming up this new law enforcement organization. I thought it would be a good place for me to be helpful."

To say he'd been injured was an understatement. But for the grace of God, he would have been like Donovan Hazard or the Swedish smith. After the battle at Cold Harbor, he'd lain unconscious for nearly a month, and the doctors had all been sure he was scoured clean. If not for Ernst's sudden appearance, he might have believed it himself. The road back had been a long and difficult one; he'd relearned everything from the beginning, right down to the childhood command words that he should have abandoned long ago.

"*Brand*," he whispered, and a tiny flame appeared at the end of his cigarillo, the blue smoke curling happily. When the words had come back to him, they'd been in Dutch, the language of his childhood. Even now, eleven years after the injury, it was easier to think in command words than to simply conjure through force of will. His superiors with the Peacemakers frowned at his apparent failure to regain the most basic of adult skills, and he knew that was a large part of what had gotten him assigned to the borderlands. The only one it didn't seem to bother was his little furry companion.

Ernst was seated on the bar, lapping idly at a small dish of whiskey that he'd managed to wheedle out of Teddy. For a creature that did not actually require food or water, he certainly liked his alcohol, and a decent aged whiskey was his favorite thing in the world. His eyes had sparkled upon seeing the treasures behind Teddy's bar, and he was certainly not above using his furry appeal to get what he wanted.

For his part, the Scot seemed rather enamored of the

little jackalope, as most people were. It was hard not to like Ernst, no matter what form he had chosen to take at that moment. Like many familiars, his personality seemed to take on the opposite traits of his partner. A stoic man would have a boisterous and effervescent companion, while a jolly man might possess a taciturn and surly familiar. Ernst, with his charming ways and optimistic outlook on almost everything, was the perfect balance to Caleb's tendency for solitude and cynicism. He often paved a smoother path than Caleb could have managed himself.

"Ye must have an amazing amount of power, Agent Marcus, ta work with artillery. And ta have the little fellow, here. I havenae seen a familiar since I came west. None that werenae tied to a red Indian, I mean."

Familiars were uncommon, it was true, and by rights Caleb should never have had one. His strength had never recovered to its former level, and yet Ernst had claimed him and refused to be budged. "You run into the Indians a lot here?"

Teddy shrugged. "Sometimes, they raid the homesteads in the foothills. Fools, the lot of them, living so close to the mountains like that. And the young braves, they get to feeling their oats now and again, and ride down into the prairie." Someone came in through the doors, and Teddy waved a greeting. "But 'til this summer, it was more that we left each other alone, and all was well."

A few more people filed in, and from the greetings it was apparent this was the usual dinnertime crowd. Teddy excused himself to pull mugs for the tables and take down the dinner orders. Caleb watched the townsfolk, even as they pretended not to be watching him. There was more curiosity in the air than hostility, and he could tell that Hector's campaign had done its job already. At least they were willing to give him a chance now.

When Teddy slipped back behind the bar, Caleb picked up the thread of their conversation. "What happened this summer?"

"Hmm? Oh, the Indians?" The bartender shook his head. "Things hae been unsettled since the battle up north. They say the Indians are stopping the rain at the mountains now, and we hae been getting small earth tremblers even out here. Turned the town well to muck for a week an' a half. We had ta truck clear out ta Warner's ta fetch water from his well." Teddy's accent got stronger with the frown on his face. "There's been raids, too, around the homesteads. The tribes are pushin' farther east than ever before."

The battle up north was the Little Bighorn, of course. Thirty Peacemakers had died or been scoured there, along with the entirety of Custer's Seventh. The great shaman Wind Walker had proven that primitive Indian magic was more than a match for the white man's army.

The land itself was a smoking crater in the ground, and nothing would grow there ever again. Caleb had seen the photographs indelibly etched in blue and white. It should have been a cautionary tale for all on the consequences of such unrestrained power, but... The expansionists, those back east who had never even seen an Indian, were calling for exterminations and land annexations. It had become the rallying point for passionate speeches and political debates. It made Caleb faintly ill.

"Has anyone been hurt?" Caleb drained his coffee.

"No. They know if they start killing folks, the federals will move in. They do just enough ta try and drive people oot." Teddy shrugged again, swiping at the bar with his towel. "Personally, I dinnae want their land, and they're welcome to it. I think there's only so much land a mon can use, and I'm happy with what I've got. Greed's one of the deadly sins, after all."

For dinner, Teddy introduced Caleb to something called a boxty—"The Irish don't get everything wrong," the Scot asserted—which seemed to be a potato pancake stuffed with some meat and stewed vegetables, and which turned out to be one of the most delicious things Caleb had ever eaten. As more people filed in and out of the bar, a few brave souls even introduced themselves to him, though the conversations were brief and no one joined him at his seat.

Caleb immediately noticed the one and only woman to appear, and she took a seat alone in a corner, exchanging small talk with Teddy and eating her dinner alone. She seemed young, no older than Caleb at any rate, and her collar was buttoned high under her chin, her dark blond hair pinned atop her head as neatly as that of any matron he'd ever seen back east.

Teddy noticed his observation. "That's Ellen Sinclair. Schoolteacher. Been here about a year. Keeps a room upstairs next to yours."

"I didn't even see the schoolhouse when I rode in."

"That's 'cause it's sittin' out behind the church in a pile a lumber." Teddy nodded. "Most of the town kids ride clear out to the Warner ranch for school, and the town here hasn't been real receptive to Miss Sinclair and her new schoolhouse."

"Seems a shame."

Miss Sinclair finished her dinner and retreated up the stairs to her room without speaking to anyone else.

Hector Pratt slid onto the stool next to Caleb just as the Peacemaker asked, "So who's this Warner? I keep hearing mention of the Warner place, but I haven't actually met the man yet."

Teddy plopped a mug of beer in front of Hector. "He'll be in around seven. Is most nights, actually. Him and his men."

The storekeeper nodded his agreement. "They stay until Teddy closes down, then ride back out to the ranch in the dark of night. Ain't no reds tried to bother them yet, so…"

"You wouldnae bother them either, nae with that Schmidt riding herd." The bartender grinned at Caleb with a glint in his eye, happy to be the first to impart gossip to a new ear.

"Schmidt?"

"Abel Warner's right-hand man. I've seen him drop a buffalo at seven hundred and fifty yards, clean through the temple." He mimed shooting at his own head. "Best I've ever seen with a buffalo gun."

"Not Kaspar Schmidt? Small man, pale blue eyes?"

"You know him?"

"Only by reputation." Caleb fought the urge to roll his shoulders as a sudden ominous itch developed right between his shoulder blades. Oh, yes, he'd heard of Kaspar Schmidt.

It was a name that had been spoken in hushed whispers throughout the Union army during the war. Not a single man stepped from his tent in the morning without a small hesitation and the sure knowledge that in the next few seconds he could be dead, and that the shot would come from far enough away it would never even be heard. Such was the legend of Kaspar Schmidt.

He was a sniper for the Confederacy, but as the story went, he felt no particular loyalty to their cause. It was merely a means of allowing him to kill as many as possible. And kill he did. Shots taken from impossibly long distances, in insanely difficult conditions. Straight shooting, augmented shooting, it didn't seem to matter. And once his reputation as a killer was established, he got creative. Arcane rounds, augmented by the shooter's own power, would explode on impact, and he used that ability to good effect. He would shatter a knee, take off an ear, amputate an arm at the elbow, anything to spill blood and cause suffering before he ended it.

Once, Caleb had heard, Schmidt shot a lieutenant's young wife who was visiting the encampment, then finished them both off as the soldier ran to help his bride. Three shots in less than seconds, and all for fun.

"I haven't heard that name since the war." Perhaps something in Caleb's mood told Hector and Teddy not to press further. *What in the world would a man like that be doing out here in the back end of nowhere?*

The hum of conversation went on. The smoke from pipes and cigars rose in a cloud to the ceiling until the room was filled with a bluish haze. Caleb watched the townsfolk go about their usual routines. There were card games, debates that had obviously just picked up where they'd been left the night before, the occasional person plinking out music on the piano. Teddy and Hector discussed the weather, the crops, the coming winter, though it was nearly six months off. Ernst, having finished his whiskey, curled up against Caleb's shoulder and snored softly, his antlers tapping the bar with every exhale.

And as the clock in the corner struck seven, the doors opened to admit a dark-haired, dark-eyed man dressed finer than anyone else Caleb had seen in Hope. His mustache was waxed, his boots polished, and he wore no gun. He didn't need to, apparently, since the four men who walked in behind him were all armed with six-guns hanging off their belts.

Those four were thugs. Caleb recognized the type, and no amount of spit and polish would make them anything but. While their boss made the rounds, shaking hands and patting backs, they claimed a table in the corner and sat, looking surly to a man. None of them was Schmidt.

"And I hear our new Peacemaker has arrived!" The dark man offered his hand to Caleb, grinning broadly beneath his elegant mustache. "I'm Abel Warner. I own a ranch just south of here."

"Caleb Marcus." He clasped hands with the rancher and felt power shoot all the way up his arm into his shoulder. Only sheer will kept him from jerking free of

Warner's touch. The muscles in his neck and jaw wanted to clench into knots, and his own power rose in answer, feeding back along those lines to surge into the rancher's hand in return. Warner raised one brow, his cheerful smile twitching at one corner.

Beside them, Ernst sat up from a dead sleep with a yelp and nearly fell off the bar, his jackalope form flickering wildly in momentary panic. Black fur sprouted, along with a sinuous cat's tail, only to give way to stubby wings with black and white feathers bristling from the coat of brown fur. Caleb moved quickly to catch him, breaking contact with Warner.

The black cat-magpie-jackalope was a quivering mess, but he finally got his appearance under control and was once again furry and be-antlered. He looked about the room with wide brown eyes, his ears flat against his head. Caleb knew how he felt. Warner was powerful. Maybe as powerful as Caleb himself had once been. *A man to be watched.* "Easy, Ernst… Have a nightmare?"

The rabbit nose quivered and twitched, and Ernst made no attempt to leave the safety of Caleb's arms. "Nasty thing, whiskey. Must be a young batch, not settled yet. Upsets the mind." The careful nonchalance might have fooled anyone but Caleb. His familiar was shaken, and though Ernst finally allowed himself to be placed back on the bar, he kept his brown eyes fixed on Warner.

"Your familiar, I assume?" Warner eyed Ernst with a smile. "I always wished I could have had one, but it wasn't meant to be."

"Ernst has been with me for quite a while." Caleb rested his hand on his companion's back, feeling the furry creature tremble.

"Well, we are glad to have both of you in Hope for the duration of your stay." As fixed as his waxed mustache, Warner's smile never changed. "I would like to invite you both to stay at my ranch if you like. The accommodations are a bit cramped here." He smiled at Teddy by way of apology, but the Scot just shrugged.

"No, thank you. I'm already settled in." The Peacemaker forced his own smile to remain as cheerful, despite the fact that his familiar was almost going to pieces beside him. "But I am much obliged for the invitation."

Something flickered through Warner's eyes, almost too quick to be seen if Caleb hadn't been watching for it. It was something dark, calculating. Warner didn't like to be told no. But the look was gone in a flash, and only the smile remained. "Well, if you change your mind, the place is about ten miles south of here."

Warner returned to his socializing, making his way toward the table where his men sat. Caleb deliberately spun his stool to face the bar, putting his back to them. Having them behind him, he could feel his skin crawl, but at least he could watch them clearly in the mirror.

Ernst whimpered, burrowing his head into Caleb's chest. "Don't let him touch me. Please don't let him touch me." The poor animal's pleas were lost in the din of the crowd, but Caleb could hear him.

"Shh. He won't hurt you, Ernst. I promise." Caleb stroked the furry rabbit ears until the antlers ceased their trembling. He'd never seen Ernst so distressed before, and that more than anything spoke volumes about Abel Warner. Caleb lowered his voice and switched to Dutch for good measure, so they could converse privately. "What's wrong? What is it that disturbs you so?"

"I'm not sure." His knowledge of languages inherited from the man he was bound to, Ernst answered him in the same language. The rabbit-like creature stood up on his hind legs, bracing his front paws on Caleb's shoulder so he could peer out at the room behind them. "He's just…wrong, somehow. Very, very wrong."

It was a declaration Caleb couldn't ignore, especially when Ernst was always the first to see good in everyone. In the mirror, he caught Warner glancing his way, his eyes not on Caleb's back but on the familiar peeking over his shoulder. Ernst ducked back down quickly. "Why don't you vanish up to the room, hmm? No reason to stay here, and I'll be up soon."

"Yes, maybe I'll do that." The jackalope sat up on his haunches so that he could look Caleb directly in the eyes. His nose quivered violently. "You be careful, Caleb. There's something dark about that man." With a small pop of collapsing air, he was gone.

Hector watched Ernst's departure with concern. "He going to be all right?"

Caleb nodded and cleared his throat before switching back to English. "I think so. He startles easily sometimes. Comes from taking the form of small prey animals so often, I think." It was a bald-faced lie. Caleb had seen his familiar stare down all manner of dangers without so much as flinching. He'd rather have the small creature at his side in a crisis than most men he knew. But he didn't know Teddy or Hector well enough yet to question them about Ernst's intuition. As much as he liked them, it remained to be seen whether they could be trusted.

He motioned for Teddy to pour him more coffee. In the mirror, Warner was very carefully not looking toward Caleb at the bar.

The bartender obliged, shaking his head with a small smile. "They never fail to amaze me, familiars, with their poppin' in and oot of places without so much as a by-your-leave. Often wished I'd had the same talent as a wee lad. Woulda saved me considerable trouble on more than one occasion."

Sipping at the coffee without really tasting it, Caleb made some sort of noncommittal agreeing noise in the back of his throat.

Abel Warner ruled the room; that much was clear after watching for about an hour. Every person who entered greeted him first, and he magnanimously bestowed toasts and free beverages on several of them. Caleb watched carefully, but Warner did seem to be paying for everything he and his men used. At least he wasn't abusing Teddy's hospitality. "The man has more money than God," Hector confided before he left to go home.

Still, there was something that set the Peacemaker on edge, something beyond Ernst's nervous breakdown. There was the face that Warner was presenting to the room, and then there was that faint glimmer Caleb had seen behind his eyes. The two didn't match. "I'm going to go get a breath of fresh air, Teddy. I'll just be outside."

Fresh air was wishful thinking, really. Though the sun was drifting down behind the looming mountains, the evening was no cooler than the day had been. The oppressively hot air sat on his chest like a weight. He lit another cigarillo with a murmured brand and leaned against the railing in front of the tavern. At the other end of the street, a yellow lantern flickered to life, revealing the form of the person lighting it, and Caleb had to smile to himself.

How different life was on the frontier than back east. In St. Louis or Chicago, the nights glowed blue, lit by the cool shine of arcane-powered streetlights. Beneath the aroma of azaleas or whatever flower might be in season, the night air would smell faintly of ozone, a scent so commonplace that no city-dweller would notice it. Crowds of people would still be traversing the sidewalks, the rustle of skirts and click of the ladies' high boots competing to be heard over the clang of transport hooves and whispery hiss of their pistons as the constructs drew ornate carriages down the cobbled streets.

Here, the streets were dust if one was lucky, and knee-deep mud if one was not. Sidewalks were raised wooden platforms, if they existed at all. The lights were yellow, more often than not, burning oil or perhaps even beeswax. In a community the size of Hope, there weren't enough people with sufficient power to use arcane lamps throughout the town. There were no fragrant flowers blooming along the sidewalks, and only one or two transports added their blue gleam to the darkness. Most folk had walked here, it seemed, and if Caleb had to guess, the five transports he saw parked at the corner of the building had to belong to Warner and his crew.

So far from home. He drew deeply on his cigarillo, letting the smoke roll around his tongue before he breathed it out, creating a small smoke ring. *So very far.*

Most of the townsfolk wandered their way toward home as the night drew down, many of them waving farewell to him as they passed his perch on the railing. Even Warner and his quartet of thugs departed, the rancher pausing to tip his hat to the Peacemaker. There was a promise behind his sly smile that Caleb didn't like.

However, he was also forced to admit that his unease could be just the exhaustion speaking. With a nod to Teddy behind the bar, he made his way up the stairs to his room.

To find his door ajar about an inch… Listening, he caught the faint sound of someone moving within. His gun was inside, as was his staff, so he summoned a ball of blue crackling power to his palm with the whispered word *"kracht"* and slammed the door open with a bang.

Ernst, on the bed, jumped almost three feet straight up with a squeal, and the young boy kneeling next to Caleb's trunk whirled and made a dash for the door almost before the Peacemaker could relax.

"Whoa! Hold on there, son!" Quickly dismissing the orb of energy, he caught the boy by the shoulders as he tried to bull his way past.

"I ain' yer son! Lemme go!" The lad aimed a sharp kick at Caleb's shin, and the Peacemaker gritted his teeth, cursing under his breath. The kid was gangly, all elbows and coltish legs, and he seemed to wriggle in seven directions at once. Caleb was hard-pressed to keep hold of him.

"Hey, settle down! You're not in trouble…yet." With a firm hold on both arms, Caleb forced the boy to stand still, fixing him with a stern stare. "Ernst, you all right?"

The jackalope snorted. "Did no one ever teach you to knock? Sparks and gears, Caleb!"

"The boy bother you?"

"I didn' touch him!" The kid stuck his chin out obstinately. "We was just talkin'!"

Caleb raised a brow at Ernst, who just shrugged. "He wasn't going to get *into* the trunk. I didn't think raising a fuss was necessary."

The Peacemaker sighed. "What's your name, boy?" The boy mumbled something sullenly. "You realize I'm the law, right? I can toss you in jail if I want."

The kid stared up through his shaggy brown hair. "For what?"

"For hindering a federal investigation by not giving me your name." Ernst snorted, but Caleb ignored him. "I'm Agent Marcus. You are?" He released the boy and offered his hand, more than half expecting the kid to bolt out the door the moment he was free.

Warily, the boy shook hands. "James Welton. Everybody calls me Jimmy."

There was power in the child, still unformed and untrained. It licked over Caleb's skin like tiny tongues of curious flame. Impressive for one so young. "And what are you doing prowling around my room this time of night, Jimmy? Won't your mother be worried?"

"Ain' got a ma. Or pa. I do what I want." Jimmy straightened his clothes, pride in the set of his thin shoulders.

"Who takes care of you then?"

"I take care of myself." The kid did his best to look

tough.

Ernst, grooming his long ears, piped up. "Teddy lets him sleep here in exchange for small tasks. And there's a widow on the south end of town who gives him clothes when he needs them." That at least explained why the kid's denim pants were rolled multiple times and he was nearly swimming in the flannel work shirt, with its sleeves folded up past his elbows.

Jimmy blushed to the roots of his hair, casting a glare at the jackalope. Obviously, that information had been given in confidence.

Caleb directed the boy to sit on the edge of the bed and moved to inspect his trunk. As he expected, it was unharmed. He passed his hand over the lock, and the warding runes flickered blue in answer. They were intact. It was keyed to his touch and would open only for him.

"This is a very dangerous box, Jimmy. Opening it could result in some very bad things happening."

"Like what?"

"Like explosions that would blow off arms and legs and leave you in tiny little pieces splattered all over the town." Each Peacemaker's special trunk was filled with things that would enhance their particular skills in times of crisis, and Caleb's talent had always been sheer, cataclysmic destruction.

Jimmy's eyes got wide. "Really?" He was, however, lacking the element of fearful respect Caleb had been shooting for. If anything, he looked more intrigued.

"Really. So playing with this is a very bad idea."

"I was just lookin'. I wasn't gonna steal nothin'." His eyes darted toward Caleb's staff, laid across the bed, and Caleb hid a smirk.

"You want to take a look at my staff?" Jimmy eyed him suspiciously, as if he expected it to be a trap, so Caleb picked up the weapon and held it out to the boy. "Have you ever seen ironwood before?"

Jimmy shook his head, eyes wide as his hands ran over the slate gray wood. "No, sir."

"That is a very old staff, Jimmy. So old that we don't even remember how to create them anymore." The ironwood staff was smooth, not from centuries of hands upon its surface, but from the sheer artistry of its craftsmanship. The wood itself was from no known tree, and couldn't be broken or marred by any tool known to modern man. The mystery of how the runes had been inscribed into the surface was one that occupied many a scholar and arcanosmith alike, and the runes themselves could be traced back to no written language that had been discovered yet.

The ironwood staves were the weapons of the Peacemakers, and rare enough that they could not afford to bind them to just one user. Each one would be passed on when its current bearer had no more need of it, often posthumously. Caleb knew that there were fifteen going to new homes because of the battle at the Little Bighorn alone.

The boy looked up from the weapon, tilting his head thoughtfully at Caleb. "How come you just let me hold this? What if I blast you with it and just take off?"

"First, I don't believe you would do that. Ernst likes you, which means that you must be a good person." Caleb reached to take his staff back, running his thumb over the dark runes on the end. "Second, because you not only have to be very powerful to use one, but you have to have special training. Only Peacemakers can use these, so even if someone *was* able to steal this from me, it would be useless to them." With just a small nudge of power, the runes glowed bright blue, casting odd shadows around the room before Caleb allowed them to fade. The look of awe on Jimmy Welton's face was worth it.

"Now, Jimmy." Caleb raised a brow. "You break into people's rooms often, just to look?"

The boy shrugged. "Never got a chance ta see a Peacemaker's stuff before. The old one stayed out at Warner's."

"And you didn't go snooping while you were at school out there?"

The kid snorted. "I don' go to school. 'Specially not out there."

Caleb sat on the bed, and the boy scooted away. "You don't go at all? Who's teaching you to control your power, then?"

"Nobody. I just... do."

Caleb frowned. "You're what, nine?"

"I'm twelve!"

For twelve, the boy was positively scrawny. And if he really was twelve, he was woefully and dangerously uneducated.

"Hold your hand out, Jimmy, palm to me." Reluctantly, the boy did, and Caleb mirrored the gesture, leaving an inch of air between their outstretched hands. "*Zoek*," he mouthed silently. *Seek.*

Caleb's power went searching, feeling across the dead space between their palms to tickle over the boy's skin. Jimmy flinched at the first tingle but didn't withdraw, and his own talent rose in answer. Soon, flickers of blue electricity were dancing back and forth between them in ever more intricate patterns.

"Are... are you doing this?" Jimmy finally asked, his eyes wide under his rough bangs.

"We're doing this." Caleb kept his eyes on the display, carefully reining in both his power and the boy's. Jimmy would be formidable when he was older, but only if he was trained before he accidentally scoured himself. "You're very strong, Jimmy. You need to learn how to harness this before you hurt yourself or someone else."

Jimmy's hand clenched into a fist, and the power disappeared with a faint pop. "I ain' goin' out to Warner's place. He's got bad men out there."

"I'm inclined to agree with you. But… have you thought about Miss Sinclair? She's right across the hall, and I'll bet she'd be happy to have a student." Someone had to take this boy in hand. Soon.

There was a rebellious set to the boy's jaw, but he at least looked thoughtful.

"Jimmy? Dammit boy, where are you?" Teddy appeared in the open doorway, and the Scot frowned. "Boy, I told you to be scrubbin' out those pots and pans, not botherin' my guests."

"We was just talkin'." Jimmy slid off the bed, reaching to pat Ernst once more. "Nice ta meetcha, Ernst. And you too, mister." He gave a nod to Caleb and wandered off with all the nonchalance in the world.

Teddy looked to Caleb. "Was he riflin' through yer things?"

"He tried. But I've got wards on the dangerous things, so no harm done."

The bartender sighed, shaking his head. "Sorry about that, Agent. Boy's got a thief's heart, and I cannae seem to break him of it."

"Someone needs to take that boy's education in hand. Before he scours himself or someone else." Caleb pushed his trunk back under his bed with one boot. "He may be strong enough to get into West Point, with proper training. And a decent education, of course."

"Really?" Teddy glanced back down the hallway after Jimmy, surprise on his face. "Never knew the lad had that much talent. Most of the wee ones here, they… well, they're nothin' remarkable."

"The group I saw earlier was still young. Maybe they'll grow into it." With a weary sigh, Caleb started to pull off his boots. "Thank you for your hospitality today, Teddy. By all accounts, I'm not sure I deserved it. My predecessor left a hard trail for me to follow."

The dark Scot gave him a grin. "You be yer own man, Agent Marcus. Folks'll learn soon enough. Good night."

"Good night, Teddy." The bartender closed the door as he left, leaving Caleb alone in his room with Ernst.

The jackalope snuggled against Caleb's side as the Peacemaker lay back and threw an arm across his eyes. "I have one question, Caleb."

"Hmm?"

"What does a rancher, out here in the forgotten armpit of nothing, need with a unit of armed men at his beck and call?"

"And a highly skilled sniper. I was wondering the same thing myself, Ernst." Caleb stroked the soft fur of his familiar. "Let's get some sleep. Since we're stuck here anyway, I may as well do some actual investigating tomorrow."

3

Something loud pounded at Caleb's skull, drawing him out of a fitful sleep. His usual nightmares faded slowly, and the sound of church bells mingled with the remembered bellow of cannon fire for long confusing moments.

"Caleb? Caleb! I think you ought to wake up." Ernst's voice prodded him fully awake finally, and he opened his eyes to find the jackalope perched on the bedside table, staring out the single window. "Something's happening. Everyone's running to the church, and the bell is pealing."

"It's not Sunday…" Caleb pushed himself upright, reaching for his shirt. He made a mental note to find out if there was a laundry in town. This shirt was on its last legs, and the one stuffed in his saddlebags was worse.

Dressed and armed with both gun and staff, Caleb followed the last of the townsfolk to their church, where a small crowd surrounded a rather shaken-looking family of five. The two little girls clung to their mother's skirts, and the boy, barely ten, did his best to stand next to his father and look manly. There was no mistaking the pallor of his cheeks or the shock in his wide eyes, though.

Abel Warner was also present, giving orders from the back of his sleek transport, calling for townsfolk to fetch food and water for the new arrivals, sending someone after the doctor, who had yet to appear. Standing at strategic intervals, their hands resting idly on their guns, his armed thugs kept wary eyes out.

Caleb slid into the crowd next to Hector, keeping

his voice low. "What's going on?"

"Anderson family. They've got a homestead up in the foothills, and the reds hit them last night. They hid until first light, then made their way in on foot. Took them more'n three hours of walking to get here."

"Anyone hurt?"

"Doesn't look like it. Just scared them to death. Don't know what's left of their place, though." Hector shook his head, his eyes grim. "Third homestead hit this month."

Caleb clapped the shopkeeper on the shoulder and edged his way through the crowd. As he got closer, he saw Ernst already clasped tightly in the smallest child's arms, the jackalope's antlers visibly vibrating with his soothing purr. The children, at least, were enchanted with the furry creature enough to forget about their harrowing experience. That was the purpose of Ernst's small, furry forms. When he was cute and non-threatening, people would embrace him easily, and he was able to soothe distress with simple contact. With the children taken care of, Caleb could focus on the adults.

Warner had dismounted and stood talking to the father. "I'll take my boys out to your place, Allen, and we'll see what damage was done and what we can recover. Until you get back on your feet again, you know you're more than welcome to stay out at my place. I've got plenty of room."

"Thank you, Abel. I… Thank God no one was hurt, but… I just don't know what we're going to do. They took the cows, and there's no time to plant new crops before winter, and…" Allen Anderson had the bleak look of a man who could only stare up at the cliff he'd just been pushed off. Rescue was far enough away to seem merely an illusion.

Warner's glance landed on Caleb as he reached the front of the throng. "Ah, Peacemaker! There you are. I'm taking a bunch of the lads out to Anderson's place. We could use a man of your skills, if you'd like to come along."

"Thank you, Mr. Warner. I think I'll do that." He transferred his staff to his left hand to shake Anderson's. "Mr. Anderson, I'm Caleb Marcus, the new Peacemaker for the region. I'm very glad your family wasn't harmed."

"Thank you, sir. So am I." Power flickered between the two men where their hands touched. Anderson's fear was augmenting what would normally be a mediocre ability at best into something spiky and unpredictable. Spurred by the man's highly emotional state, it was nearing dangerously overloaded levels. Anderson would have no idea how to control that much power.

Caleb narrowed his eyes in concentration, feeding back along the channels to smooth the jagged edges in the other man's power, bleeding off the excess energy through Caleb's own body. The last thing they needed was the homesteader exploding out of sheer nerves.

Tension went out of the other man's shoulders, and he gulped air like he'd been running for miles. His grip tightened on Caleb's, squeezing hard. "Thank you," he whispered, glancing toward his wife and children. "I don't know how much longer I could have held on. The children are in the same state, and I couldn't…"

The Peacemaker nodded, patting him on the shoulder. "It's all right. That's why I have Ernst."

The jackalope flicked a glance toward Caleb at the sound of his name, but never stopped his chirpy little purr. They'd done this before, the pair of them, and Ernst knew just what needed to be done for the children during such a tragedy. The sparks of bled-off power were visible at the ends of his fur, dissipating in tiny snaps of static electricity. The longer the children stroked his silky coat, the calmer they became, their fear and agitation channeled away through the body of Caleb's familiar.

"I'll get my transport, Mr. Warner, and I'll meet you back here." He paused long enough to speak to Mrs. Anderson and give smiles to the little ones. The presence of the jackalope seemed to have bolstered them, and some life came back to their wide, staring eyes. "Ernst, are you coming with me or staying here?"

"I'll stay with the children if that's all right."

Caleb hesitated, mentally mapping out the distance he intended to cover that day. If his bond with Ernst had a limit, they had yet to find it, but he still felt uneasy about being too far apart from his familiar for long. Still, the children needed all the comfort they could get, and he would be able to feel the connection to the little jackalope even at great distance. It would be nothing for him to simply pop to Caleb's side if necessary. "I'll call you if I need you."

The hauler-turned-transport raised some eyebrows among Warner's men, but Caleb just shrugged. "My transport is being repaired. This was what was available for rent."

Warner frowned at that. "Isby? You're having Isby repair your transport?"

"He *is* the smith."

"The man is scoured, Agent Marcus. Surely you realized that. You can't be an arcanosmith without power." The rancher sidled his transport closer to Caleb's. "You bring your transport out to my ranch. I have my own arcanosmith there."

"Thank you, sir, but if Mr. Isby says he can repair it, then I believe him."

Warner's lips thinned. "Suit yourself."

With a bit more organizing, the scouting party was off. Caleb found himself surrounded by at least fifteen of Warner's men, all of whom looked like they would just as soon knife someone in a dark alley as not. A handful of the townsmen also rode out with them, giving Caleb the comfort of additional witnesses, but he regretted Ernst's absence. An extra pair of loyal eyes would have been welcome.

He paid special attention to a slender man on a gleaming new transport who caught up to the group about a mile outside of town. Though it was hard to tell with the man mounted, he looked to be a good foot shorter than Caleb and as rail thin as a youth. Beneath the wide brim of his hat, his face was smooth and soft like a boy's, and even shadowed, his eyes were so pale as to be almost colorless. The cold, empty gaze flickered across Caleb for no more than a heartbeat and dismissed him just as quickly, but that brief encounter gave the Peacemaker shivers despite the early morning heat. Even without the buffalo rifle strapped to his saddle, there would no mistaking Kaspar Schmidt. The man fell in at Warner's side, and the group never slowed their pace.

The ride would have been long even if Caleb had been on a proper transport. As it was, the hauler's girth was exceedingly uncomfortable, and when they'd progressed into the foothills after an hour, the thing's cumbersome bulk made travel over the rocks and hills more difficult than it would have been with a lighter mount. At least it was cooler in the hills, with the searing heat of the prairie left behind them for the moment.

The purple mountains loomed over them like giants who had just noticed the insects crawling around their feet. As Caleb carefully navigated his mount through the brush and branches, he had the distinct feeling that they were being watched, and that the watcher did not approve of their presence. He took a tighter grip on his staff, resting the butt of it in his stirrup.

He was not the only one unnerved. Most of the men loosened their guns in their holsters, flickers of blue light dancing over the bullets in their cylinders. More than a few murmured under their breath, their eyes searching the thickening undergrowth for hostile natives.

The wildlife scattered ahead of the wheeze and gasp of the arcane-fueled gears and the incessant tromping noise of their transports' metal hooves. They deserted their perches and hiding places in flocks and droves, fleeing from the band of invaders. Even the wind stilled until the only sound was the steady snap and crackle of mashed branches and twigs. Anyone could have been there in the shadows, and it would have been impossible to tell. Caleb resisted the urge to send a seeking surge out through the trees, not certain he truly wanted the answer.

Whatever watched them—be it red Indians, brave and curious wildlife, or the mountains themselves—it left them alone. They followed a barely visible wagon track into the trees, climbing steadily upward for another forty-five minutes before they came upon the Andersons' homestead.

The house itself still stood. That much was a blessing. Perhaps even the Indians were loath to burn the place in the tinder-dry forest.

"Higgins, Randolph, take watch. I don't want anyone sneaking up on us." Warner dismissed two of his men, who circled wide around the cleared area, presumably taking up watch posts. Schmidt dismounted, collecting his rifle, and surveyed the trees that towered over them. There was no mistaking the calculating look in his cold eyes as he also chose a place to perch and watch.

Caleb swung down off his mount, his muscles complaining loudly about their mistreatment, but he was careful not to grimace or limp. Maintaining any sort of authority was going to be tough enough around Warner, who was obviously used to being obeyed without question.

The Anderson family had a small house, obviously made out of logs hewn from the very spot on which it stood. There was a little outbuilding to the north, surrounded by a fence, where presumably they had kept their cows. The fence itself had been largely destroyed, with lengthy sections of wood splintered into nothing and posts yanked out of the ground entirely.

Their garden to the south had likewise been trampled. It had taken painstaking work to cut fertile ground out of the rocky soil, and there was a clear path to a nearby stream where they had run metal piping to bring water to the parched plants in an effort to help them survive. All of that was in vain now, and the food plants were mashed into the dirt clods beneath. Mangled bits of metal, the remains of an arcane-powered water pump, were scattered across the garden. It was impossible to tell what the family had even intended to produce.

"Arrows here!" One of the men plucked a few shafts from the side of the house like errant porcupine quills. Several more were located, buried in the fence posts or broken underfoot in the melee.

"Let's gather some clothes for them before the reds come back." Several men disappeared into the house, while more took up positions of wariness, fingering their guns nervously.

Caleb crouched at the edge of the garden, planting his staff in the loose soil and leaning on it idly. There was another arrow at his feet, and he picked it up, rolling it between his fingers. The head was knapped from stone, precise slivers taken from each surface to give it a razor-sharp edge that shone almost like it was oiled. The shaft was straight, and Caleb let it rest on the tip of one finger, finding it perfectly balanced. The feathers and head had been bound on with cotton thread.

Frowning, the Peacemaker looked at the garden again. The tracks of the panicked cows were obvious among the slaughtered vegetables. The terrified bovines had been stampeded through the garden multiple times. But nowhere did he see the spoor of any horses. Transport tracks were visible where they'd ridden in moments before, but those were heavier marks, perfectly round. Horses left more oval-shaped tracks, uneven and chipped where their hooves had worn away. He rose and walked the full length of the garden to be sure, then went to inspect the corral, too.

Evidence of the cows was everywhere, from their dung to their tracks, but there was nothing to show that the Indians had ridden through. Only their arrows, and one lonely tomahawk found embedded in the side of the Andersons' wagon.

They came in on foot. Approached silently in the dead of the night. It was possible. Though everything Caleb had learned of the local natives—the militant Dog Soldiers of the Cheyenne—indicated that they were a formidable cavalry. Why would they give up their mounts for this raid? It would sow so much more confusion having the big animals galloping around, trumpeting their shrill cries.

Investigating more of the recovered arrows showed that each of them bore the same fletching. *They're supposed to be unique, a different style for every brave.* And they were tied with cotton thread, not sinew. *They could have stolen it from anywhere. One of the other raided homesteads.*

And where were the Andersons' transports? They had a wagon; they had to at least have one hauler. Indians wouldn't touch the transports, from what he'd been told; they were as cautious with the entrapped energies as any other sane people. On the west side of the little homestead, he found plate-sized hauler tracks and followed them south until they were lost in the rocks. There were smudges in the soil and underbrush, evidence that someone had walked along with the construct, leading it presumably, but Caleb was no tracker and could tell no more than that.

If they could find the construct, they could prove ownership by matching up the registration marks, but until that time, it was well and truly lost.

He debated for a long moment on summoning Ernst, and finally decided to leave his familiar where he was. He'd never seen an Indian raid site before, and perhaps the information he'd been given in the east was faulty. It wouldn't have been the first time.

A bird called somewhere above him, the first sound of forest life he'd heard since entering the trees. Another answered it, directly to the south. It dawned on Caleb that he'd left the homestead behind in his search, so much that he could no longer hear the men's voices behind him. The bird called again, to his right this time. Two careful notes, low then high, as if the creature were questioning.

And he knew, suddenly, that it was questioning. It was a signal, asking what to do about him, the stupid white man all on his own in the wilderness. Caleb froze, waiting for the answer. The forest was eerily silent and seemed to hold its breath along with him.

They were watching him. He could feel their eyes on him, imagined he could hear the hum of bowstrings held taut. From the south, the bird called again, the same two notes. "Low-high?" The nearer one answered with a cheery trill: "High-low-high!"

The runes on his staff flared to life as he channeled into it, markings of blue glowing against the dark wood. They provided a path, forcing the chaotic power into patterns, logical forms that could be used with exquisitely fine control. "*Schild.*"

Like the tumblers of a lock clicking into place, the air around him solidified into a shield, crystal clear and impenetrable. Only the sight of a few bushes curling their branches against an unseen surface indicated where the boundaries of his bubble were. His breath sounded tinny, as if his head were inside a large jar, and he knew he had a limited amount of time before his air ran out. Impenetrable meant that nothing got in, not even air.

Something moved to his left, and he snapped his

head in that direction.

She sat not ten yards distant on the back of a painted horse, the animal's brown and white markings seeming to be a pattern cast by the leaf-dappled sunshine. The large beast snorted softly, its nostrils fluttering as it tossed its head. Caleb saw that it had one blue eye and one brown, and it eyed him with the same mild curiosity as its rider. The Indian woman's raven hair was twined into twin braids, hanging forward on each side of her neck, and her garments were clearly of tanned hides, decorated in subtle patterns with yellow and green quills. Her black eyes held no animosity as she stared at him, her head tilted slightly to one side.

Caleb stared at her, the first native he'd ever seen in person. He could see her tanned legs, bare between her high moccasins and the hem of her dress, muscled and strong. No white woman he'd ever seen would ride astride, much less with her skirts hiked up above her knees, but it seemed natural here in this wild place. Her hands were clenched in the horse's mane, and the animal's ears were perked forward, obviously waiting for some command from its rider. Where the sun touched her face, her skin glowed like warm honey.

They gazed at each other for long silent moments, two worlds touching for perhaps the first time. She didn't seem angry, or even afraid, merely cautious. And the longer he looked, the more a glint of humor crept into her dark eyes. She found him amusing.

Abruptly, her head jerked up, and she stared over Caleb's head in the direction of the Anderson homestead. A heartbeat later, he heard the voices, too.

"Peacemaker?"

"Agent Marcus?"

They had come looking for him, finally.

The southern bird called again, the question taking on an imperative tone. "Low-high?"

The Indian woman hesitated for one moment, glancing between Caleb and his would-be rescuers, and something in Caleb's chest clenched. *Go! Don't let them find you here!* Almost as if she heard him, she pursed her lips, whistling an answer. "High-low-low." Nudging the horse with her knees, she backed it into the underbrush and disappeared.

Almost belatedly, Caleb remembered to dismiss his shield, letting the power trickle through the length of his staff into the ground beneath him. He could feel the spits and sparks of it die out abruptly, snuffed to nothing somewhere in the soil. There was nullstone in the mountains then, the chalky rock that could absorb and still any amount of power. It was far enough from the surface that it hadn't hampered his abilities, but it was there nonetheless.

"Agent Marcus? Can you hear us?" They were getting closer. Caleb could hear several men crashing through the bushes, no doubt obliterating the tracks he'd so carefully followed to this spot.

"Yes! I'm here!" He glanced one last time to the tree where the Indian woman had sat watching him, but there was nothing to show she'd ever been there. Turning, he began the climb back up the hill.

They were townsfolk, not Warner's men. Jack and Peter were very happy to see him, both of them eyeing the trees around as if they expected an entire tribe of Dog Soldiers to come barreling down on them at any moment.

"You shouldn't wander off like that, Agent Marcus, not alone. The reds are all over this territory. I heard they can call down rockslides and flash floods to knock you clear off the mountain if they want."

Caleb allowed them to herd him back toward the homestead and the safety of numbers, but his mind was on the woman and the simple curiosity in her dark eyes. He had the distinct feeling that he'd been weighed and measured somehow. Had he passed whatever test she'd imposed on him? *Oh, Ernst, how I wish you'd have seen her.*

"Ah, there you are Agent Marcus!" Warner and his men were already mounted, and Caleb was certain they'd have gladly left without him if not for the townsfolk's insistence. "We were starting to get worried."

"No worries. I was just doing a little scouting of my own." He pointed in the vague direction he'd taken, hoping that no one would investigate. "I think they took the hauler toward the south, but I lost the trail in the rocks."

Warner smirked. "Then let us hope they blow themselves to kingdom come with it. It's no less than they deserve for terrorizing good and decent people like this." He walked his transport to the head of the column that had formed, and Caleb found his own mount now hitched to the Andersons' wagon. "I hope you don't mind, but since we had a hauler, I thought we could take more of their belongings if we used the wagon."

"No, not at all. I'd have suggested the same." He clambered into the wagon, settling his staff in the seat beside him. Driving the contraption was far preferable to riding the huge hauler. "Back to town?"

"The Andersons were going to be taken to my place, and I've offered to feed the men lunch for their efforts today, as well." Warner smiled, smoothing his mustache. "That includes you, of course."

"A meal would be much appreciated. Thank you." And he could get a look at the nearly fabled Warner ranch.

As they slowly made their way back down to the plains, Caleb almost felt guilty for taking such an instant dislike to Abel Warner without just cause. The man obviously went out of his way to help the people of Hope in their dire straits. But the tiny voice in the back of Caleb's mind warned him to listen to his instincts and Ernst's. Something was not as it seemed.

A cool breeze followed them out of the mountains, as if the land itself breathed a sigh of relief at their departure.

4

The Warner place was actually the A-bar-W Ranch, as seen branded into the flanks of the grazing cattle they passed. The herd was carefully watched by a pair of armed men on transports who waved as the small procession rumbled past.

The ranch was nearly a town unto itself, surrounded by a fence of tightly stretched wire. Approximately every ten yards or so, another armed guard stood, and the blue arc of power could be seen hopping from fence post to fence post, powered by the men stationed at each one. *An arcane-powered fence. Interesting.*

The house was a sprawling two-story construction, ringed all the way around with a covered porch and many high windows. As they rode in, Caleb noted which windows contained dark shadows, the silhouettes of yet more armed guards. He added those to his mental tally of Warner's men, feeling more uneasy as the count continued to climb. Why on earth did Warner need this many men, and a trained sniper on top of that?

Schmidt disappeared the moment they arrived, and the Peacemaker spent the rest of the visit feeling the skin crawl across his shoulders. Somehow it was worse that the silent man hadn't even acknowledged Caleb's existence. Was he truly beneath the hired killer's notice, or was Schmidt just biding his time? *Or awaiting his master's orders?*

There were several outbuildings in sight, a smokehouse—so noted because of the fragrant aroma emanating from it—and a large building with metal pipes extending from its sides, clearly the housing for the pump that drew water for the entire community. People came and went in the dusty lanes, going about the daily tasks of running a large cattle ranch. Caleb recognized only a few of them from town; the rest were obviously permanent residents of the A-bar-W. Transports were scattered all over, everything from fleet one-person rides to massive haulers twice as tall and broad as the one Caleb rode. It was easy to pick out the smithy, a line of partially dismantled constructs ringing a forge of glowing blue coals.

A small pack of blue-tick hounds came boiling into the yard from their kennels with sharp baying cries until Warner spoke a single word, then they nearly tripped on themselves to fawn over him. Warner was clearly king of his own domain out here.

Shepherded by a severe-looking man with pince-nez eyeglasses perched at the end of his long beak, a passel of children paused to let the wagon by. The schoolmaster, if Caleb had to guess, and the majority of Hope's children. They ranged in age from nearly seven to twelve, which stood to reason since older children would be helping with family businesses during the day. To a one, they kept their eyes turned down,oddly subdued for children so young. Caleb turned in his seat to watch them until they rounded a building out of his line of sight.

Allen Anderson and his wife were waiting on the house steps when Caleb brought the wagon to a halt in front of them. The woman's eyes lit up seeing the load of their belongings the party had managed to salvage. "Oh, thank you, Abel!"

Warner dismounted to receive a hug from Mrs. Anderson, patting her back soothingly. "It's the least I could do, Lily. We got as much as we could haul, thanks to Agent Marcus's mount."

That earned Caleb a teary hug and kiss on the

cheek, too. "Bless you, Agent Marcus. Just… bless you. You and that furry angel with antlers."

He couldn't help but chuckle. Ernst as an angel? "Is he still with the children?"

She shook her head, patting loose tendrils of hair back into place to compose herself. "He left as we arrived here. I assumed he'd gone to you. Is he all right?"

"I'm sure he is. He often goes wherever his whim takes him." Inwardly, Caleb regretted the lack of his familiar. He could have used Ernst's eyes and ears here. He reached out along the connection that bound him to the creature and felt distance between them. Ernst had returned to Hope, he'd wager, and he let the bond go without summoning him. If Ernst didn't want to be here, Caleb wasn't going to push without reason.

Lunch was to be served on the veranda, in the meager bit of coolness the shade offered. Above them, a large fan creaked back and forth, powered by arcane pulses from the touch of the servant standing unobtrusively against the wall.

Their vantage overlooked a large man-made pond which, Warner assured him, held the area's best catfish. "Around dusk, you can watch the eagles swoop over the water and snatch up the fish that come to the surface. Magnificent."

"It's a wonder that the drought hasn't turned it into a baked mud hole like the rest of the prairie."

"Well, it's a mite smaller than it once was; that's true. But I believe the spring beneath it is strong enough to survive this summer, and when the rains return, it will be back to its former glory."

While the meal was being prepared, Warner and the other men lounged in chairs, smoking and generally exchanging small talk. Caleb lit his own cigarillo with the whispered word *"brand"* and savored the sweet smoke as it curled over his tongue. He felt the moment Warner's gaze sharpened on him, and inwardly cursed, knowing that the man had caught his use of childish command words.

"So, tell us a bit about yourself, Agent Marcus. You're from the east if I had to guess." Warner rocked his chair back on two legs, at ease as he stroked the head of one of his hounds.

"Pennsylvania." Caleb inhaled slowly, trying to decide how much to say. As little as possible, he ultimately decided, unless he was directly asked. He owed no one an explanation. "I graduated from West Point just in time to join the war. I served in the Union artillery until I was severely injured at the battle of Cold Harbor." The men made noises of approval. Kansas had, after all, been a Union state. "And after the war ended, I asked for admission into the Peacemakers."

"This is your first time out west though." Warner grinned apologetically. "I can tell you're still not comfortable out here."

Caleb nodded, chuckling. "It's true. I've only been riding this circuit for about three months. I was assigned to Chicago before, and St. Louis. East of the Mississippi River."

"Ah, a man of culture." Warner raised his class of brandy in a small toast. "We could use more of those out here."

"I'm not certain how cultured I am, but thank you for the assumption." Caleb raised his glass in return and drank. His contained only water.

"And how do you like our fair state?"

Caleb's eyes were drawn to the prairie beyond the ranch, its tall grasses burned brown and dry by the unrelenting summer sun. "I think there's a beauty out here. It feels very raw and primal, like the land itself has a life and will of its own."

The majority of the men chuckled, but Warner smiled his approval. "I have always felt the same. That's why I chose this place."

"Now if we could just get rid of the damn reds!" One of Warner's men punctuated the complaint with a wad of tobacco juice spit off to the side, and he earned a chorus of agreement from the other men.

"Do you have a lot of trouble out here? This is the deepest into the borderlands I've been in the circuit so far."

"It comes and goes," the rancher offered. "Things are usually quiet in the winter. No one wants to get out and cause trouble then. The heat has everyone riled up this summer, I'm afraid." Warner blew perfect smoke rings, watching them rise until they drifted away. "And of course, after the battle up north, no one feels safe anymore. It was a damn shame to lose so many fine men up there."

"To fallen soldiers, then." One of the other men raised his glass in a somber toast, and it was answered by the rest. Caleb joined them. He'd lost friends at the Little Bighorn, both dead and scoured.

As they all sat in contemplative silence, a woman rounded the corner of the house. Caleb flinched slightly, certain for a heartbeat that this was the Indian woman from the mountain. But no, this was an older woman, with faint lines showing at the corners of her mouth, though her dark skin was still flawless. Her raven hair was bound up in a tight bun just above the high collar of her calico dress, and she stood with her back straight and shoulders square. This was a proud woman. Warner grinned at the surprise Caleb could not conceal.

"Agent Marcus, I'd like you to meet Mary Catherine. Once a heathen, she has now found her way to God and lives here at the ranch."

Caleb rose to his feet and gave a slight bow, much to the amusement of the other men. "Ma'am." She only stared at him evenly, little expression on her elegant face, then turned her gaze to Warner.

"Cook say lunch soon. Wash up."

Warner chuckled. "Ah, yes, we've been scolded, boys. As you say, Mary Catherine. Thank you."

The woman returned the way she'd come. Just once, she glanced back, unseen by Warner and his fellows. Her eyes locked with Caleb's for a moment, then she was gone. Caleb dragged his attention back to his host.

"Her English is still poor, but several of the men here speak Cheyenne, so we've been able to continue her education on the good Lord's word."

"You are a kind man to take her in. Not many would have."

"Well, she wasn't always here willingly. She was left behind, injured, after a raid. It took us some time to convince her that we merely wanted to help her to heal, and to lead her to the Lord." Warner pursed his lips thoughtfully. "She tried to escape three times, though she could barely walk, and surely would have died on her own before she could find her own people. Her will is astounding."

"How did you convince her to stay?"

"Persistence, Agent Marcus." The rancher smiled. "We overcame her with kindness."

The little gathering rose as one to go wash up at the water pump. Warner walked at Caleb's side. "I maintain that a man, or woman, becomes what he makes of himself, Agent Marcus. Accidents of birth can be overcome, if one is simply willing to walk with the Lord. That is why I offer employment to a great many men who were born barren or became scoured through terrible accidents."

Once Warner pointed it out, Caleb could finally put his finger on what he'd been sensing all along. Certainly, the men who stood guard powering the fence were normal; that was obvious. But there were others moving around him who lacked the customary aura about them, the sense of the power residing within. Caleb could feel even a man with weak power at a few yards if he truly tried, and yet he saw face after face where his arcane sense wanted to just slide across without notice, where no power was to be seen. Barren or scoured, it was impossible to tell without Ernst's help. He realized he was staring at a man across the compound and quickly adjusted his hat to cover his inadvertent rudeness.

"It's noble of you to offer them a place. Too often, I saw men back east who were reduced to begging and crime just to survive once their powers were gone."

"That is what the frontier is for, Agent Marcus. A new land full of opportunities that would not otherwise be available. If a barren man is willing to work for it, I see no reason why he should be denied the same bounty as the rest of us." Warner slowed his pace, forcing them to fall back behind the group. "May I ask you a favor, Agent Marcus?"

"You're welcome to ask, of course. I can't promise anything."

The rancher waved his hand dismissively. "Oh, no, of course not. But if there was any way for you to get word back to your superiors... I fear this Indian problem is going to get much worse before it gets better, and I would hate to see anyone here or in Hope harmed. If they could see fit to send more Peacemakers to the region, or even some troops to harry the reds back into the mountains... Incidents like the Anderson raid have become all too commonplace, and I dread the day we wake to find that someone was killed."

"I give weekly reports on situations here. I'm sure if they deem additional forces necessary, they'll send them."

Warner smiled a bit and clapped Caleb on the shoulder. "We'll just wait for word, then."

Caleb washed his hands and splashed water on his face like the rest, but his thoughts were troubled. Warner said all the right things, did all the right deeds, and yet it felt false, something hidden beneath the gentlemanly exterior. He was reminded of the sickly sweet smell of decay covered by the aroma of blooming roses. Even Ernst said there was something wrong with the man, and the small creature had never been wrong in Caleb's experience. It sat uneasily somewhere in the pit of his stomach, and he couldn't wait to finish the meal and be gone from the ranch.

Thankfully, lunch was a largely silent affair, if a bit more elaborate than was called for. There were stuffed quail in an herbed sauce, as well as some candied sweet potatoes and a pot of lentil stew and freshly baked bread. Warner was more than happy to boast at length about his well-stocked larder and his overly expensive tastes, until Caleb escaped for the ride back to Hope.

The ten-mile trek gave him time to think, and when he arrived at Hope, he went straight to the general store. Hector looked up with a broad grin as Caleb strode through the door. "I see the telegraph lines come here, Hector. How might I go about getting a wire out?"

"Well, you'd have to see the telegraph operator." The gangly man stood up from his usual seat. "Which would just happen to be me."

Caleb grinned. "I was hoping you'd say that." He laid down a scrap of paper where he'd composed his weekly report on the ride home. "It needs to go to the branch office in Kansas City."

"We can do that! Just let me get my glasses on." Appropriately bespectacled, Hector sat down at the telegraph in the back corner of the store, reading over the paper. "Um… Agent Marcus? Do you mean to send this gibberish at the bottom as well?"

Caleb leaned on the counter. "Yup. It's just some markings that prove this is an authentic Peacemaker missive, and that I'm not under duress. Send it just as I wrote it."

Hector's eyes grew round behind his owlish glasses. "Like a secret code?"

"Something like that." Caleb chuckled to see the old

shopkeeper straighten his lanky shoulders with a newfound importance. "Our secret, all right?"

"Yessir. As a telegraph operator, I swore an oath. All messages are strictly confidential."

The weekly report was largely inconsequential. Caleb reported his arrival in Hope and the difficulties with his transport, mentioned the recent Indian troubles in the area, and gave an estimated time for his departure. The final few sentences, however, appeared to be just small talk, but were in fact coded phrases directed to the agent in charge of the western territories.

Graeme Tolliver was not only the district chief for all Peacemakers based in the borderlands, but he had been Caleb's best friend since they both attended West Point together. It was not the first time Caleb had used their boyhood code to send messages, and he hoped that Graeme would be able to find out more about Abel Warner in Kansas City than Caleb could out in the middle of nowhere.

He watched idly as Hector tap-tap-tapped out the telegram. Tiny bursts of blue power sparked from the gangly man's fingers to the taut wire with each metallic click, the arcane energies traveling down the miles and miles of wires to a receiver in a distant city.

Caleb felt the incoming presence a split second before the air next to him gave a soft pop, and Ernst materialized on the glass counter. "There you are! I was about to send out a search party."

Caleb chuckled, stroking the creature's soft ears. "You knew right where I was. Did you learn anything today?"

The jackalope's eyes glanced toward Hector and back; the message was clear. *Later.*

The bell over the door jingled merrily, heralding the arrival of the schoolteacher Ellen Sinclair. Hector glanced up and smiled. "I'll be with you, Miss Sinclair, just as soon as I finish this."

"No hurry, Hector. It's not like I have anywhere else to be." She sighed, pushing a stray lock of hair out of her eyes. Dirt smudged her cheek and the apron she'd thrown over her dress, and Caleb debated whether or not to point it out. "You're Agent Marcus, yes? The new Peacemaker?"

"Yes ma'am." He took his hat off belatedly. "And this is Ernst." The little creature sat up and preened for her, his furry paws stroking down his long ears. If the familiar were any cuter, Caleb thought he might become ill. "And you're the schoolteacher."

She grimaced faintly. "Well, I'd like to be. If anyone would let me."

"And speaking of teaching, the books you ordered came in on the mail stage today." Finished with the telegram, Hector bustled behind the counter to fetch a large bundle wrapped in brown paper.

"Now, if I just had somewhere to teach and students to educate." She smiled, gathering the package into her arms. "Thank you, Mr. Pratt."

Ernst gave a small startled gasp a split second before the ground lurched beneath their feet, setting the doorbell tinkling and sending items tumbling from the store shelves. At the door, Ellen fumbled to keep her balance and her grip on the heavy books. Caleb moved to catch them before they hit the floor, bracing himself over her in the doorway. In mere seconds, it was over.

"Everyone all right?" Hector answered in the affirmative, and Caleb looked down at the woman still nearly pinned to the doorjamb by his body. "Miss?"

Finally, she nodded, visibly pulling herself together, and only then did Caleb move back. Ellen patted her hair back into place, trying to pretend that she wasn't shaken. "That one was stronger, I think."

Hector agreed. "They've been getting stronger all summer. Damn reds. They won't be happy 'til the ground opens up and swallows us all alive."

Ernst appeared at her feet, huddling in her skirts with every indication of being terrified, and she scooped the furry creature up into her arms. "Poor little fellow... Are you all right?" He immediately set up his chirping purr as Caleb rolled his eyes. Ernst was nothing if not a shameless flirt.

"He's fine now, trust me." Somehow Ernst always wound up in the lady's arms and Caleb found himself playing hauler. "Look, I'm going back to the saloon. I can carry these for you, if you like."

She laughed softly. "It's been a long time since someone offered to carry my books for me. But I'll take you up on it. Thank you."

Giving their farewells to Hector, they stepped out into the late afternoon sunshine. Caleb donned his hat again to shield his eyes from the brightness and grabbed the reins on his transport. "How long have those earthquakes been happening?"

"Oh, they started around the first of the year, I guess. Faint at first, so we weren't really sure of what we were feeling. Lately, they've been stronger, and more frequent."

"And do you think the Cheyenne are causing them?" He shortened his stride to stay at her side, the arcane construct pacing on his other side with a faint wheeze-sigh of powered gears.

She frowned in thought, stroking Ernst's fur. "I don't know. Most likely they're just a natural phenomenon. But if anyone would have reason to cause something like that, the Indians would. They haven't been treated well."

"Nor have you, from what I understand." He almost instantly regretted saying it, but she only chuckled.

"No one has been unkind to me here. They're just... set in their ways. And Mr. Warner's school has served them well for years. I can't really fault them for not wanting to change."

"So why stay?" Caleb stepped up to open the saloon door for her.

"Because I love this place." She smiled. "I came west because I wanted to truly make a difference in children's lives. I packed my bags, hopped on the stage at Kansas City, and when I saw the name Hope, it seemed prophetic." She deposited Ernst on the bar, and he gave a disappointed little sigh. "Thank you, by the way, for sending Jimmy Welton in my direction. I've been trying to reel him in for months, and I don't think he'd have come to me if you hadn't said something."

"The boy's got potential. He needs to be taught before he scours himself accidentally." Caleb relieved himself of his burden and waved to Teddy as the bartender appeared from the kitchen.

"I agree. And I think he alone proves the water theory to be wrong."

"Water theory?"

Teddy set two glasses of lemonade on the bar, beads of sweat already trickling down the sides. "They say it's the nullstone in the mountains. That it gets inta the water and makes the children barren."

Caleb frowned. "Barren?" The Anderson children had most definitely not been barren, and they'd been living atop the nullstone deposit he'd sensed for presumably all of their young lives.

Ellen nodded, taking a seat on the barstool and arranging her skirt neatly around her legs. "Even the ones who weren't born barren have had their talents wane and die. It's sad, really."

"Ernst?" Caleb looked curiously at his familiar.

The jackalope shrugged. "The Anderson children are just fine, for their ages. And the other little ones that petted me yesterday were perhaps a bit weak, but they are also very young. Their power hasn't had time to develop yet."

"That little group hasn't started school out at Warner's place yet, either." Ellen frowned. "If it's in the water, I maintain it's out there. Rebecca Carter was a little firebrand until she started going to that school, and now there isn't a spark to her."

"Hush, Ellen," Teddy warned quietly. "You'll get yerself in trouble, lass."

"Oh, hush yourself, Theodore MacGregor. You may all cower and shy when Abel Warner deigns to glance your way, but I will not! Just because he throws money around like water and half the world kisses his boots as he walks by doesn't mean that he's lord of the manor." Color rose in her pale cheeks, and she all but stomped her foot for emphasis. Even when the tavern door swung open to admit one of Warner's men, she would not be quieted. "Warner can blame the barren ones on the Indians if he likes, and the earthquakes, and the drought, and whatever else he can come up with. But the fact remains that the little ones are fine before they start school out there and are nearly scoured within the first month."

The hired gun—Higgins, Caleb thought—raised a brow and sauntered over to the bar where they were gathered. "Now, see, I think this is why women oughta be seen and not heard."

"And I'm pretty sure you're not paid to think." Ellen slid off her bar stool, glaring at Warner's man with her hands on her hips.

The scruffy thug snorted. "I get paid for a lot of things. Like making sure big mouths get shut." He stepped close to the schoolteacher, looming over her as she held her ground. Unfortunately for him, that put his back to Caleb.

The Peacemaker tapped Higgins on the shoulder. "Excuse me, but that sounded suspiciously like a threat." When the thug turned to look at him, Caleb smiled cheerfully. "I know I misunderstood. Because only a complete imbecile would threaten someone in front of an officer of the law."

Higgins's eyes narrowed as he turned to face this new opponent. "You're just a travelin' law dog. You best be movin' on."

Ernst mumbled to himself as he hopped down behind the bar. "Shouldn't have said that…"

Teddy eyed the two men with a frown, bringing an old shotgun out from under the bar. "I dinnae want my place torn up, lads. If ye'd be so kind as to take it outside?"

"That won't be necessary, Teddy." Caleb rested his hand on Higgins's shoulder. "Mr. Higgins is a smart man. I trust that he understands his small place in this very large world."

Higgins shrugged off his touch, clenching his fists at his sides. "I'll show you small place…"

Caleb felt the power build, the hairs on the back of his neck standing up in response. Higgins was focusing into his fists, tiny sparks of power gathering around his knuckles. His weight shifted to his back foot, his shoulders tensed to swing. The blast would be strong enough to stop a heart, burn flesh.

And Caleb simply expanded his awareness, opening up to not only his own power but the other man's as well. *"Trechter."* *Funnel.* What Higgins was drawing into himself was suddenly funneled through Caleb instead. The sensation of it coursing through his veins was enough to make him catch his breath, but he held his focus and directed it downward. The power was siphoned away, trickling down through Caleb's connection to Ernst behind the bar, through the wooden flooring, and into the earth beneath. Higgins was left gaping in amazement, his face going paler by the moment as he tried to grasp his power only to find it repeatedly slipping through his fingers.

"You… you scoured me!" The thug actually staggered, and Caleb caught him by his elbow to steady him.

"No, I simply redirected your energies elsewhere. It's not permanent." Fear was spiking the man's abilities in erratic directions, and Caleb gritted his teeth as he had to adjust his own capacity for the fluctuations. "Once you have agreed to calm yourself, I'll restore your abilities to you."

It was the most precious of a Peacemaker's abilities, and the hardest one to learn. Very few actually had the strength to take on not only their own power but someone else's, much less direct it in any controlled fashion. In a very odd way, his old war injury helped with that. It had left a gaping hole in his capabilities, and where his own power was missing, it was more than happy to take on someone else's. Caleb breathed deeply, attempting to regulate both streams of energy running through him. Beside him, Ellen was creating similar spikes, her fear and anger hissing and fizzing like a Chinese sparkler. He couldn't handle all three threads, even with Ernst bleeding off as much excess as he could.

"Teddy, if you could take Miss Ellen to her room, please?"

It was obvious that both of them could feel the immense amount of power swirling around inside the Peacemaker, and when the bartender hurriedly escorted Ellen to the stairs, she did him the courtesy of not protesting.

Once they were alone, Caleb smiled at Higgins. "Now, in the future, I expect you to show respect to any ladies that you speak to, as well as law enforcement officers that you may encounter. Because it is fully within my authority and ability to scour you if I deem you a danger to society."

"You can't!" he gasped.

"I can. And I will if I must. You might want to relay that to your companions."

The door swung inward again, revealing the slender Schmidt standing in the orange rays of the setting sun. Beneath the low brim of his hat, his eyes fixed on the two men. Caleb could almost see the gears and bearings whirring in his mind. He was weighing the situation, determining risk and likelihood of success, methodically calculating his next action before he took it.

"Mr. Schmidt! If you could help Mr. Higgins back to the ranch, please? I think he's had a bit of a scare." Caleb clapped Higgins on the shoulder with an easy smile, nudging the ashen man toward the door.

Whatever conclusion Schmidt came to, he said nothing, merely standing aside as Higgins stumbled past him out the door. Caleb's control over his power lasted only until the man walked off the stoop, when distance thinned it to the breaking point and Caleb released it. It rebounded with an audible snap and the smell of ozone.

For a split second, he felt hollow, with a great aching space where Higgins's power had once been. It was so tempting, at times like that, to keep it. To draw as much as he could, then add more, drinking until he was sated. He drew his focus inward, wrapping his own energy around him like a prickly cocoon.

Still standing in the doorway, Schmidt slowly tilted his head to one side, as if he were seeing the Peacemaker for the first time. There was no change to his smooth face, no quiver of lips or twitch of brows, but Caleb knew somehow that he'd finally come to the sharpshooter's notice. That was definitely not a place Caleb wanted to be. After a long moment, the pale-eyed man simply turned and departed.

"You sure know how to make friends, Caleb." Ernst reclaimed his seat on the bar, his brown fur bristling with static electricity and tiny sparks emitting from the tips of his antlers.

"What can I say? It's a talent." Grimly, he watched

the door, half expecting Higgins and Schmidt to return. They did not. "I think we'll spend the evening down here with Teddy, Ernst. Make sure things stay calm."

5

Abel Warner and his men did not make their usual appearance at Teddy's saloon that night. Caleb, who sat up until the last patron had left, was certain the conversations had been livelier, the faces more relaxed without the rancher and his squad of armed thugs. It made him feel a bit more confident in his gut impression of Warner. Ernst wasn't the only one who was wary around the rancher, no matter what pleasant face the locals put on. If he had to guess, he'd say they felt beholden to the wealthy landowner, and such a feeling of debt sat heavily.

Still, his unease followed him into his dreams that night, not an uncommon occurrence.

It was impossible to tell whether it was mist swirling around his feet or the smoke from the bellowing cannons and their explosive shells. A high whine announced the arrival of another round, and he gathered himself, summoning the power of the two men on either side of him, yanking it from them when they lacked the strength to give it willingly. Through the power of his will alone, he summoned a shield, or more precisely, a large net. The cannonball hit with all the force of the men who had propelled it here, and he took that, too, drank it in. Using its own momentum, he guided the plummeting projectile into a graceful arc, slinging it around his position until it was pointed back at its senders.. All power was subject to the laws of inertia, the conservation of energy. A person with the proper strength could simply capture the existing force, turn it back on itself. With a heave that left him staggered and both men with him drained, Caleb launched the cannonball back at its originators. He lost sight as it disappeared somewhere over the chaotic battlefield, trailing blue arcane energies behind it.

"Captain! They're coming around the left flank!" someone yelled, and Caleb turned, yanking the corporal on his right up by the scruff of his coat. The man was barely conscious, his power thready and weak. It wasn't enough.

He felt the blast coming, felt the concussion of the cannonball's launch through the soles of his feet. And as in so many nightmares, he felt it descending on them, and he could do nothing. There was no power to draw on but his own; his aides were drained or possibly scoured. And one man alone could not stop an augmented blast.

In his dream, he tried to push the corporal ahead of him, tried to get the man to run. In reality, the blast had come without warning, the cannon before them exploding into jagged pieces of red-hot shrapnel. The noise was deafening for all of one heartbeat; then he could hear nothing, his eardrums shattered by the force. Something white-hot scored his face as he fell, agony spearing through his right eye. His head bounced as it hit the ground, and his vision grew red with blood.

In the dream, he lay there for hours, perfectly aware and awake, though in reality he knew that he'd been unconscious for the duration. Men trampled his body without thought as they retreated from the advancing Confederate forces. Blood splattered across his skin, starting out hot and quickly cooling to something thick and sticky. A fly crawled across the staring, unseeing eyes of the dead corporal next to him.

Somewhere amid the thump of silent cannon fire, through the haze of smoke and fog, someone was watching him. No matter how he tried, he could not force his eyes to move, could not raise his head, but he felt them nearby.

Something rested against his back, a light, gentle touch through the blood-soaked wool of his uniform. "Agent Marcus?"

Caleb came awake with a gasp, blinking in the light of new dawn, clutching the sweat-soaked sheets like a lifeline.

"Agent Marcus?" The knock came at his door again, and he realized he must have been hearing it for some time. "Agent Marcus, are you awake?"

"I… gah, yes, I'm awake! I'll be right out!" He ran a hand over his face, finding it covered in clammy sweat. Damn the dreams. Was he sentenced to relive the war every single night? "Just… let me get dressed," he mumbled as he climbed from the bed.

Ernst sat in the window watching him silently.

"Not a word, Ernst."

"I didn't say anything." His deep brown gaze returned to the world outside. "Warner is in town."

Caleb frowned as he struggled into his pants. "This early? What the hell's he want?"

"I think that's why they're waking you."

More or less dressed, with his gun strapped on and his staff at his side, Caleb opened the door. Ellen Sinclair and Jimmy waited in the hallway. Ellen looked relieved to have finally wakened him. "You have to stop him. He's going to kill them."

"Stop." Caleb held up a hand. "Who's going to kill who?"

"Mr. Warner," Jimmy piped up. "I heard him say they found the reds that raided Mr. Anderson's place, and they were going to go take care of it."

Caleb cursed under his breath, earning a raised brow from the prim schoolteacher. "Ernst! Come on!"

Warner had managed to assemble quite a mob by the time Caleb got mounted up on his transport and met them on the outskirts of town. There were at least twenty of Warner's own men there, including the ever-silent Schmidt and a good ten or fifteen of the townsfolk, and they were armed with everything from pistols to rifles to a few staves that were less powerful replicas of Caleb's own. This was not meant to be a peaceful excursion.

"Mr. Warner!" Caleb pulled his transport to a halt in front of the throng. "Might I remind you that the law frowns on vigilante justice?"

Scowling, the rancher reined his transport up short. "Then I suggest you accompany us, Peacemaker. Because justice will be done this day whether you like it or not."

With angry shouts of encouragement, the mob kicked their mounts into motion and rode around Caleb with little regard. Cursing, Caleb wheeled to follow them.

The hauler was not built for speed, and the lighter transports quickly pulled ahead, leaving Caleb to follow as best he could. They were headed west, toward the mountains again, but north of the track that had taken them to Anderson's homestead. *But the raiding party, at least the hauler, went south.*

"Ernst, can you get ahead of them, see where they're going?"

The familiar was clinging tenaciously to the back of the hauler with all four paws. "Not without Warner knowing I'm there. He's cast a net, watching for me."

"He did what?" Caleb relaxed his senses as much as he could, letting his eyes see into the arcane spectrum. He expected to see pulses, flashes as Warner's power went seeking outward from the man, but instead he saw a shimmer in the air, a heat wave that followed along in a steady rolling motion. *Sweet Lord, to control that much power on a moving transport...* He wasn't sure he himself could have done it, and the thought disturbed him. "Just means he's going to do something he doesn't want me to see."

Well before they entered the foothills, Caleb found the rest of the transports halted in the tall grass. The men had obviously gone forward on foot. He dismounted, gathering his staff and freeing his gun from its holster. "Stay close to me, Ernst. I need your eyes." Though the jackalope vanished the moment his furry feet touched the ground, Caleb could still feel him near.

Their trail through the dry and brittle prairie flora was not hard to follow. Creeping over a slight rise, Caleb found the posse spread at the top of the next, clearly eyeing something down the other side. Warner and Schmidt held center stage, the rancher giving very quiet instructions to his hired gun. Caleb crept up to Warner's left, shouldering aside another man to take his place, lying flat on his stomach.

Below them, a small teepee had been erected, barely more than a crude framework of hides over branches. It was nothing like the well-constructed dwellings Caleb had seen in his briefings. A small fire burned in an area carefully cleared of dry grass, and a lone rabbit roasted on a stick over it. Two horses stood tethered a few yards away, grazing peacefully. Belatedly, Caleb noticed that Warner had approached from downwind to avoid spooking the animals.

In front of the haphazard shelter, a small child sat playing with a doll. If the girl was more than three years old, Caleb would eat his hat. Her dark braids framed a cherubic face, but there were shadows beneath her eyes. She was hungry, perhaps. The rabbit must have been a precious treat.

One of the horses stamped and snorted, and Caleb saw another child slip from between the two beasts, coming to join his sister. The lad was around nine, though if they had been hungry long, he could have simply been small. Bared to the waist like he was, his ribs were painfully visible. The boy checked the rabbit, turning it, then called out in a language Caleb did not understand.

A woman emerged from the teepee, tying a leather thong into her dark hair. She smiled fondly at the boy, mussing his hair, then picked up the little girl, chattering at her in their musical language.

These were the raiders of Anderson's homestead? A half-starved mother and two young children? Caleb looked at Warner to find the rancher's eyes fixed on the scene below.

"Are you out of your mind? They can't possibly be the ones who raided the homestead," Caleb hissed softly. The little family went about readying their meal, oblivious to their danger. "Don't you think, if they had two cows, they'd be eating them instead of that scrawny rabbit?"

Warner turned to look at the Peacemaker, his dark eyes hard and cold. "Even if they aren't, that boy will someday grow up to scalp good and decent white folk. Better to get them now."

So. Those were the rancher's true colors. Caleb felt faintly ill.

On Warner's other side, Schmidt was already taking aim down the long barrel of his buffalo rifle, a tiny glimmer of blue energy fizzing at the primer.

Abruptly, the tiny flicker of awareness that was Caleb's connection to Ernst vanished from his side and reappeared down below. Unseen, the familiar prowled between the horses.

The Indian woman bent to set her daughter on the ground, and Schmidt's finger tightened on the trigger slowly. Silently, Caleb willed her not to stand up, to stay down, but of course she could not hear him. *Ernst, whatever you're going to do, make it quick.*

One of the horses let out a piercing scream, tossing its head and kicking its hind legs frantically. The other animal caught the first one's panic, dancing at the end of its lead, the whites of its eyes showing as they rolled.

The mother and son both jerked their heads upright, looking for the danger for only a split second before the boy grabbed his mother's hand... and the entire family disappeared. Nothing remained but the spooked horses and one rapidly charring rabbit.

"Damn you!" Warner grabbed Caleb's shirt as they both got to their feet. "Just what the hell do you think you're doing?"

Caleb gripped Warner's wrist tightly but made no aggressive move. Inwardly, though, he had a tight grip on his power, ready to thrust it in any direction necessary. "The horses spooked, Mr. Warner. It happens. That's why we use transports and haulers."

"Your furry rat was down there. I saw it." Warner seemed to gather himself, releasing his hold on the other man's shirt. "You may be able to get away with being a red-sympathizer back east, Agent Marcus, but out here it's going to make you a very unpopular fellow."

"Noted." Several of the hired guns gave Caleb ugly looks as they got to their feet and started the walk back to their transports. The Peacemaker returned the glances with flat neutrality, making certain they were all on their way back before he made his own way down the small hill.

He'd gone no more than two steps before a gunshot rang out, echoing off the distant mountains, followed quickly by another. Sick dread knotting his guts, he spun to see Schmidt fire off two more rounds, reloading faster than he'd thought possible, the augmented bullets streaking blue across the distance to drop the second horse in its tracks. Both animals screamed in agony, their front legs shattered.

Schmidt shouldered his rifle with no expression, never even glancing at Caleb as he passed on his way down the grassy hill.

Ernst appeared out of the tall grass, huddling near Caleb's boot. "That man has no soul."

"Literally or figuratively?" Caleb looked down

when his familiar didn't answer. "Or do I want to know?"

"Probably not."

With a sigh, Caleb turned to look over the now-empty encampment. The two downed animals were making the most blood-curdling noises, thrashing their immense bulks about in the tall grass. "We can't just leave them like that."

"I know."

Caleb made his way down the hill slowly, unsure what the injured animals might do, but neither horse seemed to register his presence, so far gone were they into their pain. He drew his pistol from its holster, checking the bullets more for an excuse to delay than out of any real necessity.

"Do it, Caleb. Don't let them suffer, please." Ernst's antlers sparked with his distress.

The Peacemaker took careful aim at the first animal and fired, not even bothering to augment the shot. The bullet took the horse in the temple, and the great beast lay still. Another shot quieted the second, and with the screams gone, the prairie seemed eerily silent, as if the world had stopped to notice the passing of the two beautiful creatures.

"Is the family safe, Ernst?"

"I think so. They're gone, at any rate."

Caleb shook his head, adjusting his hat down over his eyes. "I don't know what power that woman has, but it's a damn lucky thing. How the hell did they just disappear like that?" Holstering his pistol, he started back up the grassy hill, with Ernst hopping along behind.

"It wasn't her. It was the boy."

Caleb whistled low. "And they wonder why we lost at the Little Bighorn." The Indians were endowed with powers no white man understood; that was a given. But if even their children were capable of vanishing in plain sight, it boded poorly for further expansion into the west.

The hauler was just where they'd left it, though

Warner and his vigilante mob were long gone. Caleb mounted up and turned the construct back toward Hope, barely kicking the thing into a walk. Ernst popped into view on the rump, settling himself with a sigh. "What do we do, Caleb? They're all going to be like this, you know. Every town we visit out here, every rancher, every homesteader."

"I don't know, Ernst. I just don't know."

He didn't belong out here. He knew that much. The borderlands required a harshness, a ruthlessness that just wasn't in Caleb's makeup. He simply could not see the world as black-and-white, but the sun that blazed down over the seemingly endless prairie offered no shades of gray.

He knew he'd been destined for the borderlands, though, even before the tragedy at the Little Bighorn. Though the fire in Chicago could not have been quelled by anyone, it had gone down as a black mark on all the Peacemakers who had tried and failed. His next assignment had been St. Louis, which would have lasted only until someone else needed the position. Then where would they have stuffed him? Kansas City maybe? Or straight into the borderlands then?

Even crippled as he was, his once-awesome talent stunted and limited, he was still too powerful for them to dismiss him outright. They needed him. Even if he was limited to control words and simple logic exercises like any grade school child.

"I wouldn't send you out there, Caleb, if I had anyone else." Agent Chief Sheffield did manage to look sorrowful over the heavy oaken desk. "We're scrambling to cover those territories now. Thirty men…" He had to pause and swallow hard, the enormity of their loss still staggering, even a month later. "Dear God, thirty men lost." For a long moment, he stared out the window, his watery eyes haunted by the ghosts of dead and scoured

Peacemakers.

"You called me back to Washington to tell me you're demoting me to a borderland circuit." Caleb kept a calm voice, but his jaw ached as he bit off his bitter words. His hands clenched into fists behind his back as he stood at attention, and he let his gaze fall on the other man in the room.

Graeme Tolliver had been his best friend since West Point, and though he didn't avoid Caleb's glance, there was unease in the set of his shoulders that spoke volumes. His familiar, Tan, in the form of a lean spotted cat, watched Caleb with unblinking green eyes, and Caleb wished that he'd brought Ernst. It would be nice to have someone present who was on his side. "Not a demotion, Caleb. A temporary reassignment. You know I'm hurting for agents in the borderlands after... what happened. Once we get some new recruits trained, I'll send you back east, I promise."

"No, you won't. Don't lie to me, Graeme. I'm an embarrassment to the department."

The agent chief at least tried to protest, but the color coming to his cheeks betrayed him. "You know we have always had the utmost faith in your abilities. Recovering after an injury like yours, you're fortunate to have any power at all, let alone to the degree that you've regained them. You should be proud."

Caleb's smile felt chipped and brittle at the edges. "Of course. A grown man who can't even light a fire without mumbling incantations like a toddler. How proud I must be."

"You could be scoured, Caleb," Graeme reminded him.

"Maybe I'd have been happier that way. At least then I'd know my place."

Sheffield stood up from his chair, bracing his hands on his desk. "Listen, Caleb. You're too well-known in your current circles. Your reputation has preceded you to every city I could possibly assign you to. Maybe… Maybe going out west will be beneficial to you. Find people who don't know about… your condition. Maybe you can find a nice girl, get married, settle down…"

"A favor? Is that what you're doing? Granting me a favor?"

"It isn't intended to be a punishment." The old man took his seat again, picking up a pen to sign off on the paperwork in his neat penmanship. "How you choose to see it is up to you."

Even now, months later, Caleb winced at the memory. On Chief Sheffield's advice, he'd been trying to see it as a good thing, ever since he got off the stage at his first stop. But there were times when it was difficult. He kept telling himself that anything was better than being scoured, even the remedial abilities he'd been left with after Cold Harbor. He was still stronger than most men he'd meet on a daily basis out here in the back end of nowhere. "Except Abel Warner."

"Hmm? What was that?"

"Nothing, Ernst. Nap a bit. I'm going to take the slow way back to town." He flipped the catch on the accelerator lever and let the hauler lumber mindlessly in its current direction.

It was tempting to keep riding, leave Hope behind, hit the next town on his circuit. If he hadn't been on a rented mount, if his trunk hadn't been back in Hope, he might have done just that. Deep down, he knew that even then he wouldn't have, but he might have entertained the thought a little longer. *You're too damn honorable for your own good, Caleb.*

With the hauler plodding along at its slowest pace, the sun was well past its zenith when Caleb happened to spot a familiar figure perched on a rock alongside the trail of flattened prairie grass. He brought his mount to a halt and couldn't help but smile as he looked down at Jimmy Welton. "Now, what in the world are you doing clear out here?"

The boy shrugged, banging his heels on the boulder he was sitting on. "Nothin'."

"Nothing, hmm? You weren't trying to follow that posse, were you?"

Jimmy snorted. "If I was tryin' to follow them, I'da been home already. They passed this way hours ago." He scratched idly at a scab on his elbow. "Why wasn' you with them?"

Inwardly, Caleb chuckled. The boy had been worried about him, obviously. "Just decided to ride back on my own. You want a ride back to town? I don't know about you, but I'm about dying of thirst."

Jimmy made a show of thinking about it, then nodded and stood up on the boulder, allowing Caleb to maneuver the hauler close so he could scramble aboard. "Hey, Ernst."

"Hey, Jimmy." As broad as the transport was, there was more than enough room for the jackalope and boy. Jimmy sat cross-legged on the hauler's rump, and Ernst happily crawled into his lap, purring and sparking.

Caleb nudged the hauler into motion again, setting it at a smooth gait so it wouldn't dislodge the duo on the back. "So I hear you're taking lessons with Miss Sinclair, Jimmy."

"Mmph. When I feel like it."

"And how's that going?"

"She's real nice, I guess. Not sure about this stuff she's tryin' ta teach me, though."

"Oh?" Caleb turned in the saddle to look at Jimmy. "Like what?"

"Like these words she keeps wanting me to say. 'Fire.' 'Wind.' 'Spark.'" He snorted. "Never needed anything like that."

Caleb chuckled. "You won't need to say them forever, Jimmy. It's just a way to get your mind to focus on what it needs to do. You say 'fire,' and your mind goes through the steps to make fire appear. When that becomes second nature, you'll only have to think it, and your mind will respond." *Well, usually anyway.*

"I just feel stupid saying stuff like that."

Caleb grinned a little. "You know you don't have to use normal words, right?"

"Hunh?" Jimmy narrowed his eyes suspiciously. "How do you mean?"

"I mean, if you wanted your word for fire to be 'sarsaparilla,' you could do that. Just so long as when you say 'sarsaparilla,' you think about making fire. Sometimes, using foolish words can make it a bit less boring."

"You can?" He looked thoughtful. "So… what if I wanted to make it a different word? Like… 'dammit'?"

"I'm guessing that won't go over so well with Miss Sinclair. And if you do it, don't you dare tell her I told you to." Jimmy flashed him a wicked grin, and Caleb turned back to the front, chuckling.

For the rest of the ride, he could hear the boy murmuring soft words to Ernst, the pair of them deciding just what the proper command words should be for Jimmy's next lesson.

The town was bustling as they rode in, or at least as bustling as Caleb had ever seen it. Some of the people called greetings to him. Most did not. It was almost certain that the men from the posse had already related the tale of his perceived betrayal.

"Agent Marcus! Agent Marcus, a moment, please?"

Caleb turned around in his saddle to find a distinguished looking man trotting down the dusty street after him.

"Dr. Elm, yes?" Hector had pointed the town physician out the night before. "How can I help you?" With his back turned, Caleb almost missed Jimmy sliding down the other side of the hauler and making quick tracks into a nearby alley. The sight of the nimble urchin retreating made him chuckle. No doubt the good doctor had tried to corral Jimmy, too, in the past.

The wiry doctor frowned, pushing his spectacles back up on his nose as he craned his neck to look up at the mounted man. "Would you be willing to come look at one of the children with me? I would like the opinion of a person with more talent."

Caleb exchanged a glance with Ernst, seeing that the jackalope was just as mystified as his human counterpart. "I don't have any medical training, Doctor, but if you think there is something I could help with… Let me leave my transport at the saloon, and I'll come to your office."

"Thank you, sir." The immense relief in the doctor's voice made Caleb frown. What in the world would a doctor need to consult with a Peacemaker on?

A few minutes later, Caleb found out.

The little girl sat on the examining table, hands clasped tightly in her lap. She couldn't have been more than eight, old enough to be displaying talent and learning how to control her budding abilities.

"She was learning real good; she got the fire starting real easy and wasn't having any problems controlling it." The mother was nearly in tears as she tried to explain again to Caleb and Dr. Elm what had gone wrong. "Then she just… stopped. I didn't think she was using enough to get scoured, or I'd have stopped her. And now…" Her words were lost beneath choked tears.

The good doctor put an arm around the sobbing woman's shoulders. "I'm sure it was nothing you did wrong, Sarah. I'm going to have the Peacemaker and his familiar look at her, all right? Maybe they can see something that I can't."

Ernst didn't wait for an invitation. He hopped onto the table and cuddled into the child's lap, starting up his little chirping purr. The little girl hugged him so tightly it was a wonder he could still breathe.

Caleb watched his familiar, but also expanded his senses to envelop the child, relaxing until he could see with his power, not his eyes.

Everyone in the room glimmered with their innate power. Dr. Elm was stronger than Caleb might have guessed, but it was to be expected of one in the medical profession. The mother, Sarah Emerson, had mediocre talent, but it was at least there. Ernst glowed like a beacon, nearly blinding in his brightness. Caleb shone as well, with light pulsing along the now-visible veins in his hands with every heartbeat.

Everyone glimmered, that is, but the girl. Little Emily Emerson was matte against a world gone glossy. Where Ernst touched her skin, the familiar's power tried to trickle into her, tiny threads reaching, searching, but fading out before they'd gotten centimeters into her body. Ernst continued to do his own brand of examination, but for all that Caleb could see, the girl was powerless and always had been. Barren.

The mother was watching him closely, and he was careful to keep his face neutral, his eyes on Ernst. Maybe, just maybe, the jackalope could sense something he could not.

Ernst was silent, save for his purring, for long, tense moments, and when he spoke, he did not even open his eyes. "She is not scoured."

Sarah burst into more tears, and no one could speak again until Dr. Elm had calmed her.

"Then what's wrong with her?"

"I think she's been exposed to nullstone." Ernst raised his head and nuzzled the child's cheek, carefully avoiding her with his antlers. "It seems pervasive. In her skin, rather than on it. If she is exposed to no more, it should work its way out of her system, and she may recover completely. Or… she may never be able to touch her power again."

"They said it was in the water, but I didn't believe them. We get our water from the town well, like everybody…" Sarah pressed both her hands to her mouth to stifle more sobs.

"Sarah, if it was in the water, we'd all be losing our talents." Dr. Elm's voice was confident, but he cast a glance at Caleb for confirmation.

"Dr. Elm is right. I don't think it can be the communal water supply." He patted little Emily on the head, and she gave him a shy smile. "And I don't think it can be the water at Warner's place, either, else he and his men would be showing signs."

No, it couldn't be the water, but what else could be out there? Caleb didn't have a good grasp on how much land Warner actually claimed, but if there was a nullstone deposit somewhere there? Perhaps if the recent earthquakes had brought a vein to the surface?

The doctor frowned in thought. "Something that only the children get into, then?"

"How many children are affected like this, Doctor?"

He thought for a moment. "I've only seen four, but there are at least seven more. No one wants to admit their child is barren, so they don't bring them in to see me."

Caleb crouched down so he had to look up to see little Emily. "Sweetheart, can you tell me any places that all of you like to go play? Maybe secret places the grown-ups don't know about? Especially around Mr. Warner's house?"

The child shook her head, biting her lower lip, and Ernst redoubled his purring efforts. Sarah came to sit next to her little girl, stroking her hair gently. "It's all right, Emily. No one is going to get in trouble. We just want to make sure no one else is going to get sick."

After a few more moments of squeezing the stuffing out of the purring jackalope, the child finally offered, "We don't get to play at Mr. Warner's. The schoolmaster doesn't allow it. But there are a few other places that we go. It's hard to tell you, but I could draw a picture."

Caleb smiled and nodded encouragingly. "If I found a map of the area, do you think you could show me on there?"

"Maybe."

The doctor was already out the door in search of a map.

6

By the time a suitable map could be found and Emily Emerson drew her notes and instructions on it in painstakingly careful print, the afternoon was waning, and there would be no time to ride out into the grassland to investigate. Grudgingly, Caleb planned his excursion for the next day.

He spent the evening at the bar, poring over the piece of paper with Hector and Teddy, trying to figure out which of the locations was most likely to pose a hazard.

"Almost all of these are right here around the town. If there was nullstone there, we'd hae noticed."

Caleb nodded his agreement with the Scottish bartender. "I was thinking of exploring these two here"—he pointed at two locations between the town and Warner's ranch—"since they pass by those every day on their way to school. After that, I'll head north." And if that search proved fruitless, the next course would be to search Warner's place. He didn't see that going over well with the rancher. "How often do you really think they pack up and ride out this far?"

"Durin' the summer, probably near ta once a week or more. Whole gang of them go oot there, with the older ones keepin' watch. They take picnics."

The northernmost point was very near to where they'd encountered the hungry Indian family, as close as Caleb could guess. Was that a coincidence? If the Indian boy's magical strength was any indication, there was nothing out there to harm anyone. "Can you pack me some food for the road tomorrow, Teddy? I don't know how long I'll be out."

"O' course. And some whiskey for yer wee friend." Ernst favored him with an ecstatic purr.

None of Warner's men had returned to town after the posse that morning, but Caleb watched the regulars anyway and kept his voice down. "No one needs to know that I've gone poking around. I don't know how some folks would take that."

Hector and Teddy both nodded, the shop keeper adding, "Sure enough, we don't know a thing."

"Thank you both for all your help. I'm not the most popular fellow in the county right now, and I know you're risking some ill will with your neighbors by helping me."

"The way I see it is this, Agent Marcus," said Hector. "Most folks are decent. Just sometimes, someone shouts a bit louder, and they all forget what's right. Deep down, they know, and they'll act right when it really matters." He nodded his head on his tall, thin neck.

Teddy was a bit less philosophical. "And Warner's a horse's ass. Murderin' women and children, when everybody knew they couldnae hae been the ones what raided that homestead. I dinnae mind makin' the reds pay for what they're doin', but ye cannae tell me that family did anythin'." His face was red beneath his beard by the time he'd finished, his accent almost thick enough to be unintelligible. "What kinda monster kills children?"

"More whiskey, please." Ernst sat up on his hind legs, his front paws pressed primly to his chest.

Successfully diverted from what was sure to be an angry rant, the barkeep hurried to serve his new favorite customer. "Here ye go, a dram before bedtime." He poured a shot of alcohol into the shallow dish, and Ernst set to lapping it up eagerly. "Never seen a creature like his whiskey so much. Except my old grandda."

Caleb smiled fondly at his familiar. "I smoke; he drinks. On the whole, we're quite the pair of reprobates."

Hector leaned down to peer closely at Ernst. "Does he actually get drunk?" The jackalope looked up, licking drops of whiskey from his whiskers with his tiny pink tongue, and Hector sat up so fast he nearly toppled from his stool.

"A gentleman is never drunk," Ernst stated stiffly, which was followed by a miniature belch that completely ruined the effect.

"Speaking of bedtime…" Caleb gathered his staff and his hat. "If we're going to spend tomorrow riding that god-awful thing around the county, I should get some sleep. You coming, Ernst?"

The creature eyed the bottles of whiskey behind Teddy's bar thoughtfully. "I'll be along presently. You go on."

Caleb rolled his eyes. "You'd better start charging him, Teddy, or he'll drink you out of house and home."

The room was stuffy and hot, and opening the window did nothing but let in the night-flying insects and dust. Still, Caleb made the attempt, lying on top of the quilt in a vain attempt to get cool. He did his best to get comfortable, laying one arm up over his head, pounding the hard pillow a dozen times to try to get it just right. It was a lost cause, and he finally just lay in the dark, staring up at the ceiling. On the table next to him, his pocket watch softly ticked off the minutes, dragging on into hours.

He didn't expect to sleep well, if at all, so when the dreams began, he was genuinely surprised even in his semiconscious state.

The air scorched his lungs as he breathed in, and, he slapped at the burning cinders that had fallen into his hair, his hat long since lost in the chaos.. The soothing blue glow of the streetlamps had given way to the ominous red haze, until it appeared that the clouds above them in the night sky were smoldering.

"Here! There are more in here!" Ernst appeared around his feet, the familiar taking the form of a nimble black cat, nudging him toward the location of more trapped residents. Caleb found his path blocked and put his shoulder against the charred beam, trying to heave it out of the way.

Rufus appeared out of the smoke, coughing and hacking, but between the two men, they cleared the doorway. Inside, voices were calling for help, screaming out in terror. "I'll get them. You clear me a path."

Caleb nodded and reached for the fire all around them. It lurked in the ceilings of the building they were in, curling hungry tendrils around the floorboards under their feet. He could feel it, angry and seeking, and he grabbed hold, pulling all of that destructive energy into himself. It railed inside him, imprisoned in a form it was not meant to take. Another day, well rested, he might have been able to feed that extra power out through his familiar, but that much control had been lost sometime in the previous hours, and so he would hold it himself. A moment's lapse in concentration, and it would find a way out. His skin would curl and burn from the inside. He'd just seen it happen to two other Peacemakers.

"Smeul," he whispered. Smolder. The walls around them snuffed out suddenly, wisps of smoke replacing tongues of flame. "Hurry, Rufus. It's getting stronger."

The other Peacemaker bolted into the dark hallway, charred floorboards creaking ominously under his boots. Caleb could feel the power behind the fire looking for him, furious that something had stolen its energy. He would be able to hold on only so long.

"Go, go, go!" Rufus herded a soot-blackened family past him, carrying the youngest child in his arms. "Give us thirty seconds, Caleb, then get the hell out!"

He tried to count to thirty, but the flame inside him

would not let his mind find the numbers. It was hungry, it was angry, and it wanted to be free. Ernst was butting his furry head against his knee, urging him to let go. Finally, he was forced to release it, and he could only pray that Rufus had gotten the family clear.

The flames roared back to reclaim their territory and then some, and Caleb felt his brows and eyelashes singe to nothing as he staggered for the stairs. It followed him, drawing in a breath deep enough to flutter the tatters of his shirtsleeves, then bellowed out a gout of flame and ash that would easily incinerate him.

A shield sprang up around him, and the fire whipped around the globe, raging when it could not find entry. Caleb breathed the artificially pure air in great gulping lungfuls until he staggered into the street, collapsing at Rufus's feet. Ernst appeared right next to him, the tip of his long black tail smoking.

The blond Peacemaker, whose hair had long gone as dark as Caleb's own with soot and sweat, dropped the shield he'd put around his partner and yanked him to his feet. "This block is lost, Caleb. We have to go!"

Reluctantly, Caleb let Rufus drag him from the scene, and the building gave a ponderous groan as it collapsed behind them. There were other men moving in the smoke around them, passing buckets, and sparks of power flared where people tried futilely to direct the flames around their homes or businesses.

"George! George, over here!" Rufus waved to two other Peacemakers as they crossed the street a block away. "Where are we supposed to be making a fire break? We got separated from Daws about an hour ago."

George was supporting his partner with one arm, the other man sporting a vicious gash over one eye. He barely paused to answer. "It jumped the river. We're pulling back! It's lost!"

"Dear God..." Rufus's eyes were wide and staring,

the whites showing brilliantly against his ash-blackened face. "They can't just let it burn…"

"There's no letting it, man. It's going to do it whether we want it to or not!" George staggered off as fast as he could with an injured man in tow, leaving Rufus and Caleb alone in the middle of the charred wreckage. Even the hardy water brigade had abandoned their positions, leaving their buckets lying next to empty water barrels.

Chicago was burning.

Caleb knew they had to move. He knew, as with the rest of his dreamed memories, that the building to their right was going to collapse in another moment, the rain of debris trapping Rufus beneath it. He knew that the beam would crush his partner's life from his lungs, and that he would be forced to leave the body or burn along with him.

He knew it, and he could not prevent it, could neither move nor speak a warning. Such was the way of dreams.

In the alley to their left, a woman's voice wafted forth, humming softly. It was a soothing melody, lilting, and it had no place amid this frequent terror of Caleb's nights. Even in the dream, he was able to frown in puzzlement.

The shadows moved in the alley, at first easily mistaken for the swirls and eddies of smoke. But there was no mistaking the dark eyes he found looking back at him, framed by twin black braids.

The Indian woman tilted her head curiously, her skin and clothing remarkably free of ash and char.

"No… no, you can't be here! The building is going to fall. You have to run!" She obviously didn't understand him, and she smiled softly. "No, don't smile! Run! You have to…" He suddenly remembered Rufus, realized that he could speak again. "Rufus, you have to run!"

But Rufus was gone. There was no one standing in the street beside him. The flames seemed to have halted their inexorable advance and merely flickered in the windows and rooftops, waiting.

"Ernst?" The black cat was gone, too, and there was no sense of his presence nearby. "What...?" He blinked, wiping sweat and blood from his face as he stared around in confusion. "What's happening?"

The Indian woman never answered, merely turning to walk down the street in the opposite direction, humming softly. Every so often, she glanced back to see if he was following.

Numb, perplexed, he did. In his daze, he stumbled over the rubble in the street, fell...

And opened his eyes to find himself lying flat on his back, staring up at a high ceiling. There was a low sound of life around him, the constant quiet bustle as people passed by with hushed conversations. The blanket beneath his hands was warm, dry, but scratchy, and the smell of antiseptic stung his nostrils. The calming blue lantern on the table beside him cast a soothing aura, but, trapped beneath a heavy bandage, his right eye saw nothing. He explored it with his fingers, recognizing the careful folds of gauze and linen.

He knew where he was. This was the hospital outside Washington. How long ago had Cold Harbor been now? For four days, the dead and injured had lain on the field, waiting for the cease-fire. But he was safe now. Why was he dreaming of the hospital? He never dreamed of what came after.

The heavy weight on his chest stirred, and he realized a large ferret was curled up with him, watching him with heavy-lidded eyes.

"He won't leave your side, you know." One of the nurses smiled as she came to sit on the chair next to his bed. "He's been most adamant about waiting for you to wake. He was the only one who was certain you would."

He reached to stroke the creature's ears and was rewarded with a deep vibrating purr, a sound a real ferret shouldn't be able to make. "He...?"

"He says his name is Ernst." The nurse patted his shoulder. "I'm going to go tell the doctor you're awake."

Caleb dropped his head to his pillow, trying to grasp what was happening. Why was he back in the hospital? And why did he feel like he'd been following someone? And where was that humming coming from?

A woman was humming softly, no doubt to one of the other injured soldiers, but he couldn't remember ever hearing that before in this particular memory. As he craned his neck to locate the source of the lullaby, he caught a glimpse of a tall woman with raven black hair walking past the doorway at the end of the ward. Her knee-high boots made no sound on the floor, but even from a distance, he could hear the rustle of the beads on her leather dress. And stranger still, no one else seemed to notice the Indian woman walking calmly in their midst.

"This isn't right. This isn't how it happened." When he looked down for the ferret's confirmation, Ernst was gone. As were the people in the beds on either side, and the nurses who had been patrolling the aisles. Only the humming remained, soft and delicate.

"Why are you doing this?" he called, without really expecting an answer. "You have no right to just walk through my memories like this!" Because that was what she was doing. Somehow, with a power he could not fathom, the Indian woman had walked into his dreams and was sorting through them, sorting through him.

She appeared at the end of the walkway, tilting her head to the side.

"You can't do this. You have no right." Caleb sat up in his hospital bed. He was, after all, injured only in memory. "I don't know what you're looking for, but you can't just do this. These are my memories. You've no right to them."

Perhaps she understood him. Her eyes grew sad,

and she offered him her hand, inviting him to take it.

"No. I'm not going anywhere with you. Go away now. Leave me in peace."

She stood with her hand out for a long moment before finally deciding he meant it, and then she dropped it with a sigh. She pointed to herself, then out the door, and Caleb nodded.

"Yes. Go. Please."

A look of frustration crossed her face, and she actually stamped her leather-clad foot. Stubborn as a mule himself, when he felt the need, Caleb crossed his arms over his chest and glared back at her. For one moment, he thought she would relent, but instead of leaving, she took a few quick strides toward him, reaching out to touch his face. Though he flinched back, somehow she caught him, resting her warm palm against his cheek.

He blinked...

The wind blew through his long hair as he rode on horseback through the tall prairie. The sharp grass slipped past his leather leggings without hurting him, but it would have cut his bare chest to ribbons at this speed. His horse's legs were already flayed and bleeding, and still the loyal animal raced toward the column of black greasy smoke that rose on the horizon. Sick dread settled in his stomach; he already knew what he would find.

The village was gone, the teepees reduced to smoldering heaps. Cookfires were scattered, drying racks lying in jumbled messes, the precious meat on them ground into the dust. Everywhere the bodies of men, women, and children lay where they'd fallen. Black hair was dull with thick clotted blood. Dark eyes were glazed and cloudy, their spirits long fled.

"No... Oh, please, no..." He slipped from the horse's back before it had even stopped, falling to his knees next to the body of a young woman. Her head lolled on a broken neck. "Oh, no... Little Raven, oh, no..."

Tears burned his eyes as he gathered her into his arms, rocking her gently. His little sister, his beautiful beloved Little Raven...

In the churned mud, the perfect circle tracks of the skyfire horses were visible. How many had come, with their skyfire guns and mechanical monsters? How many of his people had been cut down trying to flee, shot in the back or trampled into the earth?

A roar of rage built in his chest, rising from his throat as a scream of primal agony. Why!? They'd been peaceful! They had refused the Dog Soldiers; they had avoided the white towns and homesteads. Why would the white men do this?

Hot tears streamed down his face as he laid his sister down, arranging her body peacefully. He was no medicine man, but he would perform the rites for them. Then he would find his weapons in the ruins of his home, and he would go join the Dog Soldiers. The white men would pay.

Soft humming caught his ear, and he snatched his knife from his belt, turning with full intent to fight to the death if need be.

A young woman stepped from the trees, her eyes full of sorrow as she gazed over the carnage. And though he knew he had never seen her before, he felt he should know her. "Will you... help me? I cannot do this alone."

She nodded with a sad smile, and made a sweeping gesture with her right hand.

Caleb woke. For a few brief moments, he was uncomfortable in his own skin. He ran his hands over his bare chest, finding it unchanged. His trousers were still the same cloth they'd always been, no leather or beads to be found. His hair was still shorn close to his head, and the thick scar still graced the right side of his face. The thin thread of power that tied him to Ernst told him that his familiar was still downstairs, so he couldn't have been asleep very long.

His body could still feel the sensation of the horse moving beneath him, though, its sensitive hide responding to every pressure from his knees, something he'd never done in his life. The hot tears of grief and rage still lingered at the back of his throat, threatening to choke him until he swallowed them down. He could still recall the weight of the dead woman in his arms, the grayish pallor that had taken over her dark skin, and the stench of charred leather and ozone lingered in his nostrils.

"Dear God, what is happening to me?" he asked the darkened room.

7

Sleep after that was obviously not an option. Caleb felt decidedly unclean, like all the events of his life had been rifled through. And the last dream… that had not been his, and that disturbed him, too. He had no right to walk through other people's thoughts, either.

A small voice inside chided him for superstitious nonsense. Dreams were dreams, and nothing more. No doubt the plight of the Indian family had plagued his mind as he drifted off, resulting in the strangeness of his dreams. "That'll teach me to eat haggis an hour before bed."

"Haggis isn't actually food, you know." Ernst hopped from the windowsill to the bed in one graceful bound. "It's what you eat when there isn't any food."

"How would you know? You don't eat." Caleb buttoned his shirt and carefully pinned his badge over his heart. "Besides, it was kind of Teddy to make us one of his traditional dishes. He was being hospitable."

The jackalope snorted and scratched furiously at one ear with his hind foot. "He fed it to you because no one else in this town will eat it."

Caleb went about the mundane business of gathering his belongings for the day, letting the silence drag out as he sorted through his own thoughts. "Ernst? Can I ask you a question?"

"You can ask anything you want. But you know I don't always know the answer."

"Can you walk into people's dreams?"

The little creature seemed a bit taken aback by the question, and it took a long time for him to formulate an answer. "No. I could see yours, if I wanted, but that's because you're mine. But I couldn't see anyone else's, and I couldn't walk into them."

"Do you know of anyone who can?"

Again, it took a long time for him to answer. A familiar's origin was often shrouded in mystery, even to the creature itself, and sometimes it took a while for Ernst to sort through the myriad of knowledge he held in his furry little head. Finally, he sighed. "I have met no one, personally, who has that ability. But that does not mean it doesn't exist." He shrugged his furry shoulders. "I am part of you. My powers are limited to the breadth and scope of yours. Other cultures, other peoples… who knows?"

Caleb nodded. It was no less than he'd expected. He holstered his gun and gathered up his staff, leaving his heavy coat behind in deference to the already sweltering heat.

"Caleb?" He stopped at the door and looked back. Ernst hadn't budged from the bed. "They're your dreams. If you don't like them, you have the power to change them."

"I'll keep that in mind." He put his hat on, pulling it low over his eyes. "You coming?"

Ernst hopped off the bed and followed him out into the hallway.

Teddy had made good on his word, and packed several meals' worth of food up for Caleb's excursion, along with a small flask that was clearly meant for Ernst. "Watch yerself in the sun, Agent Marcus. Ye'll get heat sick before ye realize."

"Thank you, Teddy."

His next stop before actually leaving town was the smithy, where he was informed in no uncertain terms that he was early.

"I tell you come back in one week! Not four days!

You count, ja? All fingers and toes?" Sven glowered at him, not even bothering to come out from behind the forge to berate the Peacemaker.

Caleb eyed his transport. The rear end was in some chaotic state of disassembly, with gears and wires and bearings all hanging out for the world to see. The thing had been reduced to simple hunks of metal held together with hopeful thoughts. The transparent windows were dark and still. He couldn't help but wonder how the scoured man had managed to safely bleed off all the energy so he could open the casing to make repairs.

"Hi, Agent Marcus!" On the far side of the transport, Jimmy's head popped up, a smudge of grease near his hairline (and probably in his hair, too, judging by how it stuck up at erratic angles). "I found the problem!"

He flipped something silver to Caleb, who caught it by reflex. The Peacemaker examined the tiny gear, finding two teeth chewed to mangled nubs, and smirked. "This one tiny thing caused all that trouble. Figures."

Jimmy came out of the shop wiping his grubby hands on a rag. "It was way down in there. Mr. Isby needed me ta get it, 'cause my hands are smaller." He took the broken gear back, rolling it over the backs of his knuckles with a grin.

"Do you help Mr. Isby often?"

The boy nodded. "Yup. I got the spark, he's got the know-how."

Caleb raised his head at the smith, who just shrugged and said, "Boy has gift. Should learn honest trade with it."

Eyeing the disabled transport, Caleb suddenly had a chilling thought. "You don't let him… I mean, that's a lot of power to be grounded. You didn't let this boy…"

Sven snorted, his white-blond brows furrowing over his eyes. "I look stupid? Boy risk being scoured like that. No, that I leave to others who help now and then. Adults."

He muttered to himself in Swedish, no doubt saying some very uncomplimentary things about Caleb, and returned to his work.

Jimmy snickered. "Mr. Isby's a grump, but he treats me good, and he pays me." Fishing in his pocket, he displayed two shiny quarters. "He says I could be a good arcanosmith someday."

Caleb nodded his agreement. "He's right, if you get the right education. You should tell Miss Sinclair; she could guide your studies in that direction."

The boy shrugged, blushing faintly. "I might keep goin' ta see her. Might not. Depends on how busy I am."

Caleb managed to hide his amusement. "Of course."

Jimmy eyed the hauler, laden with Caleb's staff and the packs of food. "You going somewhere, Agent Marcus?"

"Just out for a ride." He winked at the boy. "But if anyone asks, you didn't see me today, all right?"

"All right!" That seemed to perk the kid up, and Caleb could see visions of a vast and secret conspiracy whirling in his eyes.

With Ernst perched on the hauler's rump, Caleb lit out at a choppy canter to the south, intent on investigating the first two places on his haphazard map.

The first was a few miles outside of town, just off what passed for a main road between Hope and the A-bar-W. Perhaps it had once been part of an army of towering oaks marching across the plains, but now it was merely a solitary dead tree adrift in a sea of tall grass. The old roots had long since given way on one side, causing it to list until the branches themselves touched the ground. The floor of the resulting cave had been trampled free of grass years ago by many tiny feet as they clambered in and around the half-fallen giant. How many wars and battles had been fought there, with all the combatants cheerfully going home for dinner at the end of the day?

Caleb crawled in, through, and over every surface

he could find, seeking any trace of nullstone with tiny pulses of his own power. After two of those resulted in small fires in the deadwood, he stopped. "Ernst?"

The familiar was higher in the tangled branches, where an adult's weight would be a liability. "Nothing. There's no nullstone here. None within at least five hundred yards."

"Then we move on."

The next stop was little more than a mud hole, where little Emily had insisted there was water during all but the hottest of summers. Caleb crouched at the edge of the cracked, dry pond while Ernst made slow progress out to the vaguely damp center. "Anything?"

Ernst sniffed at the remnants of the once-vibrant spring, his furry nose twitching for a long moment before he shook his head. "No. And this spring's been broken. It'll never hold water again after this summer." He thumped the crust of hard-baked mud with one hind foot. "Been cracked all the way down to the bedrock."

"Was that from the heat or the earthquakes?"

"Both." Ernst hopped back up on the hauler, getting comfortable again. "North then?"

For a moment, Caleb hesitated. They were close to Warner's, and he truly wanted to search the ranch proper, but he was certain the rancher wasn't going to sit idly by and let that happen. Best to eliminate all other possibilities, he finally decided, before he kicked that particular hornet's nest. "Yes. North."

They rode wide around Hope on their way back north, so it was just past noon before they located the trail from the morning before. It was easy then to follow the bent and broken grasses to the site of the abandoned teepee.

The two horses still lay where they'd been felled, the carcasses swollen with gases, a noisy cloud of black flies going about their gruesome but necessary work. Caleb walked around the small camp, but nothing appeared to be disturbed. Everything was just where it had been left when the family disappeared. He crouched to pick up the little girl's doll, forgotten in the dirt. "Someone is missing you, I'll wager." He dusted it off and absently tucked it into his pocket, eyeing the rest of the waste grimly. "Why didn't they come back for their things once we were gone? Or to butcher the horses, at least? They were nearly starving; that could have been a lot of meat for them."

"Perhaps they were too frightened."

"Maybe."

It was impossible to tell from the scribbles on the map just where the town's children liked to take their picnics, but the camp seemed as good a place as any to start. Caleb placed his bare hand flat on the ground and whispered, *"Zoek."* His power went seeking through the parched soil, finding dry roots that shriveled away from his touch, scuttling bugs taking shelter deep within the earth and a small warren of hardy prairie rabbits that had denned up against the heat of the day.

He followed the pulse outward as far as he could, until it dissipated into nothing. Nowhere did he detect the nullifying effects of the white chalky stone. "Ernst, I'm going to try another one. Be on the lookout for fires, all right?"

"Will do."

Caleb took a deep breath, gathering up as much power as he dared use in such a tinder-dry clime. It pulsed out through his palm and into the soil, an ever-widening circle of sensation, the obstacles in its path reflecting back to Caleb in blue afterimages behind his eyelids. Rocks, plants, animals, insects at varying distances. A small stream, deep within the earth to the north, burbling its way from somewhere even farther without ever breaking the surface. And almost directly to the west of his position, a large circle of nothingness, a void that his power found and spread around but could not touch or read.

His eyes sprang open. That hadn't been nullstone, which would have absorbed and swallowed the seeking pulse. Something—or someone—was trying to hide their presence from him. "Ernst, three hundred yards to the west. It might be the family that belongs here, so go gentle."

The jackalope blinked out without being asked, and Caleb ran to catch up. The tall grasses sliced at the backs of his bare hands, and he was disturbingly reminded of his dream, riding a horse through this very same prairie.

They obviously heard him coming. By the time he was even close, he could hear the mother calling out in their language, frantically herding her children away. "Wait! Wait! I won't hurt you!" Where the hell was Ernst when he needed him?

The woman was trying to run with her daughter on her hip, pulling her son along by one hand as fast as they could go in the tall grass. With his long strides, Caleb caught up easily, but when he reached to stop her, the boy whirled with a knife in his small hand, swiping at the Peacemaker.

"Whoa!" He jumped back, just in time to avoid the rough blade, and held his hands up to show they were empty. "Easy, son. I'm not going to hurt you. Please, you don't have to run from me."

The child obviously did not believe him, and still facing down the man twice his size, he said something to his mother. *He told her to take the girl and run. He's going to slow me down so they can get away.* Caleb knew it from the look in the boy's eyes, a grim determination that should never be on the face of one so young. "Ernst… I could use some help here…"

The little jackalope popped into view, grumbling to himself. "I'm coming, I'm coming. Tell me to go somewhere, then take off running… It's hard to keep up!"

The Indian boy's dark eyes grew very wide, and he called something to his mother. The woman returned warily, torn between watching the jackalope and keeping her eyes on the large man her son was menacing. She finally settled on looking at Ernst, asking him something in her own language.

"Can you understand them, Ernst?"

The familiar took a few cautious steps forward and seemed relieved that the Indian family didn't bolt. "Not so much. I may know a way, but it's going to be very taxing."

The Indian woman looked at Caleb this time, asking the same question as before. He held up one hand, imploring her to wait. "This better work, Ernst."

"Hold on to your hat," the familiar mumbled, and hunkered down into a little brown ball of fur on the ground.

For a long moment, nothing visible happened. The humans present exchanged puzzled glances, all of them uncomfortable, but none yet willing to flee the scene entirely. Caleb tried to offer the woman a small smile, but she only watched him, her body tensed to bolt at the first untoward move on his part.

The boy exclaimed suddenly, pointing at Ernst.

The furry little form was growing transparent as Caleb watched, the dry grass behind him visible right through his body. "Ernst? Is this supposed to happen?"

Suddenly, the Indian woman pointed with a gasp to their right. There, huddled in the grass, was Ernst. Or, at least it was another jackalope, as transparent as Caleb's familiar. Both the creatures shivered in unison, and raised their heads to speak.

"I can't keep this up for long. Being in two places at once is difficult," the leftmost jackalope informed them in English, while the one on the right parroted the words in the other language.

Caleb swept his hat from his head, crouching down to look at Ernst. "If this is too hard, forget it. I don't want you to harm yourself."

Again, the two jackalopes spoke in unison. "I'm

fine. Just hurry." The Indian woman babbled something at him, pointing emphatically at Caleb. "They wish to know what you want."

That made Caleb sit back on his heels and think for a moment. What *did* he want?

"Ticktock, Caleb. Grains through the hourglass and all." The two Ernsts' noses twitched in perfect unison.

"Why are they alone? Where are their people?" That seemed as good a place as any to start.

The question was relayed, though Caleb found it disturbing to hear Ernst repeating his own words back at him. The woman drew herself up stiffly, holding her daughter tightly and pulling her son close.

"Five days ago, I took my children to gather greens away from the camp early in the morning. Sometime before noon, we heard gunshots and screaming, and we hid away. When things were quiet, we returned to find that everyone had been killed and our teepees burned. We took what we could salvage, and our horses, and we are going south to find my sister's people."

The memory of Caleb's dream haunted him, the bodies tossed about negligently as if they'd been no more than debris in the way. "Who did this?"

"The white man. We saw the tracks of the skyfire horses." He could hear the accusation in her voice, even if he could not understand her words directly.

"Which white men? From the town?" He pointed in the direction of Hope.

"I do not know."

"And you have no idea why?"

She shook her head. "We were peaceful. We did not venture into the plains to taunt and raid like the Dog Soldiers. But they came anyway. A woman of the People led them."

Caleb frowned. "A Cheyenne woman was with them?"

It was the boy who answered this time. "I saw them days before the attack. They moved among the rocks, and she spoke to the spirits of the earth, asking them questions they did not want to answer. She forced them, and the ground shook."

The earthquakes. "Do you know what she was asking them?"

The boy shook his head. "Foolish questions that made no sense. Seeking rocks within the earth."

Ernst's form wavered, growing thinner by the moment. "Hurry, Caleb."

"Why did you not butcher the horses if you are hungry?"

This time, the mother spoke. "The man with the dead eyes has been known to poison carcasses and leave them. We did not dare touch them."

That could only be Schmidt, and Caleb hated him a bit more knowing that. "Tell them to wait here, Ernst. I'll be right back." He didn't wait to hear the message relayed.

His transport was right where he'd left it, with the packs of food attached. He lead the construct back to the little family, and unpacked what would have been his lunch and dinner. "Here. It may not be what they're used to, but it's food. Hopefully, it'll last until they can find their people."

The woman looked grateful, if suspicious. "Why are you doing this?"

"Because it's right." He gave the little girl a small smile, and she hid her face shyly against her mother's shoulder. "And I have something that belongs to you, I think." He produced the tattered doll, and the child's dark eyes lit up with delight.

"She says thank you, Caleb." The jackalope's voice was fading, as if he could hardly catch his breath.

Caleb knew he had only moments left before Ernst had to end whatever it was that he was doing. "Travel at night if you can. And don't fight them if they find you. Just disappear like before." He looked at the boy. "You take care of your mother and sister, you hear?"

The child nodded, and Ernst gave a sad little moan, his doppelgänger disappearing like mist. Once more solid, the original Ernst flopped onto his side, his chest heaving. Caleb knelt to gather him into his arms, feeling how slight and frail he now felt.

The boy grew brave enough to move close, peering at the animal in Caleb's arms and asking a question.

"I think he'll be all right. He's just very tired." Caleb held very still, holding his arms out toward the boy. "You can touch him, if you like."

After glancing at his mother once, the child extended a hand, stroking Ernst's soft fur lightly. The exhausted familiar managed a tiny purr, only for a few seconds, but the young warrior was obviously entranced.

Caleb let both children pet the jackalope for a moment, knowing how much Ernst enjoyed it, then carefully deposited the animal on the back of the hauler. As Caleb swung into the saddle, the woman came to look up at him, questioning him again. Though he didn't understand her, he could guess what she was asking.

"I'm going to see what they were looking for." He pointed toward the mountains.

She nodded, and said something that had to be "Be careful."

"I'll try." He gave a small smile and kicked the hauler into motion.

The small family disappeared in the tall grass behind them, and the mountains loomed large before him. Caleb glanced back once to check on Ernst and found the creature snoring softly. "You get some rest, buddy. Hopefully, I won't need you anytime soon."

8

The afternoon was already waning by the time Caleb found the charred remnants of the Indian village. He'd have found it faster if he'd simply followed the memory from his dream, but he'd resisted, taking a few wrong turns along the way out of sheer stubbornness.

"What the hell am I doing here?" he wondered aloud, very aware that being in Indian territory, alone, near nightfall, was virtually suicidal. No doubt, had Ernst been awake, the familiar would have had some commentary on the subject, but he slumbered on, snoring faintly from time to time.

The village looked much like Caleb recalled it from his dream. The teepees had been reduced to lumps of blackened, charred leather, but were no longer smoldering. The bodies had been moved, arranged with dignity in low tree branches and wrapped in whatever cloth had been salvaged from the wrecked homes. The smell was pervasive, the sickly sweet odor of death and decay, and Caleb tried to breathe through the fabric of his shirt to keep the taste out of his mouth.

Beneath the reek of corrupted bodies and burned leather lingered the faint tang of ozone, the remnants of the magic that had been used here. It was more than the amount needed to fire augmented bullets. They'd used it to set fire to the teepees, to send bolts after fleeing victims. There were more than a few places where the soil had been melted into a slick, shiny surface, spider-webbed with cracks from the intense heat. They'd been frivolous with their power, the men who came here. Frivolous and arrogant.

For one split second, Caleb was certain he heard the whistle of descending cannon fire, the distant boom of a shell as it hit, the crack of rifles all around. He closed his eyes and gritted his teeth until the dizzying sensation went away.

"All right. What was so important that you had to destroy an entire village to get at it?" There was no doubt in his mind that the woman the child had seen had been Warner's Mary Catherine. But what had she been looking for?

Caleb pressed his palm to the blackened earth. "*Zoek.*" *Seek.*

The area of the village proper was devoid of all life. Even the worms and grubs had deserted the scene of such carnage, driven from the place by the taint of so much magic. The tree roots were curled and blackened in their earthen beds, the smallest ones near the surface burned to ash. Only the oldest of the trees would survive in this location, the ancient roots sunk deep within the bedrock.

Almost directly below him, his sparks of power snuffed out abruptly, leaving a void that showed clearly where a vein of nullstone passed beneath this camp.

Caleb opened his eyes, frowning thoughtfully. Aside from the nullstone, he could sense nothing unusual within the earth, and even the nullstone was too far underground to be of any harm or use to anyone. There weren't even any underground water sources nearby that might carry a taint down into the prairie.

"Maybe… the vein surfaces farther up the mountain?" He glanced at Ernst for the jackalope's opinion, to find him still sound asleep. "Well, only one way to find out."

He reached for the nullstone with the next seeking

pulse, feeling along its edges, following its jagged path farther into the bedrock. It climbed, almost unbroken, higher into the foothills. It was never thicker than Caleb's wrist, and though it was fractured in many places, it remained almost a solid line, pointing west.

Caleb continued the pulses, pushing higher and deeper, mapping the lay of the vein in his mind as surely as if he'd seen it himself. And just when he was about to give it up as a lost cause, something pulsed back.

It was barely a brushing of power, more residual than directed, but Caleb's eyes snapped open, and he yanked the rest of his scattered power back into himsclf. For a long moment he waited, senses alert to feel the first tickles of someone else's power moving against him, but there was nothing. Perhaps his intrusion had gone unnoticed after all.

"Ernst. Ernst!" He shook the jackalope until the little creature opened one eye. "I'm leaving the hauler here. Can you keep up with me on foot?"

"Mmph. Heartless man." The furry creature stretched and yawned, displaying a tiny pink tongue and rather vicious-looking sharp teeth. "I suppose I'll have to. Someone has to keep you out of trouble."

Caleb eyed the darkening sky, which was already painted in shades of purple toward the east where the sun had long since abandoned its post. "I'm more worried about getting lost in the dark."

"You could just wait until morning, you know."

"No. There's someone up there right now. I want to know who."

The pair set out on foot, able at first to follow trails broken by the Indians and even game paths when the cut trails exhausted themselves. But ultimately, as the night settled in, Caleb was forced to light the end of his staff with a murmured *licht* just to keep from walking headlong into one of the many trees that clung tenaciously to the mountainside.

He kept the blue glow as small as he could, not wanting to alert anyone else of his approach, and it made for slow going in the thick underbrush and rough terrain.

Ahead of him, he could barely see Ernst dimly outlined in the light, and the little creature sat straight up, ears pricked and alert. "Ernst?"

"Shh! Listen!"

Caleb crouched next to his familiar, straining to hear what the small creature's better ears had detected. For a long moment, there was nothing but the slightest of breezes, rustling the leaves around them. Not a bird sang; not an insect chirped. The forest was silent.

The noise, when it came, was barely more than an impression of sound, something felt through the bones as it bounced from a distant source. Once Caleb caught it, he could focus on it more, and it grew clearer to him. It was the distinct sound of metal on stone.

"How far ahead?" he asked Ernst in a whisper.

The jackalope's whiskers quivered as it scented the air. "Another hundred yards upward. Douse the light."

Caleb cut all power to his staff, leaving them in darkness. "If I break my neck, I'm blaming you."

"Hush. Follow."

For a six-foot-tall man, following a barely two-foot-tall creature through thick underbrush was easier said than done. And doing it quietly was virtually impossible. After the hundredth time Ernst had shushed him, Caleb was ready to skin the creature and make gloves. His face was bleeding where branches had scratched him, there was God only knew what crawling in his short hair, and he'd barked his knees against more trees than he could count.

He was so intent on keeping himself in one piece, he nearly stepped on Ernst when the small animal froze, ears quivering at full height. "Hsst! Get down!"

Cautiously, Caleb lowered himself to the ground,

peering over the edge of a small ridge to see what had attracted his familiar's attention. A warm orange glow emanated from the hillside ahead of them, too steady to be an open flame, but the wrong color to be from any arcane source. The incessant pinging noise was louder here, and as his eyes adjusted to the new light, he could see why.

Lanterns adorned the trees, hung on posts, anywhere they could give off a bit more illumination. The brightest light seemed to come from within a cave, barely a jagged crack in the mountain's face, and there men were bustling to and fro, some of them pushing heavy carts, others with picks and shovels over their shoulders.

At the edges of the lanterns' light, other men stood guard, armed with rifles and handguns, their eyes scanning the dark forest all around them.

"Are they looking for us or just looking in general?" Caleb whispered.

Ernst shook his head, his antlers rustling the bushes. "I don't think they heard us. I think they're just on watch."

"What the hell are they doing?" Caleb silently cursed having left his binoculars with the transport.

"Obviously, they're mining." Even in the dark, Caleb could see Ernst's disdainful look.

"In the dark. In Indian territory." Caleb looked for a clear path that might take him closer, but found none. There was a trail carved through the brush, no doubt put there by the miners and their guards, but it was completely open to view from the mine, and there was no way Caleb would avoid being seen.

"Maybe they're shy."

"Can you get closer without being seen?" Caleb shielded his eyes a bit in an attempt to see if he recognized anyone at the site.

"Not a chance. Can't you feel that? The place reeks of nullstone."

Once it was pointed out to him, Caleb could indeed

smell it on the air. Though it shared no other properties with the harmless substance, nullstone always smelled like sodium bicarbonate. Reflexively, Caleb snorted softly, trying to clear the scent from his nose. "Why would they risk working around so much nullstone? They have to be totally cut off from their powers by now."

Ernst edged forward, nose twitching. "They're scoured. Or barren. Every one of them. Not the guards, they still glow, but see how they're staying away from the mine?"

It was true. The armed men kept a careful distance from the mine and the miners alike, lest the nullstone sap them of any ability they might possess. Caleb counted six guards, and at least that many miners. There was no telling how many were still within the mine. Here, then, were Warner's barren employees. "Wait… Is that Schmidt?"

Despite the bandana covering the lower half of his face, there was no mistaking the cold-eyed gunman. The slender man stood in the shadow of a large tree, separate from the other guards, and he was still enough that only the gleam of light off his rifle betrayed his position. In spite of himself, Caleb held his breath for a few heartbeats, expecting to see the sniper shoulder his weapon and take aim at him at any given moment.

His attention apparently focused on the mouth of the mine, Schmidt never moved.

"Why in the world are they digging up nullstone?" Caleb muttered to himself.

Before Ernst could offer up any more theories, the earth beneath them gave a great heave, almost like the mountain itself had taken a deep breath. The shaking followed immediately after, and Caleb could only duck his head, protecting it from the falling branches and twigs that rained down on him. The quake was hard enough to rattle his teeth in his head, and he got the impression that the mountain was trying to shudder them right off its skin, like the unwanted parasites they were.

Rocks large enough to crack a skull bounded down the mountainside, narrowly missing Caleb and his familiar, but still peppering them with pebbles hard enough to bruise. The smell of nullstone grew stronger, and Caleb did his best to cover his mouth and nose with his shirt. Ernst burrowed against his side, taking shelter from the largest of the debris.

At the mine, the men were shouting, their voices raised in fear. When Caleb could lift his head again, he saw them scrambling from the hole in the earth, coated top to bottom in white dust. One of the carts had overturned, spilling its load of chalky white stone into the clearing, and the guards shifted anxiously into the trees, avoiding the weakening effect. One of the lanterns had overturned, and several men beat at the flames frantically until they were smothered.

A tall figure appeared at the mouth of the cave, staggering out ahead of several of the workers. Clearly a woman, judging by her dress, but ghostly because of the nullstone powder that covered her from head to toe. Only then did Schmidt move, snatching her by one arm. He dragged her away from the mine entrance, flinging her to the ground negligently once they were clear of the nulling cloud. She lay there for a long moment gasping for air.

"Mary Catherine. I knew it." Despite the nullstone dust that made her appear an apparition of her true self, there was no mistaking the tall Indian woman. Caleb's moment of triumph was short-lived, however. Schmidt pulled the bandana from his face and aimed a kick at the downed woman, who curled up to avoid the blow.

"I not do! I not do!" The woman sobbed, protecting her head with her arms. "Please do not!" Schmidt kicked her again with no expression at all. Her pleas received no response. When he drew back to kick her again, she made a gesture with one hand, and a tiny dust devil rose beneath the raised foot, white with whirling nullstone dust and peppered with pine needles and fallen leaves. Unbalanced, Schmidt landed on his rump, and the dust devil broke apart, drifting to the earth.

Caleb blinked in amazement, certain that his eyes had played a bizarre trick on him. The woman, covered in nullstone dust to the point of being ghost white, had conjured the very wind to do her bidding. It wasn't possible. There was no one in the world with enough power to overcome that much nullstone.

The gunman sat for a moment merely looking at the Indian woman with his emotionless eyes, then rose to his feet and dusted off his clothing. The next kick was to her head, and she slumped to the ground.

Caleb took a better grip on his staff, preparing to rise. He couldn't sit and watch a woman be beaten.

"Are you insane?" Ernst poked him with his antlers, hard. "You can't fight all of them, even if most of them are scoured."

"Schmidt has to be breathing in that dust. There's no way he's at his full ability. If I can take him out…"

"And do what? Kill him? Kill all of them? You're a Peacemaker, Caleb. You don't kill." Ernst put a paw on the staff, and it might as well have been made of solid granite. Caleb couldn't have picked it up if he'd wanted to. "Wait, and watch. There has to be a better chance than this."

Curse the little creature, but he was right. There was no way to intervene without it ending in bloodshed.

Schmidt left off abusing the Indian woman, gesturing for one of the others to help her up. They dragged her to her feet, depositing her on a fallen tree at the edge of the light, where she wobbled drunkenly. Two guards moved to stand over her.

One of the nullstone-coated miners approached Schmidt, careful to keep a safe distance. "The left tunnel is collapsed. It's going to take at least two days to dig out to where we were. We may have lost that vein."

They were carrying men out of the mine now, the red blood of the wounded standing out vibrantly against white skin, even in the dim lantern light. Most were walking under their own power, but two were not moving at all and never would again. Even at his distance, Caleb could see that their skulls were crushed. The mountain had taken its due.

"I don't understand, Ernst. Why would they risk all this to mine nullstone? It's not that valuable."

"I'm more concerned with what they're doing with it once they get it out of the earth. If they're taking it back to the ranch, that might be where the children are being exposed."

Ernst was almost certainly right. Caleb felt it in his gut. "Then he has to know what he's doing to them." It couldn't be a mistake. What kind of monster *was* Warner?

"Hsst! Look out!" Ernst ducked deeper into the bushes, and Caleb froze as the miners and their guards made their way down the rough path. They pushed the cart of nullstone ahead of them, struggling to keep it upright on the rocky trail, and four carried the bodies of their fallen companions. At the end of the procession, Schmidt herded a groggy Mary Catherine along, keeping a tight grip on her arm.

The Peacemaker remained still long after the sounds of the miners' passage had faded into the distance. Only when a bird in the tree above him sent out a questioning chirp and some of the night insects began to buzz around his ears did he remember to breathe normally.

"They must have haulers down the mountain to get the stone out. But I still can't fathom why. And Mary Catherine… How did she do that trick with the dust devil, all covered in nullstone like that? I wouldn't be able to find my head with both hands, covered in that much stone."

"Caleb?"

Ignoring Ernst, Caleb gathered his staff up. "I think I need to look around up there a bit more."

"Um, Caleb?"

"Don't worry, you don't have to come, and I won't go in the tunnels." He clambered to his feet, shaking leaf litter from his clothing. "I just need to see what is so important about this mine."

"I don't think they're going to let you."

"You don't think who's going to let me?" He looked down at Ernst, only to find the animal staring down the hill behind them.

"You might want to put the staff down."

Slowly, Caleb turned.

How they had approached so near without even Ernst hearing them, Caleb would never know. But the seven Indian braves were almost within spitting distance, each of them with a drawn bow trained on Caleb.

None of them said a word, but Caleb gave a small nod and bent ever so slowly to lay his staff next to his feet. It didn't cripple him, by any means, but it was at least a visible indication that he didn't intend to fight. He raised his empty hands, just in case they didn't understand.

"What do they want?" he asked quietly.

Ernst shook his head. "I don't know. And I can't translate again, not so soon."

"This creates a problem, Ernst."

"I'm aware of this, Caleb."

The men in the trees looked young and strong. Not one arrow wavered from fatigue, and their eyes never left the Peacemaker. Most of them had paint on their cheekbones and feathers tied into their dark hair.

Caleb knew he could get a shield up without the aid of his staff, but it would last only until his air ran out and he fell unconscious. Not a pleasant thought, under the circumstances.

The silence dragged out for an excruciatingly long

moment. Finally, the one in the center lowered his bow and snapped something at Caleb in their language.

"I don't speak Cheyenne. Do you speak English?"

The tall Indian only barked the same phrase at him, obviously a command, and the two men closest to him approached Caleb warily.

"Ernst, stay close. This may get a bit messy." Caleb took a deep breath, drawing power inward, feeling it pool in the center of his chest. From that store, he could accomplish almost anything. Without his staff, it could only be destructive.

Suddenly, someone laughed. It was an eerie sound, high-pitched and frantic, off to Caleb's left. The braves paused in their advance, glancing back toward their leader.

A furry head pushed through the bushes at the leader's side, and a large coyote trotted into view. It yipped once, looking up at the leader, and the man frowned darkly. The coyote yipped again, and there was no mistaking the note of command in the animal's tone.

"Ernst, is that…?"

"I'm… I'm not sure." The jackalope huddled closer to Caleb's boot, eyeing the large predator. "I've never seen a familiar like that before."

Whatever the creature wanted, it was not to the liking of the band of warriors. They grumbled among themselves until the coyote nipped at the leader's hand, growling softly. Finally, the men acquiesced.

The leader pointed at Caleb and snarled a short command. One of them reached out to grab Caleb by the shirt, giving him a slight shove, and another collected the staff.

"Where are we going, Ernst?" Caleb stumbled over the rocky terrain as the braves closed in around him, taking him down the mountain.

"Wherever they want us to, Caleb."

And they were marched into the sultry night.

9

It was easy to guess at the amount of time they'd been walking. Caleb placed that at nearly an hour. It was next to impossible to guess the distance.

The first time he noticed the anomaly, he thought his eyes were merely playing tricks on him in the darkness. They were walking along a narrow path bordered by low bushes—buckbrush, he thought. He raised his hand to wipe a spiderweb from his face, and when his vision was clear again, the path had changed, becoming rockier and almost fenced in by small saplings of various types. He got only a moment to glance behind before his captors shoved him onward, but the hardy little buckbrush plants were nowhere to be seen.

By the third such strange shift in scenery, Caleb realized that it was being done deliberately, and through no power he himself possessed. "Ernst, what are they doing to us?"

"I'm… not sure." The valiant little jackalope was hard-pressed to keep up on his short legs, and the Indians didn't seem inclined to wait for him. Caleb scooped him up without breaking stride, holding him in the crook of one arm. "It's not an illusion. We're actually crossing great distance with each leap. I just… can't tell how it's done."

The brave beside Caleb jabbed him in the ribs hard, a reminder to stay quiet. The Peacemaker gritted his teeth and said nothing more, but he watched for the abrupt shifts in scenery. Notably, they always took place shortly after the coyote familiar disappeared on the trail ahead of them, almost as if the animal were leaping ahead to make sure they reached the right destination at each shift.

Caleb kept a wary eye on the other familiar every time it appeared again. While they weren't precisely rare, neither were they common, and Caleb had never encountered one that belonged to an Indian. In fact, he'd encountered none at all since leaving the East behind him, save for Graeme's Tan in Kansas City. His friend's familiar had always just been a quiet presence in the background, the tawny spotted cat as silent as his partner was loud.

Familiars should never be mistaken for docile pets or companions, though. During the war, Caleb had seen the familiars of two powerful generals meet on the battlefield, and that combat alone had nearly leveled five acres. It was never wise to underestimate the magical creatures.

It was clear, however, that the coyote did not belong to any of the men there. And since they seemed inclined to follow orders from the furry predator, it was likely that it belonged to someone important. Someone the braves were not willing to disobey, no matter how they disliked what they'd been commanded to do.

Ernst wanted nothing to do with the big coyote; that was certain. Though Caleb would have loved to know more about what made the strange familiar different, his captors started grumbling and poking him with sharp objects when he tried to speak, and he was finally forced to fall silent. The questioning would wait until later.

The last abrupt jump in terrain was the most obvious, because they went from dark forest to a brightly lit clearing, with campfires dotting the night as far as the eye could see. Truly impressive dwellings, the teepees towered overhead, and almost a hundred people came pouring out of the lodges to see what their warriors had returned with.

Men and women of every shape and size watched Caleb and his familiar with dark eyes, some hostile, some merely curious. There were no children present, he realized, and the lack stood out starkly in his mind, once noticed.Many of the people called to the men escorting him, obviously family glad to see the hunters returned.

And they said the Dog Soldiers had been broken. Caleb wondered what the military strategists back east would say if they knew of this village and just how many Cheyenne warriors still remained.

He was pushed and prodded toward a large fire at the center of the village, where it seemed people had assembled to wait for his arrival. The coyote was seated at the feet of the most ancient man Caleb had ever seen, whose black hair had gone pure white and was plaited neatly. The lines of many cares and worries were etched deeply into his worn face, but there was no mistaking the keen glint in his eyes, though, or the proud bearing of his shoulders as he stood stick-straight. His garments were thickly ornamented with quills and feathers and beads, and elaborate scenes were worked into the leather with dyes. This was a personage to be reckoned with.

One of the braves walked forward, presenting Caleb's staff to the elderly man with a noticeable air of deference. The old man looked it over with mild curiosity. The runes themselves seemed to interest him, and he traced them several times with one finger. Caleb braced himself, ready to throw up a shield if he saw the sigils light, but the staff remained dormant.

The elderly man seemed satisfied with whatever he'd discovered, and he came forward, using the staff now to walk with, though he didn't seem to need it. As he approached Caleb, the crowd murmured in agitation, perhaps worried that the dreaded white man was going to attack their venerable elder.

Caleb held up his free hand, once again displaying his intention to simply remain passive. The old man tilted his head, looking the Peacemaker up and down. His eyes lit on Caleb's gun, which they hadn't taken away, and he asked something of his braves. The leader answered with a shrug. Apparently, they didn't feel the firearm was a danger.

"Are you up to translating again?"

Ernst barely shook his head. "I don't want to weaken myself that much around that one." His eyes had never left the coyote, though the predator seemed to ignore Ernst's very existence.

The jackalope's voice drew the attention of the ancient Indian, and he tilted his head the other way, his sharp eyes examining the creature in Caleb's arms. His gaze moved from Ernst to Caleb and back again, a thoughtful frown forming in the lines of his face.

He looked to one of the braves and gave an order. The intent became clear when the young man reached to take Ernst away from Caleb.

"No!" Blue flame flared to life around Caleb's empty fist, the threat explicit. No one was taking Ernst.

The brave hesitated, glancing toward the older man. The ancient one nodded firmly, indicating that he was to proceed. Reluctantly, the man stepped forward.

"*Kracht*!" A bolt of raw force leapt from Caleb's hand, slamming into the young brave's chest and sending him sprawling to the ground.

It was not a killing blow but one meant to daze. The brave blinked his glassy eyes, barely aware when his comrades moved to help him to his feet.

Caleb continued to hold his power, and licks of blue energy flared around his fist, casting strange shadows on the faces of the watching throng. They were eerily silent, but no one made any further hostile moves. "If you have to, blink out of here, Ernst."

"I'm not leaving you."

"It wasn't a suggestion." He glanced at his familiar. "For once, just do as I ask, all right?" Ernst didn't answer.

The ancient Indian was examining his stunned brave, and to Caleb's surprise, seemed to be chuckling. With mirth in his eyes, he came back to Caleb and pointed at the power held in his hand.

"Not a chance. You threaten Ernst, you deal with me." The Peacemaker shook his head firmly.

The old man shook his head in reply, saying something in their musical language. He pointed across the clearing, past the fire, to a wooden frame with leather stretched tightly across it. It had many holes punctured in it and a few broken arrows around the base. A target, obviously.

"You… want me to hit that?"

The old man nodded, insistently pointing toward the target again.

It was easy enough to do, though Caleb couldn't fathom why the old man wanted him to. The trick would be keeping the thing from erupting in flames and igniting the entire forest.

With narrowed eyes, he brought all his concentration into the middle two knuckles of his hand, condensing the blazing power into a narrow point of light. Arm outstretched, he breathed the word *kracht* on his exhale, and power lanced forth with a sharp crack, a beam of blue in the firelit night.

The target blew apart into many pieces, those standing closest to it diving for cover with surprised cries. The old Indian laughed with obvious delight, going himself to retrieve pieces of the mangled frame and looking them over with excitement. There seemed to be much laughter in the crowd, good-natured mockery of those who had fled from the exploding target.

"They're all crazy, Ernst."

"I highly doubt that." The jackalope burrowed himself deeper into Caleb's elbow. "Look out. He's coming back."

It seemed ridiculous to be holding on to a fistful of raw power in the face of such a wizened individual, but Caleb did it anyway, bracing himself for whatever came next.

The ancient one smirked, and pointed once again to Caleb's flaming hand, then to the leader of the braves who had captured him. The brave stepped forward, his jaw and fists clenched, a hint of hatred in his dark eyes as he gazed at the white man.

"No." Caleb shook his head emphatically. "I'm not shooting at him."

The old Indian frowned and made a gesture toward both men before bringing his two hands together sharply in the middle.

"I think he wants you to fight him, Caleb."

"Why in the hell would I do that?" They *were* all crazy. *Dear God.* "Look, I don't know what you're about, but I'm not fighting someone for no reason."

"Think of it like a duel. Just... put him down quickly, without hurting him."

He looked down at Ernst. "Just whose side are you on? Besides, I'm not letting you go for anything. Lord only knows where they'd try to carry you off to."

The old man seemed to understand, and he gestured toward Ernst, then himself. The amusement had vanished from his dark eyes, and he clearly understood the gravity of what he was asking.

Caleb took a step back, squeezing Ernst until the little creature wriggled uncomfortably. "No one touches him."

The old Indian smiled gently, nodding his understanding, but looked to Ernst next, offering his hand to the jackalope instead.

"Caleb... air!" Ernst jabbed his partner with his antlers in an effort to breathe, and reluctantly, Caleb eased up.

"Can he hurt you, Ernst?" The arcane flames still crackled around his fist, and he kept his wary gaze on the old man.

"I don't think so. But their magic is not like ours. I can't feel it at all." Caleb couldn't feel it either, and it bothered him. There should have been something there, something to explain the subtle show of great power they'd been subjected to on the way there. "It's all right, Caleb. I don't think he'll let anything happen to me."

He didn't want to give Ernst over. The very thought made his stomach knot painfully, and he felt the beginnings of a cold sweat on his forehead. *He's not being taken away. He's just going to be safely out of harm's way.* Still, it took a few deep breaths before he could willingly hand his familiar over to a potential enemy.

The old man cradled the jackalope carefully in one arm, managing to scratch the animal's ears and still hold onto Caleb's staff at the same time. After a few moments, Ernst purred softly.

Though he felt like the skin was about to crawl off his back, Caleb withdrew his power, coiling it into the center of his chest again. The blue fire snuffed out. "I don't want to fight your man."

The old man never even looked at Caleb, but merely shuffled off to the side with Ernst, entranced with the charming little creature. His coyote remained where it was seated, watching the proceedings with a bored gaze.

The Indian brave said something to Caleb, and it wasn't hard to guess the sound of an insult. Caleb raised a brow. "I'm not fighting you. This is ridiculous."

The dark man smirked, saying something to his cronies. They hooted and whooped at Caleb, taunting him.

The Peacemaker held his ground, but took no hostile moves of his own. "I don't want this. I have no quarrel with any of you."

Perhaps the tall warrior had a quarrel with him.

Suddenly, the brave let out a wild whoop. He spun in a full circle, braids flying, and flung his hand at Caleb as if throwing a spear. There was no weapon present, but Caleb could see the shimmer as the narrow shaft of air hardened, crystallized, and came straight for him.

Only instinct and years of training saved him. "*Schild!*" It wasn't pretty without his staff to help him focus, and it shattered into a cloud of spent arcane motes on the first strike. But the air spear was likewise destroyed, a faint breeze stirring the clearing where it had been released.

A chorus of laughing catcalls echoed around the clearing, goading the brave on. He glowered, apparently not seeing the humor in the situation. Caleb didn't see it, either, and made a few emphatic negative gestures, hoping the other man would stop. He did not.

There was no warning cry this time. The brave dipped and bobbed in an odd little dance, then slammed his palm against the ground. Instantly, Caleb felt the vibration in the soles of his feet, and he dove to the side only a heartbeat before the ground beneath him exploded in a rain of dirt and rocks. Those spectators who also got showered with debris called disapprovingly to their tribesman.

It was a basic trick, one of the first any cadet at West Point learned. To churn the earth beneath an advancing army's cavalry, to destroy roads and train tracks, to fell trees across paths and funnel them into ambush, all started with the same source skill. But as Caleb reached for the traces of the arcane power that had to be used, he felt nothing. It was as if the ground had simply erupted of its own accord.

"Come on Caleb! Thump him one!" Ernst was the sole voice cheering for him, and he stared at the little creature in disbelief.

"Have you lost your—"

"Look out!"

Caleb's distraction almost cost him again. The tree

branch above, as big around as his waist, broke with a loud snap, plummeting downward. There was no way to dive free of the reaching limbs, and his shield would not hold against that much weight. With only a split second to decide, he shouted, "*Stoppe!*" and channeled through his upstretched palm.

Not a shield, this time, but a cradle made of energy, catching the limb in midair. The downward momentum was captured, reversed, the energy conserved as it held the tree branch up instead of dragging it down. It swayed there, barely two feet above his head, the thinnest of twigs trailing across the ground near the fire. Though he could have easily launched it some distance, he instead lowered it gently to the ground, mindful of the gathered crowd. Judging by the pallor of those closest to him, he could tell they understood what danger he'd just saved them from.

"That's enough! You're going to hurt someone!" The response was a hail of thorns, ripped from a nearby tree. "*Brand!*" They burst into flame in mid-flight, falling like tiny stars to the soil. Caleb brushed one tiny ember from the brim of his hat, straightening it. "All right. I've had enough of you."

Ernst was close enough to act as a channel, and Caleb opened up his awareness, reaching for the brave's power. He could siphon it off, feed it out through Ernst and away, squelching it against the nullstone deep beneath their feet.

Only there was nothing to grab. The brave simply wasn't there in any magical sense, and Caleb was left with a flailing metaphysical hand, grasping at empty air. And like any void left wanting, his power went seeking that which it lacked. It moved through the crowd, sweeping over man and woman, young and old, finding each and every one of them an empty void. If he hadn't known better, he would have said the entire village was barren.

The hole within him hurt. It hungered, aching for

that which it used to hold. Caleb's own power was stunted compared to its former prowess, but, oh, it remembered. Had there been more magic nearby to snatch, it would have, and what destruction he could have wrought then.

With a tremendous force of will, he wrestled it back in, closing the ravenous maw within his psyche, tying it down, muzzling it. His jaws ached as he ground his teeth together, and his fingernails had gouged bloody crescents into his palms.

The crowd was silent, and his opponent held a frozen fighting stance, hands poised to direct some new torment at Caleb. The dark gazes were wary now, not only from the braves but from the rest of the tribe as well. Somehow, despite the fact that they had no power he could sense, they knew what he'd tried to do.

Shame curled into his stomach, sick and churning. It was one thing to appropriate the energy of one person to prevent harm to others. It was quite another to go seeking it among innocents. Yes, he'd stopped and pulled back. But the fact remained that for that one brief moment in time, he'd lacked enough control to retreat.

Shame quickly turned to anger, both at himself and at the warrior who had forced him to this point. Caleb squared his shoulders. He would end this fight now. Blue flame crackled to life around both hands again.

The man across the clearing sensed the change in his opponent, and the fight was truly on.

A sharp gust of wind met a solid blast of force in the center of the clearing, almost blowing the large bonfire out. Even as the embers flickered and struggled to survive the onslaught, Caleb caught the wind, lit the tiny particles within it on fire, and shoved it back at its sender.

A waterskin hanging on a nearby teepee burst, becoming a thin sheet of moisture between the blast of flame and the Indian brave. It went up in a hiss of scalding steam, but the fire was doused.

Caleb drove his power down, into the ground, and a jagged furrow opened up as the blast powered its way toward the other man. The Indian jerked both hands skyward, and a wall of thick shale exploded from the ground in front of him, shattering into thin splinters as it took the brunt of Caleb's blow. Someone to the side cried out in pain as a sliver of rock found a home in unprotected flesh.

People were getting hurt, and Caleb had never wanted that. He pulled two large boulders from the already ravaged ground, firing one after the other like the cannonballs of the war. The brave ducked, and both rocks sheared off a tree some distance behind them, the ancient giant falling with a boom.

The Indian man threw one hand out toward the remnants of the large fire, and the flame answered, rising in one sinuous line like a great serpent, the head weaving back and forth menacingly. In the trees overhead, leaves and twigs popped softly, the sap in them boiling in an instant. The scent of burning foliage permeated the clearing. They had only moments before the entire forest ignited, tinder-dry as it was.

"No!" Horrified, Caleb watched the serpent, careful not to be entranced. Like the snake it resembled, fire could ensnare the mind, luring people to their deaths with false promises of safety if they would just remain still. The trick was not to look it in the eyes.

Regardless of where it originated, fire was pure energy, and this Caleb could grab. The hungry monster within him gleefully launched itself at the serpent of flame, gulping ravenously. He felt the searing heat of it as it entered his body, and the blue flames around his fists turned orange, singeing the hair of his forearms. The fire serpent hissed and writhed, coiling over and over itself in an effort to escape, but Caleb had a large gaping hole within himself. There was more than enough room to capture and hold it.

Dimly, he heard Ernst yelling for him to give it over, to bleed off the power that was never meant to be encased in a human form. Somewhere in the back of his mind, he knew he had to. Give it up, or burn with it. But, oh, it felt good, the heat coursing through his veins. Even with his eyes closed, he could see the world tinged in shades of red and gold and, at the very depths of his vision, the blue of hottest flame. If he let go, he could be part of it forever, his energy blended with the eternal energy of flame. He'd known, ever since Chicago, that this would be his fate.

Something struck him across the face, hard enough to jar his senses. When he opened his eyes, he found the ancient Indian standing before him, his hand drawn back to slap him again. Seeing that he had Caleb's attention, he shoved Ernst into the Peacemaker's arms, the antlers gouging him through his shirt. His blood steamed where it oozed from those scratches and others.

"Caleb, please give it to me. Please." Ernst sat up on his haunches, his quivering little nose nearly pressed to Caleb's. His voice echoed, taking on the crackling sound of a roaring fire. "You have to give it to me, or you'll burn. Please."

Yes. He'd seen men burn from within. Their fingers turned black, and their skin curled, flaking away as ash. Their fat bubbled, and they smelled like sizzling bacon. That was why he could never eat that particular food again. And to a man, they died with smiles on their faces, seduced by the very power that devoured them alive.

"Yes." His own voice was barely audible, the air in his lungs too hot for his vocal chords to handle. "Take it!" Inside, the fire roared its denial, and it scrabbled at him with searing claws, not wanting to relinquish a ready meal.

Through the heat, he could feel Ernst's forehead pressed against his, the antlers pricking painfully. The brown fur was blessedly cool to the touch, and it cleared away some of the heated delirium from Caleb's mind. The fire left him, kicking and screaming, but drawn inexorably out nonetheless. That tremendous power funneled through the tiny form that was Ernst and away into wherever a familiar put such things.

Caleb was left cold and sweating, hugging the furry form close to his chest. There was no need for him to say thanks, unless it was to the Almighty for sending him Ernst in the first place. He would be so lost without him.

Someone touched his shoulder, and he looked to find the old Indian peering intently into his eyes. After a long moment, the ancient one nodded firmly. *"Epeva'e."* Whatever it meant, he was obviously finished with Caleb. He handed the staff back.

Turning from the Peacemaker and his familiar, the old man hummed tunelessly as he gestured with his hands over the shattered earth and rocks left from the duel. His motions were oddly graceful, and before Caleb's astonished eyes, the broken soil folded in on itself, the jagged rocks sinking back to their appropriate depths, until one could never tell that anything at all had happened here. The charred leaves fluttered down from their abused twigs, fresh new buds unfurling as all watched. The fallen tree branch took a bit longer, decaying before his eyes to become a part of the loam and normal forest detritus. All that remained was a noticeable lump on the ground, vaguely the length and width of the branch.

Finished with his work, the old man—a shaman, thought Caleb—ceased his song, and the coyote familiar trotted over to resume its place by his side. The ancient one looked to Caleb once more, touching his arm gently with a gnarled hand, then pointed toward the tree line.

"You… want me to go?"

The old man nodded happily when Caleb mimicked his pointing. He rambled off a cheerful string of syllables, all the while gesturing with his hands in between patting Caleb's shoulder.

"Ernst?"

"You'd rather stay here?"

"Point taken." Still having very little idea what exactly had happened this night, Caleb walked slowly through the village, toward the dark forest. Though he kept expecting to feel an arrow between his shoulder blades, no one moved to stop him. No one even made a sound.

He raised his foot, stepping from the village's cleared circle into the brush and bracken of the wood, and the moment his boot touched the earth again, the village was gone. The light and warmth vanished as if they'd never been, and Caleb found himself alone with Ernst in the timber. The moon had set hours ago, leaving them in impenetrable darkness.

"Great. Where the hell are we, Ernst?"

"I'm not sure." The jackalope sat erect on Caleb's arm, peering about the darkness. "I think... Is that your transport over there?"

Sure enough, the dim blue glow resolved itself into the swirling casing windows on Sven Isby's rented hauler. Caleb had never been so glad to see a piece of machinery in all his life. Even better was the realization that he could clearly see the trail he'd ridden in on and that he knew his way home from here. "Next time I decide to walk into Indian territory alone, knock me in the head with something."

"Deal."

10

The long ride back to Hope on the hauler only served to emphasize every scrape, gouge, bruise, and burn Caleb had received over the length of his long, strange night. He hurt in places he hadn't known he had, and the only thing worse than riding the transport would be getting off and lying down for the night, when he'd stiffen up.

Of course, if it weren't for the injuries, he might have convinced himself that he'd suffered some surreal hallucination or bizarre dream. He was still at a loss to see what his visit to the Cheyenne village had accomplished. What had the old shaman wanted with him?

He had no doubts that had the old man wanted, he could have erased Caleb from the face of the earth. The ancient shaman Wind Walker had decimated the U.S. Army and thirty Peacemakers. One half-scoured man would prove no obstacle to someone of that power. And the old man *was* powerful. He'd healed the land in the less time than it would take Caleb to think of the proper words to say, not to mention that Caleb never had that kind of finesse. Brute force required less skill than delicate work.

"You're very quiet." Ernst was curled in front of him in the saddle this time, instead of taking his usual perch behind. His solid weight, no matter how slight, was comforting.

"I don't have a lot to say just now."

"What are you going to do about the mine?"

Caleb shrugged, and his muscles protested the

unnecessary movement. "Nothing I really can do. I could arrest Schmidt and those miners for violating Indian territory and technically breaking the peace treaties, but no court would convict them. And other than that, I don't know that they're doing anything wrong."

"You don't think they destroyed that village to clear the way for another mine?" Ernst looked up, his brown eyes shining in the dark.

"Oh, I'm certain they did. But I can't prove it, and no one back east is going to grieve for a few more dead Cheyenne." Caleb sighed, but it was a sad truth of the world.

"And the children? If Warner's stockpiling nullstone at his place, it's very likely that he's caused all those children irreparable harm."

"I need proof, Ernst. And I can't take on Warner and his thugs alone." He ran a hand over his face, feeling the sting of a few forgotten scratches in the stubble on his cheeks. "What I need is an independent medical opinion, some parents willing to let their children be examined, and a few more Peacemakers to do a search of the ranch."

The jackalope nuzzled his hand. "What you need is a few hours' sleep. In the morning, we'll send a telegram for reinforcements."

"That's the best plan I've heard all night, Ernst." He smiled, scratching his familiar's long silky ears.

The sight of Hope rising out of the prairie was one of the most welcome things Caleb had seen during the long day and night. The little outpost was dark, and even the dogs were asleep as he rode in. The sun would rise in a couple of hours, and Caleb knew he had to get what little sleep he could. First light would bring its own set of new problems.

He hoped against hope that Teddy hadn't locked the tavern door, or he'd wind up sleeping in one of the rickety chairs on the sidewalk.

Ernst rose up, paws balanced on the saddle's horn as he peered into the night. "Caleb? The light is on in the general store."

"Maybe Hector's an early riser." His stomach growled loudly, reminding him that he'd given every bite of his food away. "Maybe he has some breakfast." With a twitch of the reins, they changed course and headed toward the general store.

Before they'd gone more than ten yards, the silence of the predawn morning was shattered as the doors to the store crashed open, glass tinkling as it scattered over the wooden sidewalk. Three men bolted into the street, dashing around the corner of the building before Caleb could identify them. A fourth man walked calmly through the broken glass, pausing to glance toward the stunned Peacemaker for a moment before following his cohorts. There was no mistaking Schmidt's slight build, or cold-as-ice demeanor, even from a distance.

Caleb kicked the hauler into higher gear, but four sleek transports galloped out of the alleyway and toward the prairie before he could even think of getting close. There was no way his ungainly mount would catch them. Instead, he slid out of the saddle before the machine had even fully halted, his boots crunching glass underfoot as he headed inside. "Hector? Hector, are you here?"

Flour was strewn about the floor like a layer of fine snow, marred with boot prints and the tracks of canned goods that had rolled across it. One set of shelves had toppled over, the contents lying in a heap where it had fallen. The pungent smell of pickle brine permeated the room, and shards of glass jars crunched underfoot as Caleb stepped inside. Somewhere behind the counter, molasses was dripping forlornly, the wet splat keeping time as regular as any clock.

Unsure whether he could channel a spark, let alone any respectable show of force, Caleb drew his pistol out of the holster instead and cocked it. "Be ready, Ernst."

The little jackalope cautiously picked his way through the debris, his nose quivering so fast it was almost a blur. "I can't smell anything over the damned pickles."

"Use your ears then." Caleb himself strained for any sound, but all he could hear was the steady drip-drip of the broken molasses cask and the thudding of his own heart in his ears. A floorboard creaked underfoot, and they both froze for a long, tense moment.

Just when he had decided to take the next step, Caleb heard a soft noise that might have been missed in the rustle of his clothing had he been moving. It could have been the low bleat of a calf, far distant and barely audible, but it came again almost immediately. A man moaning.

Ernst's ears pricked straight up. "Behind the counter."

The first thing Caleb saw was two long gangly legs sticking out from behind the counter, the dark pants covered in flour and whatever else had spilled all over the floor.

"Dear God, Hector!" Quickly, Caleb scrambled to reach him.

The shopkeeper's face was almost unrecognizable, as bruised and swollen as it was. Both eyes were caked shut with dried blood, and his lips were split and purple, the spittle and other fluids serving to stick his face to the wooden floor. He was breathing, which was a good sign, but the raspy rattle in his lungs spoke of blood there, possibly from broken ribs. As Caleb knelt over him, Hector moaned again, so softly.

"Ernst, fetch the doc!" The familiar was gone before he'd finished the sentence. "Easy, Hector. I'm here. The doc's coming. Just hang on."

The four thugs had beaten the man badly. Caleb could see the imprints of boots on his forehead where he'd been savagely kicked. His hands were bloodied and scraped, with at least two fingers bent at wrong angles. Who knew what other injuries were internal, hidden by his clothes? The Peacemaker didn't dare try to move him without knowing.

Hector moaned again, louder, as consciousness started to return. "Shh, help is coming, Hector." The older man stirred feebly, trying to fend off attackers long fled. Caleb did his best to press the shopkeeper's hands down gently, trying to avoid the broken fingers. "Don't try to move. You're safe. I'm here. It's Agent Marcus. I won't let anything happen to you."

More boots thumped on the wooden planks outside, and Caleb leveled his pistol at the door just as Teddy came bursting through the opening. The bartender immediately dropped to the floor with a startled yell, and Caleb pulled his shot, sending a round into the ceiling. "Sweet mother Mary, Agent Marcus!"

"Sorry, Teddy, wasn't expecting friends." Caleb stuffed his pistol in its holster before something else could go wrong. "It was Warner's men. Did you see them?"

"Me? No. But we were looking for you."

"We?" The Peacemaker fished a handkerchief from his pocket to try to staunch some of the blood flow, but there was only so much the tiny scrap of cloth could do.

"I'm here, Agent Marcus." It was Miss Sinclair's voice, with a faint quaver behind it. "I saw them. I saw all of them, and I ran to find you, but you weren't at the saloon…"

"No… no, I wasn't." *Dammit. Damn them all to hell.* If he'd just been there… "Did they see you, Ellen? Do they know you saw them?"

She nodded. "Schmidt looked right at me out the window. I don't know about the others. I ran."

"You did the right thing. Here, come help me hold this bandage down." As she came to kneel beside him, Caleb pressed her hand down over the sodden handkerchief. "I'll be right back."

Outside, the night was still. The yellow lights from inside the store vied with the blue glow of his hauler, but other than that, the town slept on, oblivious to the violence done in their midst. And the perpetrators were long gone.

Time dragged on with excruciating slowness as they waited for the doctor to arrive. Teddy took his turn packing Hector's wounds with whatever they could find while Ellen shredded her petticoat to aid in the bandaging, but even that wasn't going to be enough. Several times, Hector tried to speak or sit up, but his words were garbled at best and his body simply wouldn't follow his commands any longer. Every time he lapsed into silence again, Caleb nervously counted the seconds between labored breaths, fearful that each one would be the last.

Just when he was about to go looking for the doctor himself, the bell above the door jangle. It was the sweetest sound Caleb had heard yet. "Agent Marcus? Hector?"

"Behind the counter, Dr. Elm!" As the good doctor bustled around the counter, Caleb stood to get out of the way and helped Ellen to her feet.

"Oh, Lord." He was still dressed in his nightshirt, but had thrown pants on inside out for the hasty trip across town. He set his black bag on the floor, immediately examining the beaten shopkeeper. "Ernst, are you here?"

The jackalope blinked into existence atop the counter. "I'm here, Doctor."

"I may need your aid, little friend, once we get Mr. Pratt moved to his bed." The doctor's hands moved efficiently over Hector's injuries, eliciting small moans of pain when he found something else that had been abused. "Did you see who did this, Agent Marcus?" Though the doctor's voice remained calm, Caleb could hear the suppressed anger there.

Caleb glanced toward Ellen, noting the pallor of her face beneath the blood smudged on her cheek. When she opened her mouth to answer, he shook his head, and she remained silent. "Not a good look, sir. They fled as I arrived." The fewer people who knew about what Ellen had witnessed, the better.

"Thank the Lord that you happened by when you did. He's been severely beaten." He spared one glance at the standing Peacemaker. "But of course you could see that. See if you can find a plank of some kind, something we can put him on so we don't jostle the broken ribs when we move him."

"Yes, sir." Hector didn't keep a lot of lumber in the store, but inspection revealed a broken shelf half hanging off the wall that might fit the bill. Caleb wrenched it free of its nails, motioning for Teddy to take up the other end.

"Will this do, doctor?" The shelf would apparently serve quite well, and with the doctor's instructions, he and Teddy managed to get Hector's lanky frame rolled over onto it.

"If you gentlemen could carry him up to his room with a minimum of jostling, I have to fetch a few more things from my office. I'll return shortly. Miss Sinclair, get him settled into his bed and find some washbasins and fresh water." The doctor bustled out, and Caleb and Teddy struggled mightily to get the shopkeeper up to the stairs without causing him more injury.

On the downhill side of the maneuver, Caleb struggled to keep the plank level, holding it nearly at chin level, with his shoulder propped under it for support. There was a great deal of grunting on Teddy's end, too. Hector was not a small man by any means, and his very height made things difficult.

Halfway up the stairs, Caleb paused to change his grip, the wooden shelf grinding splinters into his palm. Quickly, he grabbed a large one with his teeth, yanking it out and spitting it aside. Blood welled in his hand, dark and shimmering red. *Stretcher bearer! I need a stretcher bearer here!"*

"What did you say?" Caleb tried to look over the precariously balanced plank to see Teddy, but all he could make out was the top of the Scot's head as he shook it to the negative. "I dinnae say anythin'."

"Fall back! They're coming over the ridge!" Before Caleb's eyes, a battle scene bloomed. Through the smoke and the haze, stretcher bearers in Union blue uniforms dodged cannon fire and arcane blasts as they tried to get the dead and wounded off the field of battle. He could hear the whistle of the incoming artillery, smelled the sulfur and ozone stench of the augmented gunpowder, and for a brief moment, he was there again, deaf to all but the boom of the cannons and the screams of dying men.

"Agent Marcus!" Pale hands tugged at his sleeves, poked and prodded him. "Agent Marcus, you're going to drop him!" Ellen Sinclair threw her shoulder against the plank as it started to slide from his fingers, bracing it as best she could. "Agent Marcus! Ernst, help me!"

Something sharp stabbed into his calf, startling him out of the visions of battles past. Looking down, he found his familiar looking back up at him, Ernt's vicious teeth sunk through the fabric of Caleb's pants. The jackalope shrugged, mumbling something that sounded like "It was all I could think of" through a mouthful of cloth.

"I got it. Here…" He muscled his way under the slipping plank, gently nudging the schoolteacher aside. "I'm all right. I have him."

"Ye got it, Agent?"

"I got it," he repeated. "Quickly, Teddy." Before another flashback caught him. He could feel blood trickling down his leg where Ernst bit him. The little creature hadn't been teasing.

Together, he and Teddy got Hector carefully deposited on his narrow bed. The shopkeeper didn't make a sound as they transferred him from the makeshift stretcher to his blankets, and that silence worried Caleb more than any amount of pained moaning would have. There was a sickly tint to the old man's face that Caleb had seen before, in the pallor of so many soldiers—wearing both gray and blue—and it rarely ended well.

Even that brief thought brought the walls closing in, and the summer's oppressive heat seemed cool compared to the stifling oven that was Hector's small room above the store. The moment the doctor returned, Caleb escaped outside and stood on the wooden walk, gulping fresh air. He gripped the railing until his knuckles were white and throbbing.

Ernst appeared, balancing his furry little form on the rail no wider than two of Caleb's fingers. He said nothing, but pressed himself against the Peacemaker's arm, purring softly.

The townsfolk came out of the dark, most still wearing their nightclothes, asking horrified questions as they entered the store. Word traveled fast in a small town, even in the dead of night. None of them seemed to pay Caleb much mind, concerned as they were for Hector's well-being. Someone quickly organized a cleanup of the store, and several women returned to their homes to begin making breakfast for all involved.

His eyes fixed firmly on the ground, Caleb saw them come and go by only the hems of their dresses. The dry, dusty Kansas soil seemed a safe place to let his gaze linger. Surely that wouldn't conjure visions of the war and the horrors he'd seen. "When's it going to end, Ernst?"

The familiar only increased the volume of his purr. Perhaps he didn't have an answer, either.

"Hsst!"

The sound came twice more before Caleb looked up, frowning as he tried to locate the peculiar noise.

"Hsst! Agent Marcus!" Across the street, between the barbershop and the dressmaker's, Jimmy Welton's dirty face poked out of the shadows long enough for the boy to wave frantically, then disappeared.

Glancing around, Caleb stepped off the walk and crossed the street, ducking into the dark alley himself. Ernst followed closely behind with the odd little hop-walk of all rabbits. "Jimmy?"

"Shhh!" The boy popped up from behind a barrel, his eyes darting furtively about. "Don't want nobody ta know I'm here."

"And why is that?"

The boy just motioned for him to follow further down the alley. "C'mon. Got somethin' ta show you."

"Jimmy, this isn't really a good time…"

The kid stopped, looking back with as serious a face as Caleb had ever seen on a grown man, let alone a boy of twelve. "It's important."

The Peacemaker and his familiar followed along without protest after that.

The boy led them all the way to the smithy, where the banked forge glowed faintly in the predawn darkness. He motioned for Caleb to wait and slipped inside for a few moments.

Caleb let his gaze wander over the town. There were more lights on in the houses now as people began to stir, no doubt learning shortly of the attack on one of their own.

"Mr. Isby's asleep, but he'll be up soon, so I gotta make this quick." Jimmy returned, ghosting through the darkness as silent as a cat. It was eerie. He took a seat on a nearby barrel, his heels banging softly against it. "I saw them."

"You saw who?"

"The fellas that roughed up Mr. Pratt." He nodded, a lock of hair falling into his eyes. "I went out ta check my snares, see if I caught any rabbits." He glanced at Ernst. "No offense. An' I was on my way back to the saloon when

I hear this ruckus at the general store. So I go ta peek in the window. And those four fellas were beatin' the holy tar outta him."

"What fellas, Jimmy? Do you know them?"

The kid nodded quickly. "Oh, yeah, they was all Warner's boys. And Schmidt, he was there. Only he didn't do none o' the beatin'. He just stood and watched with them funny eyes."

"Did they say why?"

He shrugged. "They was askin' him about telegrams he'd sent for you. Wanted ta know what was in 'em. By the time I got there, he wasn' sayin' much anymore. Dunno what he said before that. Then they broke the telegraph into about a million pieces. That's when I heard someone else coming, and I lit out." That someone else almost certainly had to be the schoolteacher.

Caleb frowned. Warner thought he knew something, and didn't want word getting out. But word of what? An illegal nullstone mine? It made no sense. "Did they see you?"

Jimmy snorted in disdain. "'Course not. I don't get seen if I don't wanna."

That much was a relief, at least. "Have you told anyone else what you saw?"

"Naw, I was waitin' for you ta come back. Knew you'd wanna know."

"You did a good job. Thank you." Caleb squeezed his shoulder lightly. But damn if they didn't solve one piece of the puzzle to unearth about seventeen more. What the hell was going on?

"Hey, I'm not done yet!" Hopping off the barrel, Jimmy tugged Caleb toward the forge. "After they was done with Mr. Pratt, they said they was gonna go toss yer room. An' I knew you wasn' home yet, so I skedaddled back real quick, and I took yer trunk."

Under a pile of kiln bricks in the corner, Jimmy

unearthed Caleb's Peacemaker trunk, the locking sigils still glowing faintly. "I didn't figure they should have it, even if they couldn't get it open."

Caleb knelt to inspect the box, just to be sure, but it seemed intact and unharmed. He sent a silent prayer of thanks to the Lord for putting Jimmy Welton in the right place at the right time. Those weapons in Abel Warner's hands... the very thought made him ill. "You did the right thing, Jimmy. Thank you."

The boy beamed. "You can leave it here, if you like. Mr. Isby, he don't look in this corner none; he'll never know it's here."

"That might actually be a good idea. And while we're on the subject of hiding things, we need to get you under cover."

Jimmy blinked. "Me? Why?"

"You're a witness, Jimmy. And if those men find out that you can name them, you think they won't come after you? They beat an old man almost to death, I don't think they'll balk at hurting a kid."

Though the boy went pale, he stuck his jaw out stubbornly. "I ain't scared."

"Good. Because I won't let anything happen to you. But still, I think you're going to stay with Miss Sinclair for a few days and stay out of sight." With any luck, that would keep both his witnesses safely occupied.

"Nuh-uh! She'll make me take a bath!" Clearly, the horror of bathing far outweighed the possibility of being tracked down by murderous thugs.

"You could stand a good bath." Ernst sniffed the air primly, and the boy actually blushed.

"And what am I gonna do, stuck inside all day? She'll make me learn ta knit or somethin'!"

"You can use the time for extra tutoring." His hand on the boy's shoulder, Caleb steered him back toward the general store. "You're too important to risk, Jimmy. I hope you realize how much I'm going to need you in the next few weeks."

"What do I gotta do?"

"When the time comes, I need you to stand up in front of a bunch of people and tell them what you saw. Think you can do that?"

The kid thought about it for a few moments. "Yeah. I can do that."

"I knew you could."

11

Keeping an eye on the schoolteacher was easy. She was still helping Dr. Elm with Hector when Caleb and Jimmy got back to the store. Caleb put Jimmy on a stool in an out-of-the-way corner with firm orders to stay—and left Ernst to keep an eye on him—and climbed the stairs again, navigating around people bustling to and fro on errands for the doctor or just trying to be nosy.

Actually getting her alone proved to be a bit more difficult. Hector's room was more crowded than was healthy, and Caleb arrived in time to see Ellen evict everyone with a no-nonsense glare and more than a few terse words. Obviously, she had recovered some of her nerve. Caleb pressed against the wall to avoid being trampled until he was the only one left, and then she fixed her glare on him, too.

"He's the same as he was, and you can't do anything, so out!"

"I actually came to talk to you, if you have a moment."

Wiping her hands on her apron—and when had that appeared?—she stepped out of the room onto the top step. "Will it take long? I'm still helping Dr. Elm with the stitching."

Caleb sighed, running a hand over his face. "I… It might. When you're done, then? I'll wait downstairs."

She smiled, though it was obviously forced. Bless the girl, she was trying. "Of course. You should get some coffee, Agent Marcus. You look dead on your feet.”

He felt dead on his feet, now that she mentioned it. He couldn't remember the last meal he'd had, let alone sleep.

Still instructing Jimmy to stay inside the store, Caleb found a chair and dragged it to the walk outside. He found a safe nook and sat, leaning the chair back on two legs and tugging his hat down over his eyes. With the entire town coming and going, it was surely safe to rest his eyes for just a moment.

The sunrise was beautiful, in shades of pale pink and a hint of the night's lingering violet. “Red sun at morning, sailors take warning.” There was no red sun, though. No rain on the horizon. Just another day dawning hot and dry.

He wasn't even aware that he was dreaming until the Indian woman walked out of the doorway next to him, glancing about the town curiously. Her boots passed over the broken glass on the sidewalk without disturbing a single shard, and then all sound faded away, leaving the two of them alone in the morning's first light.

“You again?”

She gave him a smile, pointing toward the mountains.

“No, not this time. I don't know how you're doing this, but you either tell me what you want, or go away and leave me in peace.”

She pointed again, her smile fading into an insistent frown.

Caleb stood, and the chair beneath him vanished as if it had never been there. “No. I've had enough of your folk for the time being. Lacking in hospitality, I must say.”

A look of frustration crossed her lovely face, and she seemed to be debating something. Finally, she held her hand out to him, asking him with a pleading look to take it.

“You're not going to leave me alone, are you?

Every time I close my eyes, you're going to come walking into my dreams until I do what you want."

She stepped closer, offering both hands now, silently begging him to take them.

With a resigned sigh, Caleb placed his hands in hers.

They were in the mountains; that much was clear. Taking his hand, she led him down a rocky path that meandered aimlessly through the tall trees. She had no regard for the darkness of the night, save to smile each time she heard a night bird call.

As the trail headed steadily upward, Caleb climbed beside her, realizing belatedly that all his aches and pains had faded. He felt like he could climb the entire mountain, and the one beyond that as well. She tugged at his hand as he lagged behind in his reverie, and he walked faster to catch up.

"Where are you taking me?" She didn't answer, which was no more than he'd expected. "What is so important?"

She turned and pressed a finger to her lips, imploring him to be silent, and walked on.

It felt like they walked for hours, wending their way up the mountain, climbing through rocky crags and twisted gnarled pines by the end. Caleb could tell they were nearing their destination, because she motioned for him to stay and crept ahead, disappearing from view for some time.

When she returned, she again motioned for him to be silent, her grim face telling him how serious this was. Then she led him forward.

They crouched at the top of a rocky outcropping looking down into a vast chasm in the mountainside. A few hardy bushes clung to the steep sides, but for the most part it was a graveyard of fallen, shattered boulders, a river of jagged stone flowing through a deep canyon.

Nothing stirred. No birds flew overhead; no agile mountain goats braved the peaks. It was deathly still.

The woman reached a hand out, passing it lightly over Caleb's scarred eye. The touch was gentle, almost a lover's caress, and when she was done, she pointed again into the rocky abyss.

A giant slumbered there. He had not been there only moments before, but he was there now. Made of the same rock as the chasm itself, the behemoth slumbered at the bottom of the canyon, cradled as tenderly as any child. His face was formed of chiseled boulders, hard planes of granite and shale. The full moon caught crystals of quartz on his surface, and he sparkled. His craggy hands could have crushed an entire house with little effort, and the entire mountain vibrated with the force of his breathing.

Sleepily, the massive creature shifted its shoulders, barely moving at all, and farther down the mountain, a rocky avalanche crushed all that lay before it.

Oh, how Caleb wanted to ask her what the giant was, but he suddenly understood the danger. God forbid that thing should wake and find them there.

The woman rested her hand on his arm, her eyes asking if he'd seen enough. He nodded, and they were suddenly gone from that place, returned to the thick of the forest.

"What the hell was that thing?"

Once again, she did not answer, but motioned him to follow. Their trek this time was faster, and she stopped them in a thicket of dense foliage. Pushing one branch aside, she pointed ahead.

This time, Caleb knew just where he was. They looked down on the nullstone mine, and he could even see the small rise where he'd watched them the night before. There was no one visible, but the sounds of picks on stone were loud in this strange dream stillness, sharp enough to hurt his ears and make his teeth ache in his head. Ghostly miners, going about their tasks unseen.

Tink-tink-TINK! On and on it went, even when he pressed his hands over his ears. Tink-tink-TINK! TINK-TINK-TINK!

He felt it before he heard it, rising up through the soles of his feet, shuddering through his hips into his chest, where his heart went cold with a deep primal terror. And when the roar reached them, the trees themselves bent nearly double in fear. The great rock giant was bellowing in pain.

High above them, near the cloud-covered peak, the mountain was moving. Great sheets of shale and granite were shifting, sliding, gathering momentum as they plunged down.

"We have to run! Go, go!" He tugged at his companion, urging her to run, but she only looked at him with sad eyes. And he knew there was nowhere they could hide. "What do we do? We have to do something!"

The sharp sting on his face brought him awake with a startled yell, and he grabbed at the delicate wrist before he realized who it belonged to. Ellen Sinclair froze, eyes wide, the alcohol-soaked cloth in her hand poised just in front of his face. The people standing on the sidewalk all stared at him, and more were peering from inside the store, their attention drawn by his wild shout.

His heart gradually resumed a normal pace as he realized that there were no great waves of rock about to come crashing down on his head. Belatedly, he released his bruising grip on Ellen's wrist, mumbling an apology.

"Nonsense." As if he'd never moved, she leaned close again, dabbing at his face with the pungent swab. "I wanted to see to these scratches on your face, but you were sleeping so deeply…"

The colors of sunrise were gone, replaced by the harsh and glaring light of day. "How long did I sleep?"

"Not more than an hour." The cuts stung despite her

efforts to be gentle, but he didn't say a word. He'd nearly forgotten they were there. She paused at his scar, looking at it thoughtfully. "Does it impair your vision any?"

"No."

She made a noise of professional interest. "You were lucky, then."

He could have debated that with her, but let it pass. "Do you have time to talk now? Privately?"

She raised a curious brow, but nodded. "I suppose so."

Reaching his limit for being coddled, Caleb gently pushed her hands away and stood. "The saloon, then? Bring Teddy, too."

Inside the store, the destruction had largely been cleared up. Perhaps everything wasn't as neat and tidy as Hector might have liked it, but the volunteers had made great headway. Jimmy was still sitting on his stool in the back corner, eyeing a jar of peppermints thoughtfully. Caleb guessed they had about another five minutes before the boy grew bored enough to start pocketing the sweets.

"Jimmy! Ernst! March!" Every adult in the place flinched at his sharp commands, but both the boy and the familiar hopped to without protest. More than one person watched in amazement as the town hooligan obediently fell into line behind the Peacemaker.

At the doorway, Caleb hesitated and looked to the boy at his heel. "We're going to the tavern. Quickly, with no stops. And if I tell you to run, you move like your rump is on fire, and you don't look back, understand?"

Jimmy's eyes went wide. "You really think I'll need ta?"

Caleb shrugged, clapping him on the shoulder. "Consider it good practice, just in case."

Truthfully, he didn't believe that Warner's men would be back for witnesses. Not yet. But despite the fact that he'd ordered Jimmy to stay silent, secrets had a way of getting around in a small town. Schmidt already knew about Ellen Sinclair, and it was only a matter of time before they found out about Jimmy. There was no way they could leave two people behind who might testify.

He kept his hand on Jimmy's shoulder as they walked down the street, Ernst hopping escort on the other side. He could feel the boy's breath coming fast, see the pulse thudding in his neck. The kid was scared to death, and yet he kept walking calmly, even calling hellos to a few people who greeted them.

The tavern was one hundred paces away. Sixty. Thirty. Ten. And then they were inside, the doors flapping behind them. Caleb grinned down at Jimmy. "See? That wasn't so bad."

Teddy and Ellen were waiting already, and the bartender set a sarsaparilla out for Jimmy, and lemonade for Caleb when he refused a stiffer drink. "It's morning, Teddy, good Lord."

"After the night ye've had, I thought ye might deserve it."

Ernst flopped down on the bar with an exhausted whuff of breath, lapping at the whiskey Caleb had turned down.

The lemonade tasted better than any liquor he could remember, and he realized how truly parched he'd been. He drained the glass in a few long gulps, and Teddy filled it up again.

"What did you want to speak about, Agent Marcus?" Ellen had managed to freshen up, her hair tidied and dirty apron discarded. It was hard to tell she'd been awake most of the night, as well, but she clasped her hands together so tightly her knuckles were white.

Caleb turned his glass in his hands, watching the beads of sweat run down over his fingers. "You witnessed something terrible last night, Miss Sinclair, but you weren't the only one."

Jimmy clambered up on the stool beside him, and Caleb ruffled his hair.

"Oh, no… Jimmy?" Ellen covered her mouth in dismay. "Did they see you?"

The boy shook his head. "No, Miss Sinclair. I was real careful."

Teddy frowned. "They saw Ellen. They'll come back for her."

Caleb nodded his agreement. "Or worse, they'll have Schmidt deal with it from afar. That's why I want Ellen and Jimmy both to stay in this building, away from the windows, until I get back."

"Back?"

"Just where are you going?"

Ernst looked up as well, whiskey dripping from his whiskers, and Caleb reached out to stroke his soft fur.

"They destroyed Hector's telegraph. I can't try to arrest four men on my own. I need some reinforcements. So I'm going to ride back to Tasco to wire the Kansas City office."

"Tasco's a five-day ride!"

"I know. But it's the nearest telegraph office. I don't know enough about the system to try and tap into the lines directly from here, and without Hector's help we're out of choices."

Though Ellen looked like she might continue her protests, Teddy was a more practical man. After a moment's thought, he pulled a pack out from behind the bar and started stuffing food into it. "I dinnae have much fresh, but the bread should last a few days, and if ye can shoot a rabbit or two on the way, ye should do fine. I'll get yer canteen filled up with water, too."

Jimmy finally piped up, the words bursting out of him before any of the adults could silence him. "I could come with you! I'm light! You wouldn't even notice me on a hauler like that. And you could keep me safe that way."

Caleb smiled and mussed his already tousled hair. "You're safer here where you know the territory. You know all the good hiding places."

He was hardly mollified and grumbled to himself as he went back to his sarsaparilla.

Ellen was harder to fool. "They beat Hector because of telegrams you sent? What was in them?"

Caleb shook his head. "It wasn't what was in them. It's what they *thought* was in them. And I have no idea what that was. Warner thinks I've found something damaging, perhaps."

"And have you?" She fixed him with narrowed eyes.

"Now, Ellen… perhaps we shouldnae be askin' about things we've no concern in," Teddy cautioned, but he too cast a curious glance at the Peacemaker, hoping for an answer.

"I'm… not sure." Caleb thumped his hat against his thigh before putting it back on. "Do either of you know anything about the nullstone in the mountains?"

Ellen shook her head. "Everyone knows it's there. They say that's why the children here are barren."

"But no one tries to mine it?"

"Why would anyone want to do that? Who would buy it?"

"I've been wondering the same thing myself." He chewed his lip in thought. "It makes no sense."

Ellen stood up from her stool. "That's what you found? Warner is mining nullstone? Dear God, if he's storing it on that ranch, the danger he's posing to those children is…" Her mouth worked silently for a few moments, at a loss for words. "You have to do something! We have to tell the parents; they have to stop their children from going out there!"

For a moment, Caleb thought she was going to

march out the door and do it right then. "No! A few more days won't hurt anything, and if you confront him, he's likely to have you laid out right next to Hector."

Teddy came out from behind the bar, resting his hands on Ellen's shoulders. "Agent Marcus is right, Miss Ellen. And I dinnae wish ta see anythin' happen ta ye."

"So we're expected to simply hide away while he gets away with… whatever it is he's doing?" Color flared high in her cheeks, and her brown eyes flashed angrily.

"That's exactly what I'm asking you to do. Warner's sitting out there with his own personal army, and until I can get back here with more men, he can do whatever the hell he wants. Pardon my language. Keep your eyes and ears open. Learn anything you can that will help me tie Warner to the men who attacked Hector. More than anything, stay out of sight. Right now, I have nothing on him, even if we all know he ordered it. All I have is you and Jimmy."

He glanced toward Jimmy, who was doing a poor job of pretending not to pay attention. "And see if Jimmy and Mr. Isby can fix the telegraph. I'm willing to bet, between the two of them, they can rig something up."

The boy perked up. "I can do that! You just wait and see. When you get ta Tasco, we'll have a message there waitin' for you!"

"Agent Marcus?" Everyone in the room jumped at the sound of the strange voice, relaxing only when they realized it was Dr. Elm looking in over the half door. "Hector is conscious at times, and he's asking for you. At least, I think that's what he's asking. You might want to come see him."

"I'll be right there, Doctor. Thank you." Teddy handed him the bundle of food and a dripping canteen. Caleb nodded his thanks and fixed Jimmy with a stern glare. "I mean it. Stay out of sight and away from the windows. Be good for Miss Sinclair and Mr. MacGregor, all right?"

"Yessir."

"Come on, Ernst." The jackalope abandoned his dish of whiskey with a forlorn sigh and hopped after Caleb.

Though the crowd had largely dispersed from Hector's store, people were making a point to wander by and peer in the windows. Caleb's arrival elicited a round of excited whispers, but no one stopped him to speak.

One of the townsfolk—a Mr. Granger, Caleb thought—sat in Hector's usual seat behind the counter and nodded to both the Peacemaker and Dr. Elm as they walked through.

Hector looked worse, if possible, than when Caleb had discovered him. The cuts on his face had been stitched up, the black threads sticking up like brush bristles. His bruises were a deeper purple than before, and his eyes and nose were swollen so badly they were hardly recognizable as a face at all. His mouth hung open so that he could breathe shallowly, and the raspy wheeze was loudly ominous in the small room. Always gangly, he looked positively skeletal now.

Caleb slid onto the chair next to the bed, barely touching the shopkeeper's shoulder, afraid to hurt him even more. Ernst hopped up on the other side, carefully nuzzling the man's cheek. "Hector? It's Agent Marcus."

Hector's breathing went on uninterrupted for a long moment. Perhaps he had lost consciousness again? Finally, he stirred ever so slightly, turning his head in the vague direction of Caleb's voice. "Agent Marcus?" The words were garbled, and Caleb had to lean close to hear.

"Yes, Hector. You shouldn't be trying to talk; you should rest." The old man mumbled something unintelligible, and Caleb tried to pat his less injured hand soothingly. "Hush. It's all right."

Hector shook his head, his swollen brow creasing as he tried to convey something. "Sorry... told them...

telegram…"

"There was nothing in that telegram that was worth your life, Hector. You did nothing wrong." Lord, was this what was bothering the poor man? "Rest now. Listen to the doctor."

He started to stand, and Hector grabbed for his arm, holding him tightly despite his mangled fingers. "C… codes! Didn't… tell them… codes…" His hand dropped, his strength exhausted.

"Oh, Hector," Caleb murmured. In his line of work, it wasn't often that he found truly good men. But this one had almost died to protect a near stranger's secrets. "I'll get them for you. I promise I will."

Hector didn't answer, his labored breathing the only indication that he still lived.

Caleb put his hat back on and met Dr. Elm at the door. "Is he going to make it?"

The doctor sighed, shaking his head slowly. "It's hard to say. There are internal injuries I can't even guess at. He could be bleeding into his brain right now, and I'd never know it. Sadly, my power has… limits."

Ernst, still on the bed, moved carefully up to Hector's head, nuzzling the salt-and-pepper hair. "He's not bleeding. But his left ankle is fractured. You might want to see to that."

The doctor looked surprised for a heartbeat, then immensely relieved. "Thank you, Ernst. That information will help a lot." He gave Caleb a wan smile. "It's too bad I don't have a familiar of my own. They're very useful little creatures."

Caleb eyed the ailing man and his familiar, huddled so close, thoughtfully. "Ernst… how would you feel about staying here to help the doctor with Hector?"

Ernst's raised one long ear. "Are you sure? We've never been that far apart for so long."

It was true. They'd never been apart for more than a

few hours since the day Caleb awoke to find a magical ferret on his chest, and while they'd stretched their bond thin over distance before, it had never been so far. Caleb felt something leaden settle in his stomach at the very thought, but without Ernst's help, Hector could die. "It's up to you. You could do a world of good here, I think."

The jackalope debated, his nose wriggling as he thought. Finally, he nodded, one decisive bob of his head. "All right. You can always call if you need me, right?" If they both believed they could still feel each other across that distance, perhaps it would be true.

"Right. Be good, Ernst. And check on in Jimmy if you get a chance."

"I can do that." He snuggled down in the crook of Hector's shoulder, purring softly.

"Bless you, Agent Marcus." The doctor pressed Caleb's hand with both of his. "I hope you find the men who did this."

The Peacemaker nodded. "I hope so, too, Dr. Elm."

Half of Hope saw him mount up on Sven Isby's rented hauler and ride out of town, so there would be no keeping his absence a secret for long. He tied Teddy's bundle of food to the saddle, tucked his staff into his stirrup, pulled his hat down over his eyes, and headed east.

It quickly became apparent that one disadvantage of leaving Ernst behind was that there was no one to keep him awake. His short nap had not been enough by far, and he found himself dozing fitfully in the saddle as the construct galloped its way over the rough-hewn track.

The heat itself was draining as the sun rose to its zenith high overhead, and he regretted not bringing more water. There were no stops between Hope and Tasco, the few tiny springs having fallen victim to the ongoing drought. What he had was what he'd make do with, and he'd have to use it sparingly.

The one thing he truly worried about was the

response from the office in Kansas City. Even if they came straight away, it would be at least a week before the stage could arrive, and a lot could happen in that amount of time.

"No other way around it, though. Right, Ernst?" Belatedly, he remembered that his familiar was not there. The tiny connection that bound them together was dwindling far behind him, but he swallowed hard and pushed on. Ernst would be fine. So would he.

For nearly two hours he rode, determined to ignore the discomfort of the ungainly transport, fighting to stay mostly awake in the broad saddle. The sun beat down on him with the force of a dozen hammers until he could feel every pounding hoofbeat lancing up his spine into the back of his skull. His lips were cracked already, and reluctantly, he reached behind him to retrieve the canteen and his store of precious water.

Half turned in the saddle as he was, he saw the blue light first, a speck no bigger than a bumblebee streaking across the prairie at him. His instincts registered it faster than his mind, but he still couldn't get the shield up before the gunshot echoed in his ears.

He flung himself backward off the hauler too late, and it exploded beneath him in a ball of raging arcane fire. The ethereal blue flames billowed around him, filled his ears, his eyes, and only when he saw the ground rushing up to meet him at great speed did he realize that he'd been blown clear of the inferno.

Then he knew nothing at all.

12

The first time he came to, all he could see was a swirl of blue energy before his eyes, bright enough to blind him to all else. Something was pounding rhythmically on his stomach until his entire body jarred with each impact. There was so much pressure in his head, he thought the top of his skull might blow off, and his shoulders were screaming in pain, his arms stretched awkwardly above his head. No sooner had he started to catalog his miseries than the jolting grew worse, pain seared through his body, and blackness once again claimed him.

The second awakening was much the same as the first, save that he thought to actually move his head a bit. The arcane glow dominating his vision resolved itself into the transparent casing on a transport, pressed against his cheek. Seemingly miles below him and yet just beyond his fingertips, he could see the dry prairie grass rushing past at a high rate of speed. It finally occurred to him that he was facedown over the saddle of a moving transport, riding hard.

The mere effort of trying to focus his eyes in his throbbing head brought a wave of nausea, and he retched violently. There was nothing in his stomach to come up, however, which was both a blessing and a curse. Mostly, it felt like his stomach was trying to turn him inside out starting from the toes up.

Nearby, someone cussed loudly. "He's sickin' up again!"

Again? How long had he been out? And where the hell was Ernst?

"We may as well stop here. It's far enough, and I want to be home before dark."

That voice he knew, somehow. If he could just clear the ringing clamor from his ears so he could think. Ernst… Ernst was with Hector. Helping the doctor. He remembered that, and reached for his familiar out of reflex, only to find… nothing. The connection was gone as if it had never been, and he jerked his head up before being reminded quite painfully that abrupt movements were unwise. Lightning and thunder crashed inside his skull, and all thoughts of trying to reach Ernst fled before waves of agony.

Mercifully, the transport drew to a halt, but the stampede in his head kept galloping along. Someone grabbed him by the belt and hauled him bodily off the back of the construct. He hit the ground in a haze of red pain, and darkness threatened at the edges of his vision again. The orange and purple sky swam above him, the sun's last rays piercing through his eyes before it dipped below the distant mountain range. *Sunset.* It had been noon when… when what? Oh, yes, the explosion.

Someone had shot his transport out from underneath him.

A slender man with dead eyes appeared in his line of sight. *Schmidt.* That explained the long shot. Ernst would have seen it coming if he'd been there. Where was he? *With Hector… remember that… He's still in Hope.*

Caleb tried to call for his familiar and got no more than a hoarse bark out of a throat parched by thirst and smoke inhalation. It sent him into a coughing fit, and agony lanced through his rib cage, curling him into a moaning ball of pain on the ground.

"Easy there, Agent. No use trying to struggle, since we have you nulled." Abel Warner knelt beside him, pushing him over onto his back. With a smile, he tapped the amulet hanging around Caleb's neck. It was a simple, unadorned lead casing, but Caleb knew the reverse side, the side pressed to his bare chest, was white and chalky. Nullstone. "You will understand of course that we could not allow you to summon your familiar. Or use any of your talents against us."

He rose to his feet, calling orders to the other men present, and Caleb watched his boots walk away.

Though he knew it was futile, he tried to reach for his power. It felt like reaching through a barrel of cold molasses for one tiny hair at the bottom. The harder he pushed, the more resistance he found, and finally a sharp stabbing pain between his eyes forced him to abandon the effort.

It occurred to him belatedly that he should simply remove the amulet, but the moment he fumbled for it, someone grabbed his wrist in a viselike grip. Another hand captured his left arm, and he found himself spread-eagled on the ground while his wrists and ankles were tied to stakes. His shoulders screamed in pain, nearly wrenched from their sockets so far did they have him stretched.

Bare-chested as he was—and where the hell was his shirt?—the dry prairie grass might as well have been scorching hot nails digging into his back. The analytical part of his mind cataloged those injuries as burns, no doubt from the exploding hauler. He could see blisters on his forearms, as well, surrounded by ugly red welts. Suddenly, he welcomed the pain. Burns that didn't hurt were the worst of all, and almost always fatal.

"Make sure you leave those feathers here, and a couple of those arrows."

"We scalpin' him, boss?"

Warner answered, "No. The local Cheyenne don't take scalps, and we want this to look authentic if anyone asks."

The rancher took his time checking the ropes and made sure the medallion was pressed stone-side-down to Caleb's chest. "I wish it hadn't come to this, Agent Marcus. I really do. Your predecessor was more than happy to take his cut and keep quiet, but somehow I don't see you being the same kind of man." He shook his head, genuine regret on his face. "It's a sad world we live in when scruples become a hazard, but there you have it."

"People… will know." His voice came out in a croak, and Caleb could taste the blood where his lips cracked and bled.

"No, they won't. They think you're bound for Tasco. It'll be at least ten days before anyone misses you." He tilted his head thoughtfully. "Unless they investigate the smoke from the explosion, but even then, they'll think the Cheyenne destroyed the hauler and took you. We made sure of that."

His nonchalance was chilling. Caleb strained at his bonds out of primal reflex, the deeply ingrained instinct of the body to remove itself from danger at any cost, and the exertion left him gasping and writhing in pain.

"Your death will not be a pleasant one, Agent Marcus, and for that I apologize. But I need the army out here to exterminate the red devils, and the quickest way for that to happen is to have a lawman killed. You understand, of course."

"The… nullstone. Hurting the children…" It was a long shot, appealing to the man's questionable humanity.

Warner chuckled. "Of course it is. How else am I going to have a ready-made workforce? That gold isn't going to mine itself, and the nullstone surrounding it makes it hazardous under the best of circumstances. Barrens will take any employment they can find, and I'm already known for my generosity to those less fortunate. They'll be more than happy to work in my mines when they're of age."

Gold! The secret mine suddenly made much more

sense. The nullstone was simply an obstacle to something larger and more lucrative.

"I intend to be mining in those mountains for years to come, Agent Marcus, with wealth to spare. If I can just get the army to eradicate the little infestation problem without finding out about the gold. Can't have the federal government laying claim to something that's rightfully mine, now can I?"

Warner fished his pocket watch out of his waistcoat, checking the time. "Oh, would you look at that? I must be going. I wish you luck in your future endeavors, of course. As short as they'll be." With a cordial smile, he rose and walked to his transport, swinging into the saddle easily.

"Told them!" Caleb jerked against his bonds again, croaking as loudly as he could. "Told them about the mine!"

Warner laughed with genuine mirth. "No, you didn't."

Within moments, Warner and his men were out of sight, and shortly thereafter even the drumming of the hooves on the hard-packed soil faded from Caleb's senses. He yanked and twisted at the ropes holding his wrists until they were rubbed raw and bleeding, and his head swam dizzily from the effort.

Gasping, he let his head fall back to the grass, fighting to hold on to consciousness, knowing that the next time he blacked out might very well be the last. *Have to…think…* After a few moments of rest, he tried flinging himself from side to side to dislodge the nullstone medal, but his arms were stretched too tightly and he had no wiggle room.

All right, take stock. As far as he knew, he had been without water for the better part of an entire day, presumably while baking in the summer heat. The sun, at least, was setting now, a minor blessing. Thunder still bounced within the confines of his head, and the burns on his back screamed every time he moved. His chest felt heavy, possibly due to cracked ribs, but craning his neck resulted in blinding flashes behind his eyes, so he couldn't assess the damage there.

With the nullstone medallion lying on his chest, not only was he unable to touch his own power, but his connection to Ernst was severed, too. Did the little familiar realize? Was he frantically looking for Caleb even now? Maybe, if he was close enough to hear… "Ernst! Ernst, I'm over here!" It set him coughing again, and he couldn't even curl up to relieve the strain on his ribs.

Some tiny biting insects, drawn by the scent of his blood, landed on his wrists and began feeding, their minor irritations only adding to his growing woes. Night was falling. How long before the bigger predators came? Coyotes, foxes, even a stray cougar come down out of the mountains for some prairie hunting.

Maybe that would be better, he thought. A quicker death surely than waiting for the sun to rise again, roasting him in his own juices.

Above him, the sky slowly faded from lavender into a serene blue and finally into the star-dotted black. The only hint of color rimmed the mountain peaks for a long time before that too succumbed to the night.

Crickets chirped softly in the tall grass around him, and there were rustlings of smaller animals going about their nightly business. To the north, he heard a high-pitched giggle, echoed shortly by four or five more. *Coyotes.* They'd be drawn to the scent of fresh meat, and at this point, that's all Caleb was. How long before they grew brave enough to approach him?

He began counting the seconds between the calls that sounded like nothing so much as deranged laughter, trying to guess the distance and how much time he had left.

Some part of him thought perhaps he should be praying. Surely, of all times, this was one when God's presence would be beneficial. But he couldn't seem to find the words within his own head. He thought instead of his sister, married and happy in Pennsylvania. With ten years' difference in their ages, they had never been close. Paulette had been married and gone almost before he could know her when he was a child. Would she grieve for him, the younger brother she'd barely known? Would her children hear tales of their uncle the Peacemaker, slain by Indians in the wild and brutal west? When had he even spoken to her last?

What of Graeme? Would he come himself when Caleb didn't report in on schedule? Would he be the one to find what was left of his friend? Would there even be anything left, once the coyotes got done with him? His last conversation with Graeme hadn't been the most cordial. Caleb had been angry and bitter, and Graeme had made a convenient target. He hoped Graeme knew that he hadn't meant the things he'd said. It wasn't Graeme's fault Caleb had been exiled to the west. In fact, it was probably through Graeme's influence that Caleb still had a position with the Peacemakers at all. Caleb was grateful, even if he hadn't shown it. Surely his best friend knew him that well after all these years. Surely he knew.

When he dragged his thoughts back from their wanderings, the coyotes had fallen silent. Either they'd given up on their human-scented prey, or they were even now stalking closer. *Or something even bigger scared them off.*

It was no surprise to him when the narrow muzzle poked through the tall grass to his left, followed by copper-colored eyes and sharply pointed ears. The coyote, a big specimen, slunk forward one careful step at a time, its dark gray hackles raised in warning.

"Hah!" Caleb tried to yell to scare the thing off, and while it did flinch at the abrupt noise, it seemed to know that he was no threat. It found a comfortable spot and sat nearby, watching him. "Go on, you! Get out of here!"

The animal did not run, nor make any hostile moves. Instead, it simply sat in silence, staring at Caleb with those deep amber eyes, as if it could see right into his thoughts. It was eerie.

"Waiting for your kin to show up?" The animal tilted its head at the sound of his croaking voice, the tip of one ear drooping comically. "Polite of you to wait until everyone's here to start eating." The thing tipped its head the other way. "Start on the thighs. They're nice and meaty. You might avoid the back, though. Seems to be a bit well-done back there." That thought spurred Caleb into slightly manic giggles, and he began to worry that his mind might be a bit unhinged.

"You might want to eat me quickly, you know. If I'm mad, it may taint the meat. Wouldn't want you getting all rabid or anything." His entire body shook with helpless laughter, and no amount of pain could make it stop. Only when the coughing overruled the laughter was he forced to stop, and even then he was riddled with sporadic giggling.

Amidst his laughter, he heard the grasses rustling again, and he looked to his left fully expecting a family of coyotes waiting to sink their sharp teeth into his extremities. Instead, he was greeted with the head of the largest animal he had ever seen. As close as it was, he had difficulty taking it all in, but the pieces of the whole—the deep brown fur, almost like wool; the large sloping forehead, ending in wickedly curving black horns; the bottomless, soulful eyes that seemed to hold all of the world's sorrows at once—added up to one thing.

A large buffalo stood over the bound Peacemaker, its warm musky breath stirring the hair on his head. The creature lowered its head to sniff at him, and Caleb held very still, suddenly beset with images of a large black hoof splitting his head like a ripe melon.

Apparently satisfied with what it had learned, the

mammoth creature lumbered around the injured man to touch noses with the odd coyote. The two animals stood that way for a long moment, sharing some kind of secret communion.

Only when a stray night breeze passed through the tall grasses did Caleb realize that the buffalo had left no sign of its passing. Where it should have flattened the prairie grass, the stalks were straight and unbroken, swaying peacefully where they stood. And if he squinted, he realized he could see the grass *through* the behemoth's body, as if it were no more tangible than smoke.

"God, I'm hallucinating." In a small way, he was relieved. Perhaps he'd at least be insensible when the worst happened. Being eaten wouldn't be that bad, so long as he wasn't aware of it.

The buffalo snorted, either at the man or the coyote, Caleb wasn't sure. Without a second glance, it turned and lumbered back out into the plains, passing through the grass without disturbing a single blade. The coyote remained, and it yawned hugely, displaying its sharp white teeth.

"Sorry that I'm boring you. I'm being remiss in my duties as host." Caleb laid his head back again, watching the stars dancing in the sky above him. It seemed they whirled much faster than he remembered, the spinning making him dizzy after a while. He closed his eyes, no longer caring if he ever opened them again.

Twice more, the grasses rustled to reveal yet another animal come to inspect the captured Peacemaker. A delicate doe nosed at his cheek, the hair on her muzzle tickling his ear until he laughed. And a prairie hen, all feathers and bluster, strutted and fussed around him, apparently oblivious to the vicious predator sitting not a few feet away.

One of them did not exist, Caleb decided. Either the coyote was not there, or Caleb himself was a figment of the imagination. And since the other animals all seemed to have some deep and interesting discussion with the canine observer, Caleb concluded that it must be him.

He had the disturbing thought that perhaps he was dead already. "If this is heaven, I'm mightily disappointed." Though, perhaps it wasn't heaven. Perhaps he hadn't been nearly the good man that he'd thought. There were so many deaths on his head, but… that was war, wasn't it? Would he be held to account for his past actions?

The mosquito bites on his wrists itched something fierce, and he next decided that he could not be dead, because allowing mosquito bites in hell was too cruel, even for Satan himself.

The coyote provided no information. It had been sitting for hours by now, perhaps simply waiting for Caleb to expire.

"Hey, since you're just sitting there…" The animal looked over at him, giving the curious head tilt again. "I don't suppose you could go get me some help, could you?" Again, the coyote tilted his head to the other side, as if considering it. "Please?"

The animal looked at him for a long time, and Caleb swore he could see the stars' own light reflected in the amber eyes. Finally, it stood and trotted into the grass without so much as a sound.

"Well, I'll be damned." That brought another fit of manic chuckling, but he quickly got it under control.

The disadvantage, he quickly discovered, was that he was now alone. Even silent and odd, the coyote had at least been companionship.

With nothing else to distract him, he became aware of how much he hurt, still, and how very thirsty he was. His mouth tasted like copper where the blood from his cracked lips had trickled in, and it was a wonder he could talk around the great swollen piece of shoe leather that was his tongue. For a few seconds, he convinced himself he was about to choke on it, and he thrashed against his bonds again, the ropes cutting deeper into his wrists.

"Warner, you bastard! You could have at least shot me like a man!" The shout went unanswered, as he knew it would.

Or had it?

Somewhere at the edge of his hearing, he caught the faintest of notes, a voice humming in the distance. Though he could make out only every third or fourth note, when the wind favored him, he found himself humming along, filling in the missing parts from memory. He knew that tune, didn't he? From where…?

It gradually swelled to fill his head, blotting out all other sounds. The soft lullaby spoke of gentle hands, loving arms, warmth, and safety. And he'd heard it before, but he could not for the life of him remember when or where.

The first time his eyes drifted closed, he forced them back open with a start. He could not afford to sleep, not when waking again was so unlikely. But it happened a second and third time, the darkness lingering a bit longer each time before he remembered to resist. It would be so easy to sleep, to rest. The song said he would be safe, and he was so very, very tired.

With the woman's voice humming softly in his ears, he finally let go and drifted to sleep.

13

Cool water trickled over his lips, and delicate touches moved over his chest and arms while the soothing song went on. It took him some time to realize that he could open his eyes if he wanted, and when he did, he found himself staring up into dark eyes set in a lovely, honey-brown face.

The Indian woman, the one from the mountain and his dreams, smiled to see him awake, and she slipped her hand behind his head to support him while she trickled more water down his throat.

Caleb gulped it as fast as he could, though he was certain even an entire river would not have been enough. When he managed to choke himself, she laid his head back down with a chiding look.

"I…" He paused to cough. "Thank you."

Smiling her approval, she gathered up some cloths and bowls and rose, walking gracefully across the floor.

Only then did Caleb realize that he was inside one of the large teepees, cheerfully lit by a crackling fire in the middle. The smoke rose in a column through the hole in the top, and beyond it he could see only darkness. It was still night, then, but the same night or another one?

An attempt to sit up revealed that he was still stretched and tied; the lodge had apparently been erected right over his place of confinement. The nullstone amulet still nestled in the center of his chest. Perhaps they didn't trust him after all. "How long have I been here?"

The woman was busily working with some pungent smelling plants on her side of the fire and barely glanced over at his voice. His answer came instead from the other side.

"Time passes differently here, so that is hard to say." From the shadows, the old shaman appeared, moving to take a seat next to the fire. It was unmistakably the same man from the Dog Soldier's village. Physically, he looked no different from the last time Caleb had seen him, though his long white braids were wrapped in dark fur this time. His face was still deeply lined with years and responsibilities, and he still carried himself with the air of a man who expects his orders to be obeyed without question.

Something was different, though, something Caleb couldn't quite put his finger on. The old man seemed... younger almost. Brighter. More alive. Even the decorations on his leathers seemed more vibrant, as if the beaded creatures were about to leap off and cavort around the fire. Everything in the teepee looked that way, he realized—too deep, too rich to be real. Too much.

The coyote familiar padded into view as well, lying down with its head on its paws and its eyes on the captive man, and Caleb abruptly realized that the shaman had spoken, and he had understood.

"You speak English now?"

The old man smiled, the creases in his face deepening. "There is only one language of the spirit, and all who are brothers may speak it in this place."

Caleb glanced around. "What, in this teepee?"

"You are in the Place Between."

"The place between what?"

"Between life and death. Between asleep and awake. Between one world and the next." The white-haired man threw a handful of something on the flames, and aromatic smoke rolled out. Sage, Caleb thought. "Coyote spoke to me of your need, and your readiness to see this place."

Caleb eyed the familiar beside the fire, but he couldn't tell whether it was the same coyote that had watched over him on the prairie. One looked very much like another. "Am I… hallucinating still?"

The old man chuckled. "It is possible. That is one way of reaching this place."

"Am I dying?" The woman returned to his side, and Caleb eyed her warily. She knelt, scooping a handful of a dark, wet substance from a bowl, and began smearing it on his burned forearms. The poultice was cool and sent tingles through his skin.

"I do not believe you are dying. Though you would have without our aid." The old man produced a long pipe and began filling it with tobacco. Caleb could smell it even under the aroma of the other herbs. "I am called Crying Elk. I am the medicine man of this band of the People. And you are a star soldier of the white man."

"Star soldier?"

The old man tapped the place above his heart, and Caleb understood.

"My badge…" It was gone, he supposed, wherever Warner had discarded his shirt.

"You are not the same as the last star soldier who came to this land. He was a man like the dark one, the one who digs into the mountain's heart and causes such pain. He was only interested in his personal gain." Crying Elk smirked with dark humor. "We would not have aided him, no matter how he begged Coyote."

That fit in line with everything Caleb had learned about his predecessor. "I feel like I should apologize for that."

The old shaman snorted, smoke curling from his nostrils to join the haze. "Each man chooses to walk his own path. His choice was not yours, so why would you need to apologize for it?"

Caleb shrugged, only to be reminded of the bonds that tied him. The woman frowned at his fidgeting, reaching to smooth some of the sticky goop over his forehead as well. "What is… what is she doing?" Instinctively, he flinched away from her touch, and she grabbed his chin firmly, giving him a glare.

"She is a great healer of our people. The poultice will take the heat from your wounds, allow them to heal. The water will replenish you."

"Why are you doing this for me?"

"I told you this already. Because you are not like the other star soldier. You spare lives when you could more easily take them, even among people not your own. You give food to the hungry and warning to those in danger." The old man grinned in the firelight. "Though your spirit guide should more likely be praised for that."

Spirit guide… Ernst! "Is Ernst all right? Where is he?"

"You cannot tell?" The shaman canted his head curiously. "Is he not a piece of your spirit?"

"The stone." Caleb jerked his chin at the medallion lying on his chest. "It blocks me from him, keeps me from reaching him."

Crying Elk pursed his lips thoughtfully. "When I was a boy, a man with pale skin and black hair upon his face came to our lands. He had a headdress and shirt made of metal, and rode a horse before we had ever seen such a creature. His own people had left him behind, but he fell in love with a beautiful woman of the People, and he chose to stay with my band. We learned much of the white man's ways through him.

"Once, in battle against another tribe, he split himself in two, the piece of his spirit aiding him much as your spirit guide does. When the battle was over, the piece of his spirit remained, separate from him, yet always a part of him. Is it not the way with all white men and their spirit guides?"

Caleb blinked in the dim light for a few moments, disturbingly certain that the old man had just described the arrival of the Spaniards on this land, something that had taken place over three hundred years ago. *Dear Lord... Three hundred...?* There had to be some mistake, some error in translation perhaps. "We don't know where familiars come from. They just... appear. Ernst just came to me."

The shaman shrugged his narrow shoulders. "Perhaps he was a different kind of white man, then."

"What about yours? Is he part of your spirit?"

The coyote cocked his head at Caleb's words, giving every impression of being indulgently amused.

"Coyote visits when he wants, and aids me when he chooses. We are friends, but he is not of my spirit." Crying Elk rested a hand on the head of his own familiar, more a gesture of respect for an equal than affection bestowed on a pet. The coyote looked up, and Caleb swore he could see the animal smile fondly in return.

Even knowing he would not be able to move past the nullstone, Caleb tried to reach out for his connection to Ernst. It was like pushing through yards of wet wool, but he gritted his teeth and tried anyway.

The woman slapped his arm lightly and shook a finger in warning. Caleb resisted the urge to stick his tongue out at her petulantly.

"You are not strong enough just now to fight the power of the draining stone. I will teach you later, when you are more yourself." Crying Elk drew on his pipe deeply, his eyes watching the dance of the fire before him. "Now is the time when we must speak of more serious things."

Caleb dragged his gaze away from the woman with her hands all over him to look at the old shaman. "What things? And you know, it's hard to have a conversation all tied up like this."

"Is it? It is not bothering me in the least." The old man blew a perfect smoke ring, amusement in his dark eyes. "Attend now. Time must not be wasted in this place."

"But you said time—" Caleb fell silent at a look from the old man. Something told him that the shaman would answer only what he chose to.

"The dark man must be stopped. The mountain sleeps for now, but if he continues to dig at the heel of the giant, it will awaken, and all will feel its wrath. Even now, it stirs fitfully in its sleep, and the world shakes."

The image of the sleeping rock giant sprang vividly to Caleb's mind, and he looked toward the woman, who had her head down over her mystery concoctions. Her eyes met his, and she subtly shook her head no. He was not to mention their little dream adventure, then, hmm?

"What happens if the… if the mountain wakes?"

"Who knows? It has not happened in all of my three hundred forty winters, nor those of my father before me nor of his father before him. But if the sleeping giant can cause the mountain to fall down upon our heads, imagine what an angry and wakeful one could do."

Caleb had to blink and allow that information to sink in. *Three hundred forty winters. He really did see the Spaniards arrive.* Granted, strong magic users were blessed with longer lives, but… Even Caleb could expect to see only one hundred and thirty years, if he was truly fortunate.

The rumors of the ancient Indian shamans had trickled back east, spread by gruesome war stories and sensationalized penny dreadful novels. Privately, Caleb had always scoffed at such tales as dramatized yarns good for frightening women and children on dark nights around the fire.

If it was true, though… No wonder the white man could not defeat the red man's magic.

"Why don't you just stop him then? Drive him off

the mountain?" Even as powerful as Warner was, this Crying Elk was more than a match. Of that Caleb was certain.

"Because if my people attack the white men, the soldiers will come just like in the north. I do not wish to lose my people, or to kill any of yours. I have no hatred for those who simply wish to live in peace, so long as they allow us to do the same."

He spoke the truth, though Caleb couldn't have said why he was so sure. Maybe it was the great weariness that lurked in the old man's eyes, that threatened to stoop his proud shoulders. "You didn't raid the Anderson homestead, did you?"

"The family in the foothills? No. That was the dark man, poorly made to look like a raid by the people. I do not allow my warriors to raid."

Caleb nodded, resting his head back to gaze up at the thick leather above his head. "I thought you'd say that."

"You do not believe me?"

"No, I believe you. I bet they're on top of another gold vein; that's why he wanted them out. The Cheyenne woman is showing him where they are somehow."

The old man nodded. "That is a sad tale. She was a daughter of the People, but now she angers the spirits greatly. The dark one has tethered her to his will, but if she were free, I think she would fight against him."

"Tethered… I don't understand what you mean."

"You will see. When you go there."

"Now, wait." Caleb tried to raise his head, the muscles in his neck quivering. "What makes you think I'm going out there? Just because you tell me to?"

"You will go, because that is the path I see before you. All of your roads lead to the dark man." Crying Elk tapped out his pipe into the fire and stood.

"And if I don't believe in your… vision?"

The old man chuckled. "We shall see. I do not see

whether you will die, but if you do, it will be a good day for it. I will find you again when it is done, Good Man." He paused at the leather flap that led outside. "Do not attempt to leave the teepee. There are things in the Place Between that are not brothers and would not be happy with your presence."

Caleb eyed the ropes still binding his wrists and ankles. "I don't think that's going to be a problem."

The old man left, chuckling.

That left Caleb alone with the woman, who was humming softly under her breath again. "How long are you going to keep me here?"

She glanced up briefly, but went back to her work without a word.

"I guess you don't talk here, either." With a sigh, Caleb laid his head back to stare at the ceiling again. The poultice was drying on his arms, itching faintly, but he could tell that the pain had receded already. If it was a hallucination, at least he wasn't suffering.

"I do not know what to say to you." Her voice was low, soft, and Caleb looked at her in surprise to hear her speak at all. She blushed faintly under his gaze.

"Tell me your name, then."

She returned to his side with more water, helping him drink as she spoke. "I am called Falcon Woman."

He swallowed the water gratefully, feeling his parched tissues suck up the precious moisture. She laid his head down gently, and began checking the packs of damp herbs covering his body. He watched her long enough that she blushed again.

"Why do you stare at me so?"

"Why do you walk in my dreams?"

She bit her lip as she bent to smear more poultice on his raw wrists. "I should not have done that. Father would be very angry if he knew. It is not polite to walk in another's dreams without being invited."

"Do many of your people walk in dreams like that?"

"No. It is a gift in Father's line. His children, their children, and so on. Many of them have grown to be great medicine men and women of our people."

Caleb glanced at the door and back. "That man… Crying Elk? He's your father?" He would have guessed grandfather at the very least, and maybe a couple of greats to go along with it.

Falcon Woman nodded. "I am one of the youngest of his children. I have two sisters who are younger still. There are many who are older. Like Tall Bear. The man you fought at the village."

"He is your brother."

She nodded with a small smile.

"I hope I didn't hurt him. I think I lost track of what happened that night."

"He was not harmed. Only shamed. He should not have asked the fire for aid. The fire is always hungry, and in the dry times, it can devour too much." She wrung a cloth out in a bowl of water, beginning to bathe some of the plaster off his chest. "You did well to contain it. I do not think Tall Bear himself could have done that. If Father had been forced to step in, Tall Bear would have been twice shamed, so it was a doubly good thing you did."

"Glad I could help," he muttered, watching her hands move over him with clinical detachment. "So… my dreams. If you're not supposed to do it, why are you bothering me?"

Her dark skin went ruddy in her embarrassment. "I wanted to see what kind of man you were. After the day in the mountains… You could have harmed me easily, and yet you protected yourself and did not attack. I wished to know why."

"And what did you learn?"

Instead of answering him, she lifted his head again. "Look at your chest."

It took some doing to crane his neck and see, all trussed up as he was, but where she indicated was a deep bruise in the area of his heart. "Damn. I must have landed on a rock."

She shook her head, her braids falling around her face. "These injuries were from the great blue fire." She touched his poultice-covered forearms, his forehead, traced her fingers over the ribs on his right side. "Because your body and spirit are one, I can heal your spirit in this place, and your body. But this…" She laid her warm palm flat over the bruised place, and still she could not cover it all. It was an expansive wound. "This is older, and a wound of the spirit alone. You fought a great battle. I saw it in your dreams. This is something only you could heal. Perhaps later you can ask Father to show you how. He has guided many wounded warriors through such a healing."

"I don't understand any of this. You know that, right? This is all… myth to me. Legend."

"And yet it is life to us." She smiled softly. "I have heard of the great lakes-with-no-shores and the large canoes belching blue fire that cross them bearing hundreds of people. That is myth to me, and life to you."

"Fair enough." His shoulders ached, stretched out as they were, but at least it was better than the screaming pain of before. "Can you untie me? Or at least take this necklace off me?"

She shook her head. "I cannot."

"I promise, I won't hurt you."

"I know you will not hurt me. You are the Good Man." She did tuck a small pile of soft tanned hides under his head so he could rest more comfortably. "But as you are both flesh and spirit, so I can affect you here. The ropes that bind you, they are part of the other world, and in this place I cannot touch them."

"So… I'll wake up back on the prairie, still tied up like a snared rabbit?"

"Yes. But if Coyote saw fit to tell Father about your need for aid, he may also see to your freedom. He is like that." She rose once again, returning to her pile of belongings on the far side of the lodge.

"I saw a coyote when I was out there. And a buffalo, and a deer and other things. Were they real or did I dream them?"

"Yes." At first, he thought she was going to leave him with that enigmatic answer, but she returned to his side with a bowl of hot broth and went on. "When I took you to see the mountain spirit, I gave you the sight to see. Do you remember?"

He nodded as best he could. "You touched my face."

"The sight will linger for a time, I think. It is possible that you saw Buffalo, and Deer, and Coyote. It is also possible that they were simply animals. A warrior's visions are his own on his quest."

He sipped the broth with her help, his stomach growling hungrily even as the salt in it made him crave more water. "I didn't go on a vision quest. I was left out there to die."

"Then perhaps the vision quest found you. Though I do not know how you could have a spirit guide before you had your vision. As Father said, perhaps it is because you are a white man and your spirit guides are different. You must be a very powerful medicine man among your people."

That thought made him chuckle, though he tried to keep the bitterness out of his voice. "No, I'm not. Not anymore."

"Then you are a puzzle, Good Man. Drink. It will nourish you."

He allowed her to feed him in silence for a long moment, his mind too rattled to even form a logical question. Perhaps he was still hallucinating, but he couldn't recall any before that had been so very real. Every detail was crystal clear in his vision, from the quillwork on her dress to the tiny feather braided into her hair behind her right ear. The firelight cast a warm glow around, and it was reflected in her ebony tresses until they nearly shimmered with flame themselves. When she leaned over him, he could smell the herbs she had used to wash, see the pulse fluttering like a hummingbird's wings in the hollow of her throat.

He closed his eyes and swallowed hard. He had not been with a woman in some time, to be sure, but this was not the time or place to be thinking of it.

A wet cloth stroked his forehead as she wiped away the poultice there, too. He could feel the water trickling through his short hair and down his neck. It tickled, and he squirmed a bit.

She giggled at him, a trilling laugh made of sunlight. "I am sorry. This is difficult with you tied so."

He opened his eyes to find her bent over him, her dark eyes alight with merriment. He couldn't help but smile in return. "It's all right. If I get out of this, it will be an interesting story to tell someday."

Falcon Woman nodded, patting his face with a dry cloth. "And we will tell it often. You will be known among the people. When Father meets with the other medicine men here, he will speak of the Good Man, and they will know that not all white men are evil."

"We're not, you know. There is good and bad in all of us. I'm sure it's the same with your people."

She nodded, resting her hands in her lap finally. "Even within the same person, yes. It is a matter of which side is stronger, I think." She placed one delicate hand on his chest again, over the bruise. "Your good side fights hard and wins. But I think you make the struggle harder than it must be."

"You know all that just from walking through my

dreams?"

"I knew that the first time I looked into your eyes. The dreams only told me why." With her other hand, she drew something from a pouch at her side and cast it into the fire. Fragrant smoke rose again in pale blue billows, and a sweet scent drifted to fill the lodge.

Caleb's eyelids grew heavy almost immediately. "What…?"

"You must rest, Good Man. The road Father sees for you is not an easy one, and you need to gather your strength." She stroked her hand down his scarred cheek lightly, and her humming filled his ears once more.

He tried to fight it, he truly did. But the smoke whispered to him to sleep, and her song spoke of safety, and it became harder and harder to keep his eyes open. "Falcon?"

"Yes?"

"My name… It's Caleb."

"Rest now, Caleb Good Man. I will watch over you until you wake."

14

It was not the morning sunlight that woke him so much as the interruption of that light as the shadow of something large loomed over his face.

Caleb blinked his eyes open to find himself staring up a very long, very furry face, one deep brown eye observing him curiously. The nose, no more than an inch from his own, breathed warm, grainy breath into his face, snuffling at him with interest.

"Gah!" His startled yell resulted in wrenching his shoulders against his bonds, and the painted horse danced away nervously. "Christ!"

His time spent in the Indian teepee had surely been a dream or fevered hallucination. There was no flattened grass, no tracks, no smoldering fire, nothing to show that anyone had ever been there. *The Place Between...*

Once his heart stopped thundering in his ears and he lay still, the inquisitive horse came back, nosing his hair and chest with strong nudges, blowing horsy breath all over him. It examined him in some uncomfortably personal places, and he tensed, knowing full well he was unable to defend himself if the animal got cranky. "Is there something I can do for you?"

The horse's ears flicked once, perking at the sound of his voice. The animal was colored in splashy brown and white spots, the white half of its face sporting a glassy blue eye in contrast to the gentle brown eye on the darker side. Someone had painted dark blue handprints on its flanks. He realized the creature was also wearing a crude bridle, the reins knotted loosely over the animal's withers. It obviously belonged to someone. Were they missing their mount?

It started nibbling at the grass, finding the shoots beneath Caleb's left arm particularly tantalizing. Caleb kept an eye on those sharp-looking hooves, waiting for one of them to lash out and end his misery. Everyone knew how erratic horses could be; that's why all civilized folk rode transports.

Something tugged at his wrist, and he realized the horse was nibbling at the rope. He froze, trying to stop even his pulse as those large white teeth snipped closer and closer to his bare skin. "Good um… boy? Just don't bite me…"

Unfortunately, the horse lost interest before it severed the rope completely, and it wandered a few yards away to look for greener grasses among the dry stalks. Caleb glared at the frayed bond for a few moments, tugging to see if he could part it any further. The remaining strands seemed determined to hold.

He rested his head against the hard soil for a few moments, only half noticing that it wasn't pounding like a brass band anymore. In fact, though the skin on his forearms was a rather cheerful shade of pink, the blisters were gone, and it felt like nothing more than a mild sunburn.

"Until I roast out here all day again." The horse seemed to be attracted to his voice, and came back over to see just what he had to say on the subject. "You're a friendly sort, at least. Any chance you want to finish dining on that rope? I promise I'll get you something nice." What the hell did horses like, anyway? He had a vague memory of sugar cubes, but that could have been just a child's story from long ago.

The horse snorted and turned its attention—*his*

attention, Caleb could clearly see from this angle—to its grazing, again finding Caleb inconveniently in its way. The animal was strong, and had no qualms about shoving the prone Peacemaker this way and that to get at the choicest tidbits.

Only when the animal wandered away yet again—though never farther than a few yards—did Caleb notice that his actions had dislodged the nullstone amulet from his chest. Though it was still looped around his neck on a thin chain, the heavy medallion had slipped back off his shoulders, nestling in the grass right next to his ear.

Caleb hardly dared to breathe. So long as the stone wasn't actually touching his skin, he had a chance.

It should have coursed through his veins like living fire, the substance of life itself burning and enticing all at once. Instead, his power was sluggish, a reluctant trickle of thick sludge. It was a supreme effort of will to draw on that murky core, forcing what little he could out the length of his arm toward the frayed rope. It almost oozed, cold and lifeless, chilling him despite the day's heat already brewing.

He let the power pool in his palm, the vibrant blue energy now clouded and almost black. He'd have one shot, and then he'd have to wait until more of the nullstone cleared from his body before he could gather enough strength to try again. That could take hours that he didn't have.

With his staff, he could have taken even the sluggish remnants of his energy and focused them into a narrow blade, a tiny point of controlled force to part the strands of the rope. Without it, he was left with brute force. He almost took comfort in that. It had always been where he excelled.

"Wish me luck," he told the horse, and squeezed his fist closed.

There was no boom, no crack of released power. It

came out instead as a sick squelch, superheated energy dripping between his fingers to sizzle in the dry grasses, sending up warning tendrils of smoke. "Come on…" A twist of his wrist, a tilt of the hand, anything to direct those dribbles onto the rope itself.

When it finally snapped in two, his arm whipped upward by reflex, the last of his power searing down his own arm before he could think to draw it back in. "Yes!" The horse started and stamped at Caleb's joyous celebration, and eyed the beginnings of the prairie fire warily.

With his newly freed hand, Caleb beat out the tiny flickers of flame before they could turn into something monstrous. His next act was to yank the amulet from his neck and fling it as far as his prone position would allow.

The horse whickered in concern at the violent movements, but was apparently too intrigued to run away. Its ears flicked back and forth, swiveling almost full circle as it watched the strange human put on a little show.

Though it took some rather painful stretching, and he got rope fibers embedded deep under his fingernails, Caleb managed to work his other arm free the old-fashioned way. It was only a few minutes more before he had his legs free.

He stood and immediately swayed on his feet, his body adjusting to being upright for the first time in almost a full day. A reaching hand found the horse's warm flank under his palm, and he gladly took the support. "Thanks."

The horse craned its neck to look at him, snuffling softly with what Caleb took to be curious noises. "Yes, I'm the crazy person talking to a horse. You should have seen me last night. I was talking to an imaginary coyote."

Slowly, the world righted itself. The morning sun was just off the horizon, casting the prairie in a brilliant yellow glare that promised to bake it dry and hard for the hundredth day in a row. And as Caleb stared around the flat grassland, he realized he had no idea where he was.

"I don't suppose you know the way back to Hope, do you?" The horse flicked its ears, but didn't say anything. "Didn't think so."

For good measure, he kicked some dirt over the nullstone amulet, grinding it into the soil with his boot heel. It was time to reach for Ernst.

He was still hampered by the residual null effects, but somewhere, deep down beneath the thick cotton batting in his head, he could feel the little jackalope far in the distance. His shoulders sagged in relief. "Ernst…" It took several tries, but he finally managed to feed a small pulse into that connection. Hopefully, it was enough to get his familiar's attention.

Almost immediately, there was a pop as the air was displaced to make room for one frantic little familiar. "Caleb! Thank everything!" Quivering with excitement, he gathered himself to leap into the man's arms, but Caleb quickly stepped back.

"Don't! I'm all over nulled. Don't touch me." The chalky stone was debilitating to any human with a shred of power. It was fatal to familiars who were nearly made of magic.

Ernst's ears perked up, and his furry nose wrinkled as he got a good whiff. "Eugh, you reek of it! What did you do, roll in it?" He noticed the horse for the first time, the larger animal giving back the same startled look. "And since when did you go native?"

"I… actually don't know where the horse came from." He had his suspicions, though. It looked awfully like the one Falcon Woman was riding the day he saw her at the Anderson place. "And you can thank Warner for the nullstone."

"He didn't!" The little rabbit-ish creature puffed up to twice his size. "Oooh! I'll scratch his eyes out! I'll put fleas in his sheets! I'll… I don't know what I'll do, but it will be bad, I tell you!" He hopped around in furious circles until he landed on the buried amulet, at which point he leapt sky-high with a pained yelp. "Ow!"

"Be careful, Ernst!" With thorough reluctance, Caleb retrieved the medallion, careful to touch only the lead casing. "First things first, which way is Hope?"

"Almost due south. You're practically in the Wyoming territory, you're so far north."

Caleb cursed softly. "Even if I had a transport, I'd have to ride the better part of the day before I got back there. On foot…"

"Well… you have the horse…" Caleb raised a brow at Ernst, who shrugged his little shoulders. "What? Indians ride them. And it has a bridle; surely it's trained."

"Regardless of how, I have to get back there. Miss Sinclair isn't safe, especially since Warner thinks I died out here." He eyed the horse, getting a quizzical look in return. The animal seemed to know that it was about to be accosted.

"There was some hubbub starting in town when I blinked out, but I didn't get to see what was going on. You want me to go back? Since I can't ride with you anyway."

Caleb nodded. "Yeah, see if it's something serious, and help out if you can. Hey, Ernst?" He caught the jackalope in mid-blink, and the animal quickly faded back to something resembling solidity. "How's Hector?"

Ernst drew himself up proudly. "He's awake, and giving Sven and Jimmy tips on repairing the telegraph."

"Good. Get going, I don't want anyone to see me make an ass of myself with this horse."

"Aye-aye, captain." And he was gone, at least physically. Caleb could still feel him, distant but there, and he took comfort in it.

"At least if I break my neck, someone will know to come looking for me."

The horse snorted its agreement.

The first dilemma was the lack of a saddle. All transports and most haulers had the stirrups built in, making mounting quite easy. The horse had no such convenient handles and steps, and Caleb walked around it a few times trying to judge the best way to get on.

Finally, he grabbed a handful of the animal's mane. "Don't tell anyone about this, all right?"

The first attempt to throw his leg over was less than graceful, but at least he didn't wind up on his rump. The horse was less impressed, shying and snorting for a few moments before Caleb could get close to it again.

On the second try, he made it aboard, where he clung to the animal's neck precariously. How different it was to be atop something with nothing to hang on to. And was a transport this high up?

The horse decided that the strange man riding him was going to offer no guidance, and lowered its head to graze again, nearly dumping Caleb off headfirst.

"Whoa! Easy there!"

He carefully let go of his hold on the mane and took up the reins. That would allow him to steer, of course, but how did he make the thing go? There were no pedals to step on, no levers to kick forward.

He must have been sitting uncomfortably for the horse, because the big animal gave a shudder, every inch of its sensitive skin shaking at once. Caleb grabbed for the mane again and clung tightly with his knees.

The horse's head came up suddenly, and it lurched forward so abruptly that Caleb was almost unseated yet again. They were off across the prairie before he even knew what had happened, the Peacemaker bouncing and clinging to the animal in a most undignified manner.

Some very painful moments passed while he got himself righted again, and it was quickly apparent that knee pressure was going to be a guiding force with the animal. Once they both understood that, Caleb got it pointed south, and they galloped toward Hope, following his connection to Ernst.

Riding a horse was very different from riding a transport. Caleb adapted quickly as he found his own body moving in rhythm with the animal's. He could feel the horse's lungs heave like bellows between his legs and see the pulse of the animal's great heart in its arched neck. He thought his own heart might have matched that beat, until they were almost one creature.

Bare-chested as he was, he was reminded of the dream Falcon Woman had given him, of the Indian brave riding across the prairie to find his village decimated. It sent a shiver of foreboding down his back, and he leaned forward more, urging the horse to run faster. Suddenly, he needed to reach Hope.

The sun was well past its zenith by the time he arrived in the small town, and both he and the horse were soaked in sweat. When he reached the saloon, a crowd had gathered, pressing close and calling out until he couldn't tell one voice from another.

Holding the reins, he slid off the horse's back and tried to make sense of the clamor.

"Agent Marcus!"

"Oh, thank God you're back…"

"You have to do something."

Caleb tried to shout over the din but was getting nowhere. The horse had better luck. Pressed on all sides by shouting humans, it suddenly reared up on its hind legs, lashing out with its sharp hooves. That effectively cleared an awed circle around the beleaguered Peacemaker.

Caleb stroked the horse's sweaty neck, hoping to sooth the agitated animal. "One at a time, please. What is going on?"

One of the women stepped forward, her hands clutching reflexively at her skirts. "He won't let the children leave. They tried to go get them, and men with guns turned them away at the gate!"

That declaration spawned another chorus of impassioned pleas, and it was a few more minutes before Caleb could restore order. "Who won't let them leave where?" He knew, though. What better way to control a town than to hold their children hostage?

"Mr. Warner! They went out there this morning, like usual for schoolin'. Then folks from the homesteads started arrivin' in town, saying that the Injuns were on the warpath, riding down outta the mountains and all. So some o' the men went to collect the children, give 'em safe escort back here. Only Mr. Warner wouldn't even let them on his place. Says it's too dangerous to have the kids out in the open if the reds are on the warpath."

"They threatened to shoot my David if he didn't leave!"

Someone finally noticed Caleb's state of undress and his unconventional mode of transportation. "You been with the Indians, Agent Marcus? Are they really comin' down ta scalp us?"

Fearful cries rang out, and once again Caleb had to shout them down. "No! The Cheyenne are no danger to you. I have a feeling that Mr. Warner's motives are not nearly so noble."

"What's happening, Agent Marcus?" They fell silent as a whole, their desperate eyes looking to him for some answers, any answers.

"I will see to your children. I need a few moments to change and gather some things, but I promise you, I will bring them back. All right?"

"Well, we'll go with you!"

"No. This has become a law enforcement matter. I'll be going on my own."

The townsfolk clamored in protest, but he did his best to ignore them. Sven Isby shouldered his way through the crowd with a scowl and yanked the horse's reins from

Caleb's hand.

"Horse run too much. Must walk." He glared at the Peacemaker and walked off with the painted horse following docilely behind. He was already gone before Caleb thought to tell him about his destroyed hauler.

"Agent Marcus!" Teddy appeared at his elbow, offering him a shirt, which Caleb took gratefully. "There's somethin' else."

"What's wrong?" He winced as he pulled the cotton garment on over his sunburned shoulders.

"Miss Ellen. I just went upstairs ta tell her you were back, and she's gone."

Caleb froze in the act of donning the shirt. "What do you mean, gone?"

"She left a note." Teddy handed over a crisp piece of paper, and Caleb glanced over the precise penmanship.

I intend to tell Mr. Warner that I will not testify against his men, in exchange for the release of the children. Agent Marcus will still have Jimmy for a witness. My testimony will not be important. I will return soon. ~Ellen

Caleb swore, and dropped the letter so he could work at his shirt buttons faster. "He was willing to kill me just for knowing about that mine, Teddy. What do you think he's going to do to her for possessing truly damning evidence?"

The Scot went pale under his beard. "She can't have been gone more than an hour."

"That's long enough to get her to Warner's." He tucked the shirt in with brusque movements. "Find Jimmy; tell him to get my trunk. Get me some water and something to eat quickly." Nodding, Teddy took off at a dead run. "Ernst!"

The jackalope popped into existence balanced on the sidewalk railing. "We're going?"

Caleb nodded. "Go ahead. Find Miss Sinclair and the children. I need to know where they're being held."

"There's nullstone there somewhere."

"Do your best, but stay safe." He reached out to scratch the familiar's ears. "I'll catch up around sundown if you're not back to me by then."

Teddy returned with Jimmy on his heels, the boy struggling to carry the large trunk by himself but proudly refusing all help. Caleb gave the boy a brief smile as he took the box from him. "I hear you're making good progress on the telegraph."

"Yessir. Mr. Pratt and Mr. Isby and me. We might get it workin' in a few days."

"Get it working tonight, Jimmy. Tell Hector to send a message to the Peacemaker office in Kansas City. Tell him to use the gibberish; he'll know what it means." The authentication codes would get Graeme moving, if nothing else.

The boy's eyes went wide. "Yer goin' out ta Warner's alone, ain'cha? Lemme go, too!"

"No. I need you to get that telegraph working and that message out in case..." In case he didn't come back. Which was highly likely. *Crying Elk said it would be a good day to die.* "Just get that machine working. If anybody can, it's you." He mussed the boy's hair and flashed him a smile he didn't truly feel. "And thank you for taking care of my trunk."

"Yessir. Yer welcome, sir."

Shouldering his trunk, he ducked into the relative coolness of the tavern. No one was inside, save Teddy, who produced a glass of water and a dripping wet canteen, as well as a plate of beef and cold potatoes. "It's the best I have on short notice, sorry."

"That's fine. I just haven't eaten in a day or so." Unless he counted the broth from Falcon Woman... if that had even happened. "I need to get my strength up for this little excursion."

"Did ye even make it to Tasco? What happened to

ye out there, Agent Marcus? Ye came ridin' in here like a red Indian."

Caleb talked around mouthfuls of food. "I didn't make it to Tasco. They shot the hauler out from under me, went up like a Chinese rocket. It was a long shot; I never saw it coming. I'm willing to bet it was Schmidt."

"Sweet Mary, mother of God. Yer lucky yer not in bits all over the prairie!"

Caleb nodded his agreement. "Knocked me cold, and when I woke up, Warner and his boys were there. They tied me to stakes and left me to die. Put a nullstone around my neck."

"So how'd ye get loose?"

"I just… did. It took me a while." There was no need to tell him about shamans or dark-eyed Indian women with hypnotic voices. "Now, I need you to listen to some things, Teddy, and tell the other Peacemakers when they get here."

The bartender nodded and leaned in attentively.

"First and foremost, Warner has my staff." It was almost impossible to destroy an ironwood staff, and Caleb had no doubt that if it had survived the explosion, it was in the rancher's hands now. "He shouldn't be able to use it, but they need to get it back from him. Tell them to take at least four men."

Teddy blinked slowly. "Ye think he's a danger ta more'n one Peacemaker, but yer goin' alone? Are ye mad?"

"It's possible." Caleb guzzled the glass of water and motioned for more. Who knew when he'd get a chance to replenish himself again? "Second, he has a stockpile of nullstone somewhere on that ranch. They need to be prepared for him to use it as a weapon." The use of weaponized nullstone had long been banned by combatants in all of the world's civilized nations. Warner was in no way civilized.

"And third?"

"Third… tell them about Schmidt. He'll kill them before they even reach the ranch if they're not warned."

"Ye honestly dinnae think yer comin' back."

"Probably not. But I have to try. He'll hold those kids to keep the town obedient, and God only knows what he'll do to Miss Sinclair." *Or has done already*, he thought with a private grimace.

"Yer goin' out there empty-handed?"

"No." Caleb wiped his mouth and tossed the napkin on the bar. "That's what the trunk is for."

The lock popped open with a click when Caleb channeled a bit of power into the warding runes, and he eased the lid up just in case the contents had become unstable during travel. Fortunately, everything looked to be in its place.

The twelve glass vials were the most important, and he checked the seal and cork on each of them carefully as he drew them from their resting places. The blue glow was serene and soothing, belying the destructive power locked within the fragile glass shells. He tucked those explosive charges into loops on the inside of his heavy duster, taking care not to clink them together.

The slender length of wood he drew out next was no replacement for his staff, but it would do in a pinch. It was barely the length of his forearm and only as big around as one of his fingers, and the runes etched into it were shallow and barely visible. It would last through two, maybe three strong blasts before the sheer force it channeled would disintegrate it. Odds were, if Caleb needed more than three shots, things would be going against him anyway. He let it dangle from his right wrist on a thong, within easy grasp.

The nullstone handcuffs he handled gingerly, tucking them deep into his duster pocket along with the lead-cased amulet. His revolver was long gone, either blasted over the prairie or in the hands of one of Warner's men, but he tucked extra rounds for it in his other pocket anyway, just in case. If nothing else, it balanced out the weight.

The last thing he took from the trunk was his badge, which he pinned over his heart. The one he'd lost on the prairie was nothing more than a tin star to denote his occupation. The one he kept locked within his trunk would not only act as a shield stronger than anything he could conjure with his staff but also lead other Peacemakers straight to him.

Teddy watched Caleb's preparations, keeping silent for a long moment before he simply had to speak. "And just how are ye goin' ta get out there? That Schmidt will see a transport comin' a mile away, especially after dark."

"He's not looking for me yet. As far as he knows, I'm dead. And he won't see what doesn't glow."

Teddy looked puzzled.

"I'll ride the horse."

The Scot shook his head. "Ye really have gone native on us."

"You have no idea."

15

Caleb waited in town until the sun was nearly down and only the last vestiges of red and purple were visible over the mountain peaks in the west. By that time, Sven Isby had deemed the horse at least semi-recovered from its day-long gallop, but the old smith was still very displeased with Caleb for taking the animal again. The Peacemaker rode out of town with dark glares from the Swede and many prayers from the other residents.

The horse, for its part, didn't seem to mind the additional exertion now that it and the human had reached some kind of understanding about things. Though Caleb would have happily paid for a saddle and some stirrups, it wasn't that bad a ride once he became accustomed to the animal's gait. Caleb held it to an easy lope on the way out to Warner's place. There was no hurry, and only the darkness would save him from Schmidt's long eye.

Standing out like a lighthouse in a sea of tall grass, the lights from the A-bar-W were visible miles before he got there. Though his skin itched terribly as he rode closer, certain he was about to hear the hiss of an augmented bullet cutting through the grass, he rode within a half mile of the ranch before he pulled the horse up and slid off its painted back.

The animal tossed its head, snorting, when Caleb removed the bridle. "Go back to wherever you came from, friend. This won't be a place for you." Contrary to orders, the animal didn't seem inclined to leave at all, though it did wander off a few paces to graze.

Caleb crouched in the tall grass, pulling out a pair of binoculars to survey the ranch. "Ernst…" The small form of his familiar appeared next to his right boot, the tips of his antlers sparking in the darkness. "What did you learn?"

"I can't see the children, but he's buried the nullstone all around the schoolhouse on the southern side of the compound. I'm guessing they're in there. What easier way to control them?"

"And Miss Sinclair?" There were men posted at the fence, several yards apart. He could see their silhouettes, and the long lines of the rifles they carried.

"She's in the main house. I couldn't get close enough for her to see me, but she appeared unharmed."

"Warner?"

"He's got them set for a siege. He's armed the barren men around the interior and set the others around the perimeter to keep watch and power the fence. I think he believes the townsfolk will rally and try to retrieve their children. He's got the guards watching the road, but he's not worried. He knows he's stronger than anyone else out here."

Caleb fingered the vials inside his coat with a grim frown. "He may be stronger, but he's not better trained. Where's Schmidt?"

"I can't find him anywhere." The jackalope's tiny form shivered, the motion rustling the dry grasses around them. "Be careful, Caleb. All the training in the world won't stop a bullet if you can't see it coming."

His power nestled inside his chest, warm and comforting. The last of the nullstone had cleared hours ago, and he finally felt like himself again. "That's why I have you to watch my back, right?"

"As long as I can."

"First things first. I need to get inside that fence. We

may have to take out a sentry or two." With any luck, he could disable them without harming them. If not… He'd deal with that when the time came, but he wouldn't like it.

Caleb began his long creep through the dry grasses, moving slowly through the drowsing herd of cows. The massive animals shuffled a bit at his passing, but not enough to raise an alarm. As he got closer, he could see the men patrolling the fence line within easy sight of each other. Flickers of arcane power danced from one fence post to the next, lighting the night with blue flashes. The pulses were steady, uniform, and he could probably slip through the fence itself, but taking out one of the sentries was going to leave a gap in the power feed, and that would be noticed.

However, at the corner near the smithy, there was one area where the building broke the line of sight. *Best to confront one man instead of two*. A scuffle would still be heard, but it was their best chance, and perhaps it would be some time before someone came to investigate the fence.

As they maneuvered around to approach in that blind spot, Caleb could see no sentry standing there. It was enough to make him pause for a long moment. The fence continued to pulse, the tiny blue spark traveling down the wires and around the corner out of sight. Why would Warner leave one section unguarded? Was it a trap? He exchanged looks with Ernst, who shrugged his furry shoulders in the darkness.

"If it's a trap, at least I know it." As silent as he could, he moved forward.

The mystery of the unmanned fence was quickly solved, though the answer left more questions. Placed carefully beneath the fence wire was a small metronome, very like the one Caleb's childhood piano teacher had used. Its arm swung slowly but steadily back and forth, and every time it connected with the wire, a small spark would jump, sending a pulse down the fence. It kept time like a long heartbeat, the same as if a person had been there to power it.

"Who…?" Caleb could only shake his head at Ernst's question. He had no idea who was aiding them, or why. *They're supposed to think I'm dead.* They both slipped under the fence between pulses, careful not to disturb the little mechanical device.

The reason for the lack of sentry became apparent when they discovered an unconscious man behind the smithy. Caleb slipped over the open space quickly, imagining a target painted across his shoulders until he could take refuge in the shadows behind the building again. His fingers found a pulse in the man's throat, but the large purpling bruise on his forehead assured him the man would not be waking anytime soon.

"I don't like this, Ernst." There was an unknown factor in this equation, and it made the skin itch between his shoulder blades.

"You're never so rich as to turn down a friend, Caleb," Ernst murmured quietly, hopping to the far corner of the building to peer around.

Caleb took the hunting knife off his belt and scraped at the hard-packed soil enough to bury one of the glowing blue vials, transferred from his coat to the dirt before the light could be noticed, then moved to join Ernst. "Try to get to Miss Sinclair; let her know help is coming. I'm going to work my way to the schoolhouse for the kids."

"Watch the nullstone. It's just barely under the dirt."

"I'm going to leave a trail." Caleb patted his coat. "If I get in trouble, you know what to do."

There was no one in view between the buildings, though Caleb could still hear the roar of the forge just beyond the wall that concealed him. The next shelter he would find would be the shadows behind the smokehouse, and there was a large patch of open ground to cross.

He counted off ten to himself, then darted out,

keeping low as he scurried to the next patch of darkness. Footsteps alerted him at the last possible second, and he pressed himself flat against the wall. One of the fence sentries passed within ten feet of him, and Caleb held himself motionless, trusting darkness and the sentry's apathy to conceal him in plain sight. The man reached the edge of his assigned patrol and turned about, his eyes giving a cursory glance around. If the man had been truly paying attention, he'd have seen the Peacemaker crouched against the stone foundation, but his thoughts were obviously elsewhere. He moved on, an irritated sigh carrying to Caleb where he hid. Apparently, Warner's men thought the extra precautions unnecessary.

And if I were dead, they most likely would be. That thought gave him a sort of dark satisfaction. He concealed another of the glowing vials before the sentry made his return pass, and when the man cleared the corner of the building, Caleb was waiting.

Pouncing on him from behind, he clamped a forearm over the man's windpipe before any cries could alert the others. He was bigger than the guard, but physically overpowering him was only the beginning of it.

There was a brief surge of power, born of fear and anger, but Caleb opened himself to it, allowing it to pass through his body and into the soil without so much as a spark or crackle. It stung, really, but not nearly as much as resisting the charge would have.

The man's struggles became stronger for a moment, thrashing in the body's last desperate act of self-preservation, then he slumped into unconsciousness. Caleb eased him to the ground and crouched there next to him for a long, tense moment, waiting to hear alarms clamoring. Nothing came. He now had limited time, though, before the gap in the fence drew attention. *Best be moving.*

He arranged the unconscious man as comfortably as he could. "You're a lucky one. Just remember that when you wake up."

Ernst was on the far side of the compound. Caleb could feel him, a tiny pull against his own power. Had he reached the schoolteacher yet?

Two buildings still remained between him and the schoolhouse. One appeared to be simply a supply shed, small with no windows in the tall walls. The other housed the kennels. Until this moment, Caleb had forgotten about the pack of bluetick hounds. If the kennel doors were open, things were going to get complicated.

Behind the shed, he planted another glowing vial, and then waited while a group of three men walked past his position, laughing and exchanging bawdy jokes. Obviously, no one had noticed the malfunctioning fence yet. They were still unaware that they had been invaded. *They're too cocky, counting on the fact that they're facing only townsfolk.*

At the kennels, his luck ran out. Before he'd even reached the side of the structure, a furry head poked out of an open door, its sensitive nose sniffing the hot night air. A low growl rumbled from a spotted chest, and Caleb froze where he was, caught in the open space between two buildings. The hound padded out, hackles raised, head turning to find the scent that did not belong. There was no breeze, nothing to carry Caleb's scent away. Unerringly, the flat head turned in his direction.

Goooood doggy...

The dog opened its mouth and bayed, instantly echoed by the rest of its pack. They boiled out of the kennels in a spotted tide, every one of them yowling at the top of its lungs.

It was already too late to shut them up. Caleb could hear annoyed voices yelling at the noisy animals, coming to investigate the commotion. And worse than that, it was clear that the dogs weren't going to settle for raising the alarm. They came at him with fangs bared, saliva spattering in all directions in their zeal.

As much as he hated to hurt a dog, he summoned force into his clenched fist, readying it to blast the hounds into silence. It was going to give away his presence, sadly, but he couldn't afford to get mauled either.

The dark shape darted past him and was in the midst of the dogs before Caleb even realized what was happening. The baying of the hounds became furious snarls, and then cries of pain as they turned on the new attacker in their midst. Something small and dark was tearing them to bits.

In moments, it was over. Three of the hounds turned tail and ran, yelping to the high heavens. One of them was never going to get up again. The others limped a wary distance away, eyeing the creature that had humiliated them.

The coyote sat licking one forepaw nonchalantly, then turned to attend an itch on its back as if it had not a care in the world.

As the shouting voices and running footsteps closed in, it occurred to Caleb that he was still out in the open. He squeezed inside the first kennel just as the guards rounded the corner.

"Gawddam coyote tore up the dogs! Lookit the smug little bastard just sittin' there!"

Through a knothole, Caleb watched, holding his breath against the stifling dog stench in the small enclosure, as the coyote went streaking back toward the prairie, bullets kicking up dirt all around it.

"Betcha that was the same one that got the chickens last week."

"Damn varmints. I'm goin' huntin' tomorrow, skin me some coyotes."

The men were barren. Caleb couldn't find them in his arcane sense, and so he could only wait for a long, tense moment as they wandered back to their posts. He could only hope that they wouldn't suddenly decide to come back, because he'd have no warning.

He rested his head against the side of the kennel, letting his heart resume its normal pace. That had been too close. If it weren't for the coyote… Or was it Coyote? Not a question he was willing to ponder, at the moment. It was merely comforting to know that he was not alone.

As he slipped from the kennel, he buried another vial at the corner of the building, with regrets for any harm he might cause the unwitting animals. Creeping to the opposite corner, he pondered his next course of action.

The schoolhouse stood apart from the rest of the buildings, no doubt to avoid contaminating anyone else with the nullstone taint. There were no lights on in the little building, so it was impossible to see if anyone lurked behind the dark windowpanes. The clear area he would have to cross to get there seemed acres wide, but there was no help for it. He gritted his teeth and ran.

He almost made it.

The gunshot sounded at the same moment that a train hit his left shoulder and rolled him head over heels into the dirt. His head was still swimming when the second report exploded the dirt in front of his face.

Instinct forced power through his badge, and a shield sprang up around him, shimmering in the darkness. As the flying dust settled, he saw Schmidt calmly walking across the compound toward him. "Oh, hell."

His left arm hadn't started hurting yet, but it was also not obeying his commands. Caleb struggled to his feet to face the sharpshooter, summoning power into his uninjured hand.

Schmidt raised the rifle to his shoulder, taking careful aim, and fired twice, reloading impossibly fast. The bullets ricocheted off Caleb's shield, sending spiderwebs of colors dancing across the surface, and impacting hard enough to make him stagger back a pace or two. Onward

Schmidt came.

The next two shots bounced off with a plaintive whine and almost knocked Caleb down even within the magical shield. He could feel something dripping down the back of his left hand, warm and thick. It left dark spots in the dust. His vision wavered slightly, and he knew if he didn't see to the blood loss, he'd simply pass out. That would be the end of his shield.

Two more shots pushed him back farther, and when his heels touched the nullstoned ground, he understood why. The power in his shield started to drain away, the shimmering globe of air flickering, shattering. He quickly stepped forward again, the line of nullstone etched in his senses now. The shield firmed, the particles of air locking into place once more. He had a matter of feet.

No more than fifteen yards away, Schmidt stopped to load another cartridge into his gun. He seemed to be in no hurry, his emotionless eyes fixing Caleb where he stood as his hands reloaded by feel. He brought the buffalo gun up to his shoulder again, sighting down the barrel. His finger squeezed the trigger.

Caleb gritted his teeth, leaning into the force of the double shot, and just managed to keep his position. He couldn't let Schmidt force him onto that nulled ground. The sharpshooter came forward again, as if out for a Sunday stroll.

The ground under Caleb's feet was getting sticky. His own blood was making mud of the soil, clumping on his boots. There was still no pain in his shoulder, but he knew it would come the moment he lost concentration. He had to end this.

He felt the power flare yards away, saw the blue spark fizzing on the gun in Schmidt's hands. The next shots would be augmented, faster, harder, more accurate, and they would explode on impact. There would be no resisting these.

In the war, Caleb had captured cannonballs out of the air, turning their momentum and energy back on their senders. How much different, then, could a bullet really be?

The sharpshooter stood aiming for what seemed an eternity. Caleb drew every bit of power he could, mindful of what trickled away into the soil behind him. His hand was wreathed in a crackling blue nimbus as he brought it up, and he let the shield fall.

The gun cracked twice so fast it seemed one sound, and overhead, lightning split the sky, casting everything in negative for a fraction of a heartbeat. The glowing blue bullets streaked through the air at Caleb, leaving a solid light trail through his vision. And he reached for it, found the energy in it, absorbed it into his own.

A bullet was no different than a cannonball. Inertia was inertia, and propellant magic was all the same. He caught both bullets, one after the other, spoke to their power, used their own momentum against them. His mind went through the forms faster than thought, faster than control words. Catch, convert, counter. He spun in place, one bullet following his glowing hand, and when he came out of the turn, it went rocketing back at its sender.

The thunder boomed loud enough to rattle everything where it stood and masked the sharp crack of the speeding projectile. Schmidt's dead eyes showed faint surprise, the first human emotion Caleb had ever seen in him, in the split second before the returned bullet shattered the barrel of the rifle, exploding it into stars of white-hot shrapnel. Schmidt fell, ever silent.

The second bullet glowed faintly in Caleb's palm, most of its energy fed into its sacrificed partner. Caleb pocketed it.

Another bolt of lightning struck as Caleb crossed the open ground between them, shaking his focus rod from his sleeve to slide into his palm. Perfect in a face mangled and bloody, Schmidt's pale blue eyes stared up at the dark sky above them. One eyelid twitched as Caleb watched, but the man's chest was still. The dead eyes went filmy, true death claiming the body as it had already claimed the soul.

Peacemakers didn't kill. They weren't executioners; they were law men. Caleb had sworn an oath. It was something to mull over later. Much later. Caleb watched a moment longer, then tucked his focus rod away again. The unused revolver on Schmidt's belt would fit well enough in Caleb's empty holster. There was nothing else to be done for the dead man now.

With the distractions gone for the moment, Caleb's shoulder hurt, throbbing in time with the stumbling steps he took toward the schoolhouse. The moment he stepped onto the nulled ground, he felt his power sucked down and away, leaving him cold and shivering. The door slammed open as he staggered into it, and he collapsed to his knees in the doorway, silhouetted against the distant light behind him. The perfect target, if someone were so inclined.

The schoolhouse, dark and silent, was empty. The desks and primers sat serene and undisturbed, waiting for the next day's lesson. But there were no children. Caleb's shoulders sagged, sending a lance of pain that took his breath away. Where the hell were they?

The distinctive sound of a gun cocking brought his head up. In the corner, a tall shadow moved, resolving into Mary Catherine, holding a shotgun leveled at his head. Her raven hair was unbound around her shoulders, and the flickering lightning outside revealed the grim determination in her dark eyes. They watched each other for a long moment.

Caleb finally broke the silence. "Are you going to shoot me now?"

"Are you going to give me cause to?" Her English had improved drastically, it seemed.

He shook his head. "No. I just wanted to find the kids."

"I can show you where they are. But you must do something for me." Thunder grumbled, and her eyes darted toward the windows once before returning to him.

For a split second, Caleb thought about rushing her, wrestling the gun away while she was distracted. He did not. "What do you want?"

"Warner has my son in a room inside the smithy. He keeps him there to insure my obedience. You have to get him." Slowly, she lowered the barrel of the shotgun to point at the floor. "The shaman's daughter walked in my dreams. She said you would come. I removed one of the guards so you could enter."

Caleb, deciding he wasn't about to be shot again, struggled to his feet, leaving a bloody handprint on a desk. He shrugged his left arm out of his coat and inspected the dark, wet mess that was his shirt. "Did you send the coyote, too?"

"Coyote is here? No. Crying Elk is near, then. He calls the storm. This will be a night of cleansing." She propped the shotgun against the lectern and came to examine Caleb's shoulder. "I am not a healer, but we must bind this before you lose more blood."

"I appear to be fresh out of bandages."

Without hesitation, the woman grasped her own blouse in both hands and ripped, buttons popping off in all directions. Caleb quickly averted his eyes. "This will do for now. I disliked the garment anyway."

She bound his shoulder in calico cloth, as tightly as possible without cutting off the circulation to his hand. He did his best not to notice her bare arms as she worked in only her chemise. "I… ow… I assume you are coming with us when we leave tonight?"

"If you can free my son, I will depart. If you cannot, I will die to retrieve him." She helped him back into his coat, and the vials on the inside clinked softly.

"Where are the children?"

"The smokehouse. And the teaching woman is upstairs in the main house. He has not been kind to her, but he treats her better than he does me." She smiled darkly. "Warner has no honor. He will die weeping."

"I'm not here to kill anyone. We have to see the children and Miss Sinclair to safety first."

The woman moved to the doorway, which still hung open, and peered cautiously into the night. "They have not come to investigate the death of Dead Eyes. Something has distracted them."

"Then it's as good a time as any to move." He took two glowing vials from his coat and handed them to her. "Find somewhere to bury these. Shallow. Many yards apart. Keep them away from the nullstone."

She took them, raising a brow. "What are they for?"

"Removing extra factors from the equation." He moved to stand near her, getting his own view of the compound.

"I do not understand what you mean, but I will do as you ask. Crying Elk sent word that you are a good man."

"Get the kids; get them outside the fence line. Maybe take them back into the pasture among the cattle. It'll be harder to see them there. I'll get your son and Miss Sinclair."

She nodded. "I will do that once these are buried." She lifted her skirt right in front of him and retrieved a knife she had strapped to her thigh. "It is a good day to die, Good Man." With an almost feral grin, she slipped into the lightning dazzled night.

Caleb took her place pressed to the doorjamb. His shoulder throbbed, but he had no time to think about it. There were dark shapes moving around in the lighted windows at the main house, and it was only a matter of time before someone missed Schmidt. No doubt, Ellen Sinclair would pay the price for Warner's displeasure once Schmidt was discovered.

"Ernst, I hope you're with her." Caleb darted from the doorway, running low and fast across the nulled ground to take shelter against the kennels once more. The hounds, if they were still present, had grown wary of the strange things creeping through the night and made no sound. He took shelter in the spilled straw bedding, smelling strongly of dog and dust. His power surged back into him, and something tight in his chest loosened as it took its place in his veins again.

"All right, Warner. Here I come."

<h1 style="text-align:center">16</h1>

Something had definitely gone wrong for Warner's men. Crouched at the corner of the kennels, Caleb watched them run back and forth across the compound, shouting to each other with panic in their voices and fear hanging heavily in the air. Under the constant rumble of thunder, he could make out no words, but the chaos had to work in his favor.

He spied Warner once, as the rancher came out onto his porch to shout orders to his men, but he quickly vanished back inside. There were at least three other men within, and probably more that Caleb could not count. Getting in there was going to be messy.

If Mary Catherine's son was locked inside the smithy, he was most likely safe. It was Ellen who was in the most danger. Caleb found his link to Ernst and tugged, calling silently.

Instantly, the jackalope popped into view at his boot. "She's upstairs, and they haven't harmed her yet. But he's put a nullstone necklace around her neck, like the one he put on you. Did you get the children?"

"No, Mary Catherine's going after them."

"Mary Catherine?"

"It's complicated. Does Ellen know we're here?"

Ernst shook his head. "I couldn't get her alone to show myself. But they think the Dog Soldiers are coming. They think the storm is the old shaman calling down the thunder."

"They're right about that much." Caleb continued to

watch the men pass weapons among one another, forming a tighter perimeter around the main house. This was going to be both good and bad. "You ready to see how many we can take out?"

The familiar cocked his head, one floppy ear perked curiously. "I can feel… six charges? Not quite a full circle, but it should do for most of them."

"Think it'll get Warner?"

"No. He's stronger than that, Caleb, and you know it. At least the nullstone should protect Miss Sinclair. What about the barrens?"

"I'm willing to bet they'll flee the moment the guards start dropping." If not, Caleb would have to deal with them, too, power or no power.

The arcane-powered guards had ringed the house. He couldn't be sure to get them all, but it was worth a shot. Kneeling, he put both palms against the hard-packed soil, ignoring the sharp pain in his shoulder at the movement. "Ready, Ernst?"

"Ready, Caleb."

There was one other advantage to having a bond with a familiar. They were a font of stored power, and they could share it if necessary.

Ernst hopped over and placed one tiny paw on the back of Caleb's right hand, purring softly. The man closed his eyes, took a deep breath, and nearly gasped it right back out again as pure energy flooded his senses. With Ernst added to his own reservoir of power, Caleb was almost his old self, very nearly the man he had once been. But this was not his power to keep. He was borrowing it for a very specific purpose.

He sent it out through the ground, seeking, finding. He knew where the dirt gave way to pastureland, could feel the roots of the grass desperately craving water. The cows stirred restlessly, spooked by the storm overhead and the electricity beneath their hooves. The coonhounds, beaten and unnerved, retreated out of his range even as he sensed them. Each man who stood on the ground left an impression, a faint echo of the power he held, beating in time with his heart. Even the barren men were there, but only as a sense of pressure against the soil where they stood.

More distant were the frantic steps of ten young children, their power muted but visible, and the blankness that must be Mary Catherine. Caleb "watched" them until they neared the schoolhouse. The nullstone there stood out as a dark place in his vision, and he lost all sense of the escaping children.

Lastly, scattered through the compound were six dots, glowing brilliantly in his mind's eye. His own power, locked into tiny vials, and sealed with corks.

One pulse, that was all it took. One strong shove, one tremor barely felt at the surface but churning through the soil mere inches down. Simultaneously, those vials cracked.

The power escaped with six explosive booms, putting the thunder and lightning to shame. It drowned out all sound for several heartbeats, and destroyed any sort of night vision with the searing blue brightness. Even prepared for it, Caleb saw ghostly images before his eyes, and his head swam in the stunning aftermath. Ernst peered up into his face, his nose almost touching, and Caleb could see the creature only in shades of black and brilliant white. The tips of Ernst's antlers sparked and fizzed, then died out.

"You all right, Ernst?"

"Never better. You?"

"I'll let you know in a moment." When Caleb could see again, he raised his head to scout the courtyard.

Bodies lay scattered, some of them moaning and stirring slightly, most of them absolutely quiet. They would be alive, barring some unforeseen medical condition, so long as they hadn't been standing directly on top of a charge. But even those still awake, unprepared for such a powerful release of power, would be stunned for hours.

Two of the downed bodies stirred, starting to rise, and Caleb knew those would be barrens. The arcane explosion wouldn't affect them the same, but it had apparently served the purpose of scaring them away, because the two men staggered off in different directions, leaving their rifles behind. Hopefully, the others would do the same. Caleb really didn't want to raise his power against barren men.

Shadows still moved in the lighted windows of Warner's house. At the dead center of the charged circle, where the concussions were the weakest, the occupants would have escaped the worst of the effects. Those men he would have to deal with on his own.

"Come on, Ernst." He emerged from his concealment and walked across the compound. There was no more reason for hiding. He stepped over the downed men in his way, making certain as he passed that each of them was still breathing. Ernst paused a bit longer by each, assessing their power to see that their threat had been neutralized. Since the familiar never called out, Caleb just kept walking.

His boots thudded as he stepped up on the porch, and he actually stopped to rap his knuckles politely against the door. There was movement inside, but no one opened it. "Mr. Warner, it's over. Release Miss Sinclair and come out."

Behind the door, Warner's response was slightly muffled. "You will understand why I am reluctant to do so, Agent. She seems to be my best bargaining chip at the moment."

"There is also the little matter of you shooting my transport out from under me and leaving me for dead that must be addressed."

"If you'd be so kind as to depart, I would be willing to chalk this up to a gentlemanly misunderstanding and forget it."

"Caleb…" Ernst whispered. "On the roof."

Caleb was well aware of the stealthy footsteps overhead. Two men had stepped from the second-floor windows and even now were creeping over the shingles to get above his position. He gripped the slender shaft of wood tied to his wrist and lit the runes. In the softer wood, the blue runes burned to red embers at the edges. It would not be able to hold his power for long. "Duck."

He dropped to one knee even as he pointed the shaft upward, mouthing the word *kracht* as he released his energy. The resulting explosion opened a hole the size of a water barrel in the roof and sent both men plummeting to the ground with startled cries that quickly turned to groans of pain as bones snapped upon landing.

"Make them sleep, Ernst." Pointing the wand at the locked door, he channeled only a trickle of power, drawn down to a pinpoint. Instantly the doorknob grew hot, glowing a cheerful red. On the other side, someone yelped in pain.

Caleb slipped another vial out of his coat, stepped back about a foot, and kicked the door in. Before anyone inside could react, he gave the glass vial a toss and dropped to the ground, arms over his head for protection.

The windows exploded, raining glass for yards, and the already damaged roof above the porch took on a dangerous tilt. Out of the dust and debris, Ernst appeared, annoyance clear on his face. "You could warn me before you do things like that, you know."

"No sense of adventure." Caleb got to his feet, cautiously peering into the interior of the house. The force of the charge had blown out the lamps, but he could make out two bodies sprawled on the floor. One was bald, the other blond. Neither was Warner. "Find him, Ernst."

The familiar blinked out, presumably to scout the upper floor, and Caleb advanced slowly, the smoldering rod clutched in his left hand. The runes had almost charred themselves black. He had minutes at most before the whole thing went up in flames.

The floorboards creaked ominously under his feet, and mortar sifted from the chimney stones as the house groaned and settled. The explosion had done more damage than he'd bargained for.

He crossed the sitting room quickly, pausing at the first open door to listen for anyone lurking within. Save the settling of the house, all was still, but in the hallway, he found a section of floor that had noticeably less dust on it and no debris at all. In fact, the clean area had a clearly defined boundary in a perfect circle. *A shield.* Footprints, both male and female, marked a path toward the kitchen in the back. Judging by the scuff marks, Ellen wasn't making it easy for Warner.

Ernst popped into view in the middle of the hallway. "Caleb, he's—" he eyed the retreating footprints. "—not here. But you already knew that."

"He'll be headed for the livery. If he gets on a transport, I can't stop him without hurting her." Caleb hurried down the hallway, wary of walking into a trap left behind but anxious that the rancher not get too far ahead.

"Not if I get there first." Ernst vanished between one bound and the next.

As Caleb ducked out the back door and into the night again, he passed two more men who were moaning and semiconscious on the ground. They were of little interest. Loud snarls and a woman's startled cries led him to dash on toward the livery.

A flash of lightning illuminated the open area between buildings, freezing all motion for a heartbeat. Warner was there, holding Ellen by one arm, a tall staff in his free hand. Ellen was struggling to free herself, one fist raised to beat on Warner's shoulder. And crouched in the livery door was the largest wolf Caleb had ever seen. The animal stood with forepaws braced, head down and hackles raised, gleaming white fangs bared in a snarl that was audible even beneath the thunder's rumble. It could have been any wolf, save for the antlers sprouting from its head, the tips frenetically sparking blue in agitation.

In the next flash of light, Ellen caught sight of Caleb descending upon them, and screamed out his name. "Agent Marcus!"

Warner whirled away from the threatening Ernst and leveled the staff at Caleb. "Hold it, Agent! You know very well what I can do with this."

The wooden rod was smoking in Caleb's hand as he came to a halt a few yards away. "That doesn't belong to you. I want it back."

"What is it they say? Finders keepers?" Warner gestured toward the ground. "Drop the rod."

"That staff is useless to you." Caleb took another step forward, and the runes at the top of his staff flared to life, blue sparks flying from the power funneled into it. He froze, and Warner grinned slowly.

"Best money I ever spent, you know? Your predecessor, Agent Hazard, was a very good teacher." He raised an expectant brow.

Caleb hesitated only a moment, then dropped the nearly spent rod. It wouldn't have held together much longer anyway. "Release Miss Sinclair."

"I think not. You won't dare strike at me, not without this staff to focus and with her in the way. I think Miss Sinclair and I are going to be spending quite some time together."

"Like hell!" With a very unladylike snarl, Ellen stomped down hard on Warner's instep and threw a respectable punch at his throat. At the same moment Ernst sprang, sinking gleaming white fangs into the rancher's calf.

Attacked on two fronts, Warner had no choice but to release his hold on the schoolteacher's arm, turning to stab at Ernst with the butt end of the staff.

Ellen instantly threw herself flat against the ground, clearing the way for Caleb's shouted "*Kracht*!" The bolt of blue power streaked across the empty space between them, crashing like the violent spears of lightning above.

Warner moved impossibly fast. The staff cracked sharply against the wolf's skull, snapping an antler off in a shower of blue sparks. Ernst let out an agonized yelp of pain. In the same motion, the rancher spun to slam the long shaft of ironwood into the ground. The runes flared to life, and Caleb's blast slammed against the instantaneous shield.

When the brightness had faded, Warner smiled coldly at the Peacemaker from behind his protective wall. "Care to try again?"

Ellen gave a small shriek and scooted away, beating at the smoldering hem of her dress. Where the shield had intersected with the cloth, a straight line had been burned through the calico.

Caleb realized that was not a shield of solidified air like the one he most often created. What Warner held was a shield of pure power, and tiny tendrils of smoke rose around the edges where it charred even the dirt upon contact. He wasn't risking running out of air. He could hold it almost indefinitely, as long as his concentration didn't waver.

"Ernst? You all right?" The wounded familiar answered with a savage snarl, the broken end of his antler fizzing and popping like a Chinese sparkler. The large animal prowled the edges of Warner's shield, reminding him what would happen the instant it dropped.

"You should go, Agent Marcus. While you still can."

"You are under arrest, Mr. Warner." Caleb drew the

borrowed revolver from its holster. He had no idea how he would get a bullet through the shield, but if he found his chance he wanted to be ready.

"As you like." In a blur, the shield fell, and Warner's left hand sent a glowing lance rocketing at Caleb's chest. The Peacemaker had only time enough to drop himself into the dust, and he felt his hair stand on end as the electrical charge passed over him. In answer, the thunder boomed directly overhead as a bolt of lightning shattered the weathervane atop the house.

Another sizzling bolt speared the ground near his right hand, forcing him to snatch it back without the revolver.

Ernst closed in on the rancher from behind, but not fast enough, and the shield slammed back into place, searing the wolf's tender nose. The familiar whined and rolled in the dirt, trying to ease the burning.

Caleb felt the fragile vials in his coat pressed between his chest and the hard ground, and a cold chill went down his spine. If those had shattered, all his worries would have been ended in one spectacular moment.

"Oh, do get up, Agent Marcus. I will not lower myself to killing a man who is groveling in the dust. Leave the gun where it is."

Something else pressed against Caleb's thigh, and he remembered the nullstone amulet in his coat pocket. Reluctantly, he left the revolver where it lay, but and as he clambered to his feet, he subtly fished the medallion from his pocket. His fingers went numb where they brushed against the chalky stone, and he let it dangle by the chain, hidden from Warner in the folds of his heavy coat. If he could break Warner's concentration for just a moment, he could hit him with the medallion, he was certain.

"Schmidt's not coming to protect you, you know."

Warner smirked. "Oh, I know. I saw. Rather impressive, that. A shame to lose such a talented hand, though. I'd ask if you'd want to take his place, but… Well, we both know you won't."

In the other pocket of his coat, the one that hadn't held the nullstone amulet, Caleb's fingers found the tiny metal forms of many bullets, the spare ammunition he would never get to use now. And among those innocuous lead lumps, there was one that made his senses tingle. Schmidt's last round, caught and held. Caleb palmed it quickly.

"I ask you one more time, Mr. Warner. Drop your weapon and surrender to federal authority."

"What authority? These are the borderlands, Agent Marcus. There's no authority out here but bolts and bullets."

"Caleb! The house is on fire!"

At Ernst's bark, Caleb spared a glance for the ranch house, seeing that flames were indeed licking along the rooftop, seeking a way down.

"There are men in there, Ernst. Get them out!"

The antlered wolf hesitated for a brief moment, obviously reluctant to leave his partner, then bolted off toward the burning building. Part of Caleb relaxed. Ernst was out of the line of fire now, so to speak, no matter what was about to happen.

Warner raised one dark brow at the Peacemaker. "You know, I'd rather hoped to get a better fight out of you, Agent. I did see you catch a bullet, after all."

"No. You saw me catch two." Ignoring the screaming pain in his left shoulder, Caleb threw the augmented bullet as hard as he could.

There was no force behind the throw, nothing to power the projectile other than the last vestige of a dead sniper's will, but when the tiny missile hit the shield of pure power, it exploded like a Chinese rocket.

The rancher cried out in pain as pure arcane energy blasted through his defenses with a blinding flash and a deafening boom. He dropped the ironwood staff, the runes going dark as soon as his hand left it.

Caleb whipped the medallion in a quick circle, and it spun through the air to wrap around Warner's outstretched arm, the delicate chain twining around his wrist several times.

"No!" The rancher's polite demeanor faded into a snarl, and he scrabbled at the chain, trying frantically to tear it away from his skin. The tiny metal links parted finally, the medallion dropping to the dirt at the rancher's feet, but it had distracted him long enough.

Caleb took the opening. "*Kracht*!" He dipped to slam his fist into the hard-packed dirt, sending his power ripping through the soil to explode beneath Warner's boots.

The rancher leapt back, further separated from the staff, and summoned a glowing ball of power into his hands. "Damn you!" With a yell, he thrust it at the Peacemaker, lighting the night bright as day for a heartbeat.

"*Muur*!" shouted Caleb. A thick wall of soil erupted, pulverized to a cloud of dust by Warner's blast, but sparing Caleb the injury.

The next bolt blasted through the haze of dust, igniting the tiny particles on the way, and Caleb grabbed for the power in the sudden wall of fire, sending it back at Warner with a snarled "*Brand*!"

The wave of heat drove Warner back from the staff again, and he countered by sending another narrow shaft of energy lancing through the darkness at Caleb. His next gesture sent the staff itself spinning off into the darkness, out of reach of either of them. Lightning ignited the top of the schoolhouse on the other side of the compound, and the thunder nearly drowned out the sound of the blast. Smoke drifted from the engulfed house, lying low and heavy in the oppressive air under the storm clouds.

Twice more, Warner took shots at the Peacemaker, and both times Caleb managed to disperse the blasts. The air was already charged with energy from the storm overhead, and every bit that Caleb scattered only added to it. The smell of ozone warred with the smell of burning wood. Something was brewing, swirling in the dark sky above them.

Caleb knew he had to end the battle before they tipped the building energy over the edge. Against his better judgment, he opened himself, reaching out to rip Warner's power away from him, hoping against hope that he could hold it all without his staff to focus it.

In his haste, he'd forgotten that Warner was not the strongest source of power. The great gaping hole went searching elsewhere, tapping Caleb into the storm. He gasped as he felt the power rush into him, lightning and fire and gale-force winds suddenly warring within his mind.

His vision shifted to see the broad spectrum of energy flowing all around and through him. His hands were painfully bright, nearly blinding him to all else. Warner seemed dim by comparison. Entranced, Caleb watched as the rancher gathered more energy to attack again, each movement taking a split second that lasted an eternity. He could see the power flowing through the other man's veins, pulsing with every rapid heartbeat. It pooled in Warner's hands, merged as he brought them together, and trickled out into the air toward Caleb.

The damaged part of him, the part that longed for what had been lost, saw that bolt only as more power to absorb, and when it hit Caleb square in the chest, it spread through his body with an almost pleasant tingle.

Warner swallowed hard, and Caleb could hear it, even through the roaring in his ears. Despite the darkness, he watched the blood drain from the rancher's face, saw the moment his heart doubled its pace. He could smell Warner's fear, rank on the storm's wind. He felt a dark smile stretch his face, and knew it was the storm's, not his own.

Warner was gathering himself for another try, and that could not be allowed. Scarcely knowing what he was doing, Caleb brought his hands together in a clap that echoed like thunder. It crashed through his body, down his arms, the wave of sound as solid as steel.

The dark-haired rancher was knocked off his feet and blown back a good twenty paces, tumbling head over heels beneath the wave of sheer force. The second blow pinned him against the wall of the livery, and the entire building groaned under the assault. Blood trickled from his nose and ears.

When he looked up, Caleb was advancing on him, and he made a weak attempt to scramble backward. "No! No, you can't! You're a lawman!"

"You tried to kill me." Dimly, Caleb knew his voice sounded wrong. It hurt his ears, stung his mouth. He tasted copper on his tongue and wondered what was bleeding.

"I'm sorry! I'm sorry! Pleasepleaseplease..." Warner's pleading devolved into incoherent babbling, and the smell of urine tainted the air. He fell to his knees, weeping at Caleb's feet.

It would be so easy to crush the life from his body, to rip him apart through sheer will. For a long moment, Caleb pondered it, even knowing that it was not his own thought. The storm inside him snarled at his reluctance, battering at his self-control.

"Agent Marcus!" In the chaos, he'd forgotten about Ellen Sinclair. She plucked at his sleeve. "Agent Marcus, don't do this!"

The storm focused on her for a moment, and that more than anything made Caleb clamp down on it, wrestle it into a modicum of submission. "I have nullcuffs in my right coat pocket, Miss Sinclair. If you would please put them on Mr. Warner."

She did so, wincing as the power he held licked over her skin even through the fabric. "The fire is spreading, we have to go!"

Feeling only a mild sense of curiosity, Caleb turned to look at the buildings. The house was fully engulfed, the charred skeleton showing through the glowing walls. The kennel roof was already smoldering where embers had made the leap, and the smithy's north wall was crawling with tendrils of flame.

Caleb paused, frowning. The smithy was important, but he could not remember why.

Ellen dragged Warner almost bodily to his feet and gave him a shove. "Move, or you'll burn, too!" Her words were nearly lost in a fit of coughing as the smoke grew heavier.

The smithy… The storm inside him saw it only as a structure to be destroyed, a creation of straight lines and right angles that must succumb to nature's fury. He had to let it go, so he could think, but to release it, he would need the staff. *Ernst.* Where had Ernst gone? He lost long, precious moments, trying to wrap his mind around that simple question while the storm thrashed inside his mind.

"Agent Marcus!"

What was it about the smithy that plagued him so?

"Caleb!" Ellen screamed in his face. "Where are the children??"

He knew this answer. "They're with Mary Catherine…" The Indian woman's face flashed in his memory, her dark eyes imploring. She'd asked him… Oh, Lord. "Her son is in the smithy!"

"Dear God…" Horrified, they watched the flames clamber up the wall and spread across the roof of the structure. The smoldering kennel gave a pop, and a long-dried knot of sap exploded in fiery stars, the sparks landing in the dried grass on the other side of the fence. Immediately, the infant flames devoured their newfound meal, the grasses caught, and fire ran the fence line in both directions.

Caleb saw it all in rainbow shades, blues and reds warring for control of his vision. Ellen shimmered, her small glow of power muted by her earlier exposure to the nullstone but spiky and erratic with fear. He gripped her arm, and the storm licked over her, testing to see whether she was a threat or food. "Get the children; get to the lake. The whole prairie is going up!"

"What about the boy?" She was shouting, he realized, because the fire was bellowing all around them. It seemed soft in comparison to the thunder inside his skull.

"I'll get him. Go!" He didn't wait to see if she obeyed.

The smithy was only across the clearing, but it seemed to take him a lifetime to cross the distance. It was nearly impossible to remember just how to put one foot in front of the other and still control the raging tempest he'd taken inside him. And still he could feel the hungry place inside him wanting more. It would destroy him in its greed, he knew.

Three walls of the smithy had already succumbed to flame, including the door. With seemingly no effort at all, he stretched out one hand and blew it off the hinges. The storm crackled within him, gleeful at the destruction. The fire, on the other hand, roared to life in the open space, resentful of the intrusion.

Someone inside the smithy was coughing. Caleb could hear it somehow, the predatory storm homing in on the sound of weakness. The power surged, and he barely managed to stop it from ripping the building to kindling. The fire roared back in response, filling the doorway with a column of flame as the two volatile powers challenged each other.

The flame weaved and danced, mesmerizing him. The roof of the building groaned, threatening to give way. Caleb knew there was only one way in.

The storm threw itself about within him as it

grasped his intent, but he reached for the fire anyway, grappling with that power, too, dragging it into the hungry part of himself, the part that would never be sated.

The smoke thickened as the raging fire was reduced to smoldering embers, its energy captured within one man's very mortal body.

Oh, God, it hurt. The fire and heat of the burning structures, coupled with the turbulent electricity of the captive storm, were enough to scorch his skin from the inside out, and his clothing smoked in response. Dimly, he remembered to shrug out of his heavy coat, lest the heat ignite the dangerous vials still hanging from the loops inside.

And he realized, belatedly, that he could either control both warring powers or he could move. He could not do both. Inside the building, a child was coughing, choking on the smoke, and he could do nothing but watch helplessly, knowing if he took even one step, something was going to break free and destroy everything within reach.

"I'll get him!" Ellen darted past Caleb into the smoking building before he even realized she had followed him. Part of him could have sobbed with relief, but both fire and storm howled inside him, wanting to destroy her and everything else they could reach. A long moment passed as the silent war raged, but finally she reappeared, half carrying an adolescent Indian boy.

They both staggered and fell at Caleb's feet, and he could do nothing more than look at them, his fists clenched with the effort of controlling all the power inside him.

Ellen looked up, her eyes huge in a face marred with soot and dirt. "Agent Marcus…"

"Run." His own breath burned his tongue. "Run for your lives!" Because he knew the power had to come out. It was killing him, and it had to escape. Soon.

The schoolteacher grabbed the boy's hand, dragging

him until he found his feet, and the pair of them stumbled off through the smoke and the haze. But there were others, men he'd knocked unconscious himself, not innocents perhaps, but no one that deserved to die in the cataclysm that was coming.

"They're gone, Caleb." Ernst appeared out of the dense smoke, once again in the form of a small furry jackalope. "The children are in the lake. It's all right to let it go now."

"You should go, too." In a few more moments, it would be done, regardless of his choice.

"No. I stay with you. Always." The creature huddled against one of Caleb's smoking boots, emitting his tiny chirping purr. "We're together, always."

Ernst was here at last. He was here, and everything would be all right. Caleb had to believe that. Tears streamed from the Peacemaker's eyes as he raised his gaze to the heavens. Somewhere above the smoke and the clouds, stars were twinkling over the prairie. He could almost see them.

With a soft exhale, he let go.

For a moment, the world was utterly silent. Even Ernst's purring seemed to pause, waiting for the next beat of a great and immense heart.

Then all at once, it exploded. A blast wave of fire and wind spiraled outward, flattening every building in sight, destroying the wooden fence, melting sand into warped, cracked glass. On and on it went, obliterating all sound, all order, in a torrent of sheer primal destruction. A secondary explosion sounded, distant and puling by comparison, as the transports in the livery went up in a billowing ball of arcane fire.

And even knowing it meant his death, there was part of Caleb that scrabbled to hang on to a shred of that immense power, part of him that did not want to let go. For a brief, blasphemous moment, he had been as a god, and he was loath to let it slip through his fingers.

The storm and inferno would not be contained any longer, and he felt them both shrieking with glee as they escaped, leaving him hollow and hurting. In the back of his mind, he knew that he'd pitched forward onto his face in the dirt, but he couldn't bring himself to care.

The last thing he saw was Ernst's brown eyes peering into his with concern. The last thing he heard was a woman's voice, humming softly.

17

Rain returned to the Kansas plains. The first tiny droplets met a swift and steamy death in the the raging wildfire that swept outward from the Λ-bar-W Ranch. But sheer numbers prevailed, and ultimately the rain beat down the flames, leaving acres of charred earth behind.

For seven days, it rained. The parched earth drank up the water until it could hold no more, then gradually turned to a thick soup that clung to all feet, hooves, and wheels that braved the swampy mess.

Caleb stood on the church porch, out of the rain, and watched Hope go about its daily business. He nodded hello to those who bothered to walk out this far, but there weren't many. The novelty of the situation had worn off, and the curious found the constant rain too daunting to go out in search of some undiscovered tidbit of information.

The Peacemaker rubbed his left arm, which was still in its sling, per Dr. Elm's instructions. The sling even matched the blue denim shirt Caleb had been given. He cut quite the fashionable figure. The shoulder itself ached abominably, but the good doctor had declared the wound clean and even Caleb could tell it was healing.

"Any word yet?" Ernst leapt up to the rail, balancing there with uncanny grace. His broken antler had repaired itself in one of his many shape-shifts and now only sparked idly.

"We'll know the moment they get here. An off-schedule stage is big news in a place like this." Caleb's stomach growled, and he grimaced. "And we're due for lunch, if Ellen wants to brave the muck today."

"I hope Teddy sends some whiskey over." The jackalope smacked his lips in anticipation.

"We're technically on duty, you know."

The familiar snorted. "You're on duty. I'm just the pet."

"Is our prisoner awake?" In a town with no jail, the church had seemed the only logical place to lock up Abel Warner. Shackled and cuffed except when taking care of bodily necessities, he'd remained isolated from the citizens of Hope. Most days he spent staring into space, though Caleb had offered him books to pass his time.

"Mm-hmm. Seems a bit feisty today, too. Maybe he knows today's the day."

"Maybe." Or maybe the man had just recovered enough to gather his wits and start mentally preparing his defense. No doubt, he'd have one.

Warner might be able to wish away the kidnapping charges as a misunderstanding, but he was going to have a hard time explaining the attempted murder of a federal officer. And with Jimmy and Ellen's eyewitness accounts, they might even be able to locate the men who had beaten Hector.

All of Warner's men had disappeared the night of the fire. It seemed likely that a few had been caught in the inferno, but in other areas of the prairie, there were a few islands of untouched grass, as if someone had created a shield there and sheltered through the raging flames.

Whoever it had been, wherever they'd gone, once the warrants and posters went up, the Peacemakers could hunt for them in any U.S. territory. Their only chance would be to flee south, into Mexico, or west into the mountains and Indian lands.

Hector himself seemed to be recovering, slowly but surely. Dr. Elm credited Ernst's intervention with a great deal of the patient's success, which seemed to embarrass the plucky jackalope. Caleb couldn't recall ever seeing his friend so disconcerted before. When asked, Ernst would say only, "I'm supposed to be the familiar, not the hero."

"Agent Marcus!" The scrawny figure of Jimmy Welton looked comical as he tried to slog through the muddy street at a full run. "Agent Marcus, they're coming!" By the time he squelched to a halt at the foot of the stairs, he was gasping for breath and covered to the thighs in brown Kansas sludge. "They... Brett saw them...'bout a mile out on the road..."

Caleb smiled. "Thank you, Jimmy. When they arrive, can you please escort them out here?"

"Yessir! I can do that!" Jimmy craned his neck to see past the Peacemaker. "They really gonna take him away?"

"That's why they came." Thanks to Sven and Jimmy, a garbled distress telegram had gone out around the time Caleb leveled the A-bar-W. Only after the Peacemaker regained consciousness had he been able to send another message, updating his superiors and requesting a prisoner transport. "I'll get Mr. Warner ready. Thank you, Jimmy."

The urchin ran back toward the center of town as Caleb turned to go inside. "Mr. Warner, your ride is nearly here."

The rancher's shackle chains rattled faintly. "I hope you realize that this will be a farce, Agent Marcus. You have absolutely no proof of any charges, and it is your word against mine."

Caleb bent to unlock the chains from the bench. "That's for a judge to decide. In the meantime, you'll be on your way to Kansas City and out of my hair."

"I have friends, Agent Marcus. Powerful friends. Just remember that."

"I don't think you're in any position to be making threats, Mr. Warner." He tugged the prisoner to his feet, careful to keep his own hands away from the nullstone cuffs around Warner's wrists.

"And we'll see just what your superiors have to say about you betraying your own kind to the red menace."

"Is that truly what you think I did?"

"Isn't it? You aided and abetted a magical attack on my ranch. Such things will not be seen in a good light back east."

Caleb ignored him. That very same worry had been plaguing his thoughts since that night, but he didn't dare let Warner know. In truth, he hadn't done anything that would technically count as betrayal. Yet. But the future was wide open, and he wondered just how far he could stretch the boundaries before they snapped back on him.

One of the sources of his unease appeared in the doorway as he herded Warner toward it. Mary Catherine had abandoned her calico dresses and high blouses in favor of returning to her native garb, leather covering her from neck to toe. Her black hair, with a few strands of gray showing at the temples, was now plaited into two braids, and one feather dangled against her right cheek.

Her dark eyes fixed on Warner with a coldness even Caleb could feel, before she looked to the Peacemaker instead. "The stage has arrived."

"I heard. Thank you, Ma— River Falls." She had also taken up her real name, and she spit in a most unladylike fashion whenever someone called her Mary Catherine.

"Once he is delivered..." She ground out the word *he* as if it left a foul taste in her mouth. "You are departing, yes?"

"Probably. Tomorrow, surely."

She nodded. "I will pack, then." In a whirl of leather and beads, she was gone.

Warner smirked. "Got yourself a squaw now, hmm?"

"Keep moving." The situation with Mary Catherine—River Falls—made Caleb uncomfortable. She had made it clear that she was following him from now on, as repayment for saving her young son's life. The boy himself had been spirited away by Crying Elk's people sometime during Caleb's bout with unconsciousness, but for her crimes against their laws, they had refused to take the woman. Her self-assigned penance was to haunt Caleb's path, it seemed, whether he liked it or not.

She had also made it very clear that should he attempt to touch her, she would make him suffer. It was not to be that kind of relationship (for which he was honestly relieved). He got the impression she intended to watch over him as fiercely as his own mother had ever done.

Others wouldn't see it that way, however. He worried about her, and how other whites would react to her presence in the towns he had to visit. He held on to the hope that he could convince her own people to take her back before they hit the next stop on the circuit.

A small procession was making its way through the muddy streets when he and Warner stepped out on the porch. Most of them were townsfolk; insatiable curiosity brought out gawkers even in the dismal downpour. But Peacemaker stars graced four long coats, and Caleb recognized the man in front, even with his face hidden by the downturned brim of his hat. If nothing else, the large spotted cat padding at his side gave him away.

"Graeme." Caleb found himself smiling, and a sense of relief released the tension in his shoulders. Deep down, he'd been afraid his longtime friend wouldn't come.

"Caleb." The tall Peacemaker stepped up on the porch to shake hands. "God almighty, could you have picked somewhere farther out in the backside of nowhere?"

"Why, Hope is positively metropolitan." He glanced down at the feline familiar with a polite nod. "Tan, good to see you."

The cat merely sat on his haunches and groomed the mud from his spotted fur with an expression of distaste. Tan had always been more reserved than the more joyful Ernst, a reversed reflection of his partner's personality. The jackalope hopped down from the porch rail to join the other familiar, and the two quickly put their heads together, communing in their own silent way.

Graeme took his hat off and ran a hand through his graying hair. Caleb frowned mentally. They were the same age. When had Graeme started to look so old?

"Is this the prisoner?"

"Yessir. Mr. Abel Warner." Caleb moved his hands so Graeme could fasten his own cuffs on Warner's wrists.

"And the charges?" With deft fingers, Graeme removed Caleb's cuffs and shackles and handed them back.

"Thirteen counts of kidnapping, and one count of attempted murder of a federal peace officer. He is also implicated in the savage beating of a man here in town, as well as deliberately nulling most of the children." He could have easily added a violation of the Aboriginal Peace Accords of 1874, but he didn't want to explain about the mine. If the government knew there was gold up there, there'd be no keeping them out of the mountains. Crying Elk's people would be extinct in a matter of months.

Graeme motioned for the other Peacemakers to take custody of the prisoner. "If you could escort Mr. Warner to the stage, I'll collect the paperwork and be right there."

The watching townsfolk seemed torn between following the prisoner back to the stage and staying to watch the two Peacemakers talk. Caleb solved it for them by leading Graeme inside the church and firmly shutting the door. Tan and Ernst slipped in at the last moment and resumed their conversation under one of the pews.

Graeme looked around the rustic church for a few moments before turning his gaze on Caleb. "You scared the hell out of me, you know that? I didn't know if you were alive or dead for about twenty-four hours."

"I'm sorry for that. In all honesty, I didn't expect to walk out of that." If it hadn't been for the two women coming back for him, dragging his unconscious body into the lake, he wouldn't have. He owed both Ellen and River Falls his life.

"You *always* wait for reinforcements, Caleb. You know that."

"There was no time. He had hostages."

"And you could have gotten them killed, too." There were lines on Graeme's face when he frowned. Being a director of the Federal Peacemakers was obviously wearing on him. "I got your first telegram, asking for more information on Warner."

"What did you find out?"

"Nothing useful. He has some influential contacts in various places. What did you expect me to find?"

Caleb sighed, leaning against a pew. "I don't know. Something to justify my gut instinct, I guess. Preferably *before* all hell broke loose."

"Well, there's nothing. And even if this comes to trial, I doubt there'll be anything. His contacts are *significant*, Caleb."

Caleb blinked. "He tried to *kill* me, Graeme. They shot my transport out from under me, then staked me out in the prairie and left me for dead."

"Prove it. You have witnesses? Testimonies? Anything but your word against his?" There was a look in Graeme's eyes, almost pleading for Caleb to say yes.

"A Peacemaker's word was always enough."

"I don't think it will be, in this case. I mean, you won't even tell me *why* he tried to kill you."

"Because he could? Because I wouldn't sit in his pocket like a good pet? How do I know?" It hurt, keeping the truth about the mine from Graeme. But at this moment, Caleb couldn't be certain if he was talking to his friend or his superior. And the worst part was, Graeme knew he was holding back. "You don't believe me."

Graeme eyed Caleb for a long moment before nodding and putting his hat back on. "Of course I believe you. I just don't know that it's going to be enough." Tan, at some unspoken command, left Ernst and came to heel at Graeme's side again. "Have you filled out all the transfer paperwork?"

Caleb handed over the thick sheaf of papers. "There are testimonies in there from the parents of the children and from the schoolteacher he held. I have my report in there as well." When Graeme reached to take them, Caleb held on for a moment. "I expect to get a telegram from you, telling me when to report to Kansas City to testify at his trial, with enough time for me to actually arrive."

The senior Peacemaker tugged the folded papers free and tucked them inside his duster. "I'll keep you posted. I promise."

"I also have requests in there for warrants on three men on assault and attempted murder, and I have two eyewitnesses if we can apprehend them and bring them to trial."

Graeme shook his head. "You don't start small, do you?"

"We don't get paid to look the other way." Caleb caught his friend's sleeve as the man turned to go. "Are you all right, Graeme? You look… worn."

Graeme nodded. "Was just a long trip out here on the stage, is all. I'm fine." His familiar slipped out the door ahead of him into the steady rain.

One advantage of using arcane-powered haulers instead of real horses was that rest was not required. The Peacemakers put Warner in the stage and immediately turned it around to head back east. The townsfolk dispersed now that the spectacle was gone, and Caleb stood alone in the drizzle watching the stage disappear into the prairie, stroking Ernst's soft fur as the creature purred in his arms.

Gradually, he became aware that someone had lingered nearby. He turned to find Jimmy Welton watching him from the steps of the general store. The boy's pants were still splattered with mud up to the thighs, but someone had captured him long enough to put a clean shirt on him and comb his unruly hair.

He glared at Caleb accusingly. "You're leaving now, aren't you?"

The Peacemaker nodded, stepping up on the sidewalk. "Tomorrow morning, probably. I'm late for my next stop on the circuit."

"But what if those men come back? The ones who hurt Mr. Pratt?"

Caleb let Ernst hop to the railing and placed one hand on Jimmy's shoulder. "I don't think they're ever going to come back here. They know they'll get caught if they do. I'm going to find them and arrest them."

The boy looked skeptical. "Maybe they're just waiting around 'til you leave."

Caleb nodded seriously. "I don't think so, but it's possible. That's why you're going to stay here with Teddy and Miss Sinclair, and if anything happens, they'll get a message to me, and I'll come back, faster than you can imagine."

"You promise?"

"Swear." Caleb offered his hand and shook on it solemnly, though he had to smile at the sparks of power that snapped and crackled between their palms. "But you have to promise to keep up your lessons. I want to see what you've learned next time I pass this way, all right?"

"Yessir." With no further farewell, the boy darted around him and vanished into the nearest alley.

Caleb looked around the dismal street, realizing that he had committed himself to riding the circuit for at least a year. It would take him that long to get back to Hope, even if he had no other delays.

"You'll miss it," Ernst observed.

"I'll miss the people." The jackalope had a distinct smirk on his furry face, and Caleb amended, "I'll miss most of the people. They're good folk out here."

The next morning, the drizzle had ended, and Caleb found River Falls in front of the saloon, her meager belongings already strapped onto a travois behind a sorrel gelding. The glass-eyed paint horse was also standing there, and it whickered when it recognized him. Caleb couldn't help but stop and stroke its silky muzzle. "I wondered what happened to you." Knowing that the animal had somehow survived the raging grass fire made him feel unexpectedly happy.

Without asking, the Indian woman took his trunk and saddlebags from him, adding it to the collection. Apparently, she was still planning on traveling with him. "I'm going to go settle up with Mr. Isby," Caleb said, "then we'll be ready to go."

She nodded, ignoring the blatant stares from early-rising townsfolk as she loaded up the two animals.

The smith was already awake, and looked to have been up for hours. He gave Caleb a scowl when the Peacemaker walked up. "Who is pay for my hauler, huh? Is in pieces, all over prairie, boom."

"Well, I've been thinking about that." In fact, he'd been thinking about it for no more than the few minutes it took to walk to the smithy, but a glimmer of a plan had emerged. "How about I leave my transport here with you? As a replacement."

The old Swede looked at him with narrowed eyes. "What you ride, then?"

Caleb smiled. "I have a ride. Do you want the transport?" He hadn't thought of it until he saw the paint horse standing in front of the tavern, but it quickly seemed like the right course of action.

The smith pursed his lips, looking the sleek transport over critically. "Is used. Repaired once already. Many miles. Not good for hauling."

Caleb knew very well that the transport was newer than anything else they had in the small town by probably a decade, and it was in excellent condition. He simply waited.

Finally, Sven nodded. "Ja. I take. No charge."

"It was a pleasure doing business with you, Mr. Isby." They shook on the deal, and the Peacemaker managed to keep the grin off his face until he'd walked around the corner and out of sight.

A crowd of children had surrounded the horses by the time Caleb got back, but the large animals were not their focus. Ernst was being passed from tiny hand to tiny hand, each child hugging him and giving their tearful good-byes. The familiar's purr was audible from yards away.

Ellen and Teddy came down off the sidewalk to meet Caleb as he walked. "The bairns are goin' ta miss that little rascal more'n anythin' else, I think."

"Ernst has that effect on people." Caleb stopped as more people began to emerge and gather around. "I didn't expect so many to come see us off."

"You've done us a great service, Agent Marcus." Ellen smiled, brushing a lock of hair out of her face. The bruise under her right eye had faded to almost nothing, but she wore it like a badge of honor. "When the rain lets up, they're going to start building the schoolhouse. It seems I'll get to make use of my books after all."

"That's good. I hope you can keep a collar on Jimmy Welton, too. He'll be old enough for West Point in about five years, if he can pass the entrance exams. I'd love to sponsor his admission."

Teddy whistled. "Can ye imagine? Somebody from Hope goin' to the Point? Who'da thought."

"I'll see that he works hard." The schoolteacher

pressed a small paper-wrapped package into Caleb's hands. "This is from Hector. To thank both you and Ernst for everything you've done."

Caleb felt the color rise in his cheeks, and he squirmed. "It's just my job. But thank him for me."

One of the horses, pressed on all sides by the townsfolk, snorted and tossed its head, instantly clearing a circle around them.

"The animals are getting restless. I guess that means it's time to go."

River Falls was already astride the big gelding, and Caleb wished there weren't so many witnesses to his clumsy attempt to mount up. To his surprise, it went better than he'd expected, the horse standing perfectly still as he slipped onto its back. He'd have to get used to riding bareback, or find someone in another town who could fashion a saddle for the animal. He patted the horse on its muscled neck, and it turned its head to nibble at his boot.

For a few moments, he looked at all the faces staring up at him. The smiles and calls for care were a far cry from the frightened looks he'd received as he'd ridden into town. "I guess… I'll be back next year, about this time. Everyone take care. C'mon, Ernst."

The jackalope left his throng of followers with one elegant leap, landing just behind Caleb. If the horse noticed, it didn't show.

The crowd parted, leaving them a clear path out of town. At the Peacemaker's nod, the Indian woman clicked her tongue and kicked her horse into a trot, and Caleb's followed hers obediently. He could hear the farewells of the townsfolk long after they left the last building behind.

"We're going south. The next stop is a town called Dusty Wash." Ernst groaned, and the strange trio rode in silence for nearly an hour before River Falls offered any conversation.

"That is her horse, you know. The medicine man's

daughter."

"Falcon Woman?"

River Falls nodded. "She pays you a high compliment, giving it to you."

"I'm honored, then." He kept his eyes on the horizon, hoping she wouldn't notice his blush.

Falcon Woman had come into his dreams every night since the inferno. The first time, he had found himself once again in Crying Elk's teepee, with the Indian woman tending his wounds and singing softly in her way. The old man was there, too, though it seemed he was merely chaperoning, and watched silently.

After that, Caleb remained safely in his own thoughts, but she would find him there, taking walks through his memories. It hadn't been entirely unpleasant, and he was embarrassed to admit that he was starting to look forward to her visits.

Aware that River Falls was watching him with a knowing smirk, he cleared his throat. "Um… does it have a name? The horse, I mean?"

"*Mo'ehno'ha.*"

"What does it mean?"

She chuckled. "Horse."

He had to chuckle, too. "Maybe I'll just call him Moe."

Coming Soon from Pirate Ninja Press

IRON DRAGON

THE ARCANE WEST TRILOGY
VOLUME TWO

1

It took Caleb a moment to recognize where he was. The vast green field of close-cropped grass was immediately familiar, but he only realized why when he turned to see the imposing brick buildings looming behind him. The realization was enough to earn a chuckle. It looked just like the day he'd left, and with that thought, the sunshine took on a spring-like shine and a cool breeze sprang up out of nowhere.

"Where is this place?" The woman standing next to him gazed around with frank curiosity in her dark eyes, and Caleb did his best not to flinch. She hadn't been there a moment before, and her arrival had been utterly silent. He should be used to it by now.

Her interest in their surroundings gave him a moment to watch her unobserved. She stood tall, balanced on her feet like she might leap into the air like a startled doe at any moment. The faint breeze stirred the feathers in her raven braids. Her tanned and beaded leathers stood out starkly against the straight, orderly lines that surrounded them. When her eyes fell on him finally, she smiled, her dark skin practically glowing in the sunlight.

"It's far to the east. It's called West Point. I came here as a young man to learn to be a soldier." They were standing on the parade grounds, the grass clipped close under their feet, and he smiled as he watched Falcon Woman kneel down to run her fingers through it.

"Do they graze horses here? To keep the grass so

short?”

“No. They have machines. They channel an arc of power between two points, and it singes the grass to the correct height.” That thought brought back images of a younger version of himself, trudging back and forth across these very grounds with the arcane-powered grass trimmer, sweating buckets under his heavy wool uniform.

Falcon Woman giggled suddenly, and pointed at him. “Look at yourself!”

Glancing down, he found himself once again clad in blue-gray wool, with lines of brass buttons running up each side of his chest. He could feel the weight of the cadet’s cap, suddenly resting on his head, and he resisted the urge to snatch it off. “Um...yes, this is what we wore. Obviously.”

She stood up again, running her hands over the heavy fabric, taking note of the braided trim around his cuffs. “It suits you.”

“Yes, well…it was hot as all get out, at the time.” Caleb swore he could feel a phantom trickle of sweat beginning between his shoulder blades, even though there really was no such thing as temperature where they were, and he shifted uncomfortably. “Why do you never have this problem? Your clothing doesn’t shift when you think of stray things.”

“We are in your memories, Caleb, and your memory of me is very strong. This is how you think of me, so this is how I appear.”

“So…if I thought of you differently, would your clothing change?” That could be…awkward.

The Cheyenne woman grinned at him. “No. My memory of myself is very strong, as well, and my mind will hold the image steady. Now, close your eyes and recall yourself as you are at this moment. Your clothing will change back.”

With a sigh, he did as instructed, trying to picture

what he'd come to think of as his "usual clothes." After a moment, the weight on his head disappeared, and when he opened his eyes, he found himself in a pair of plain brown trousers and a chambray shirt.

"See, you are getting better at it." Falcon Woman beamed at him, and he had to admit that her approval made something warm swell in his chest.

When he felt that warmth seeping into his cheeks in the form of a blush, he cleared his throat and looked anywhere but her. "This is where I met Graeme. Where we became friends."

"Then that is why we are here. Because you have been thinking of him often, of late."

"Yeah." It was true, Graeme had been on his mind a lot the past week or so. Starting, really, when Caleb had received a telegram from his friend, now boss, requiring him to leave his usual circuit and meet up with him in Silver City, near the Mexico border. It would be the first time he'd seen his old friend since the incident in Hope. Since he'd felt himself start to change inside.

"So, where are you tonight? Can you show me?"

"Hm? Oh, yes. Of course." Crouching down, Caleb made a gesture over the short grass with his hands, and a map appeared, the curled edges quivering in the remembered breeze. "I think we stopped somewhere around…here."

Falcon Woman knelt at his side, peering at the carefully drawn lines. "Then you should reach the town sometime tomorrow, yes?" Her finger traced his intended path toward the east. "This is where the tracks will converge?"

"Yeah, that's it. See, the crew from Kansas City should already be close – probably here somewhere," he pointed to a place on the map, and a small red spot appeared and stayed. "And then the Mexican crew will be coming up from the south just here." Another dot appeared, this one blue. "They'll join the rails up somewhere just north of the Mexican border."

"What if they miss?"

That thought made Caleb chuckle. "Well then I reckon someone's getting fired."

The Transcontinental Railway Project had been decades in the works, and would finally complete the first railroad line to join the east and west coasts. It was a joint effort between the United States and Mexican governments, the rail line swinging far south through Mexican land to avoid the biggest portion of the Indian-controlled Rocky Mountain range. The project had involved more blood, sweat and politics than Caleb could ever explain to his Cheyenne companion. Even now, the two governments involved stalked around each other like territorial felines, and one stray comment could bring it all to a screeching halt.

"So why do they require your presence? Does your friend expect there to be danger?"

Caleb settled down on the grass, the map vanishing as he ceased to maintain the thought of it. "Not danger, really. But any time you get that many people together, there's bound to be a ruckus. Folks will be drinking and celebrating, and I think he just wants a few of us there to make sure things don't get out of hand. Just to back up the local sheriff."

The Cheyenne woman nodded, sitting down beside him and curling her leather-clad feet beneath her. They sat in contented silence for a bit, her dark gaze roaming the buildings around them with interest before they landed back on him. "It is not the job that unsettles you so. It is seeing him again."

"Yes." There was no point in trying to lie to her. First, she was very perceptive, and second, in this place, lies had a way of making themselves known whether one wanted it or not. "I wasn't completely honest with him, about all that happened in Hope. He knows it."

Falcon Woman frowned faintly, toying with the beading on her dress. "You could simply tell him the truth. It would end your conflict."

The very thought sent a chill down Caleb's spine. "If I tell Graeme that there is gold in those mountains, he'll have to report it. And then you and your people will be wiped out."

She sniffed. "We are a strong people. We would fight."

"You would lose. You don't understand the sheer numbers that we...that they would send against you. For gold? They'd throw the entire army at you." Caleb sighed. They'd had this argument before, and he just couldn't seem to make her understand. "The tribes have won victories in the past, but that was against small pieces of a much bigger force. The only reason the Army hasn't pursued it further was because they didn't have a reason." A previously unknown fortune in gold would give them that reason.

The silence stretched out heavy between them before she finally smiled again, reaching out to brush her fingertips down the ridge of scar tissue that marred his right cheek. Even here in this dream world, his scars remained. "And this is why we name you Good Man. Because you protect, even when it hurts your heart so."

He caught her hand before she could withdraw, and their eyes locked for long moments. Caleb let himself study the delicate line of her jaw, the way the tendrils of ebony hair escaped her braids and clung to her tan cheek. The lashes around her dark eyes quivered as she gazed back at him, and he wondered again just what she saw when she looked at him that way. She was truly the most beautiful creature he had ever laid eyes on.

As usual, she broke the gaze first, a blush rising under her dark skin. When she tugged on her hand, he released her. "Father...will want to meet with you at the usual time. Will you be able, with your new duties?"

Caleb cleared his throat and did his best to rein in his wayward thoughts. "Two nights from now, right? I should be able to." Time passed differently in his dreams, but he was fairly certain it was nearly morning in the real world. "I probably won't be able to come here tomorrow night, though."

Falcon Woman nodded. "It would probably be best for you to get some true sleep. It is taxing on the mind to walk the dreams every night."

"It's worth it." He was rewarded with another blush from her, even as she gave him a chiding look. He grinned in response, and finally she chuckled again, shaking her head at him.

"You are a terrible student. I should never have agreed to teach you the ways of the dream." Her black eyes sparkled, though, as she teased him.

"I'm glad you did. Very, very glad."

For three months, they'd been practicing stepping in and out of his dreams, and occasionally into hers. Caleb had come to appreciate the young woman's sense of humor, and wickedly sharp intelligence, as well as the lessons she worked so hard to drive into his skull. There were days, long, hot days on the road, when all he could look forward to was laying his head down on his saddlebags and allowing himself to slip sideways to where he knew she would be waiting.

This thing between them… It was new and unnamed as of yet, still unformed. They were both treading carefully, too afraid that the differences between them would prove insurmountable. But every time the Cheyenne woman smiled at him, Caleb felt himself tumble a little further down that slippery slope. At some point, he knew he'd have to make the decision to stop himself, or just let go and fall freely.

A sharp pain in his right arm brought that train of

thought to a screeching halt, and he winced, rubbing the invisible bruise. "And I think that is my wake up call."

Falcon Woman laughed quietly. "Tell her that I send my greetings. And to Ernst as well."

"I will. Ernst is still very disappointed that he can't seem to come here and meet you himself."

"You must bring him to visit, the next time your journey brings you to the mountains."

"I will. I promise." His circuit wouldn't bring him back to the Rockies for months still. By then, maybe Caleb would know what to do about his feelings for the lovely young woman.

The pain sparked in his arm again, and he threw up his hands. "Ow! All right! I'm coming!" With Falcon Woman's giggle in his ears, he closed his eyes and stepped...

...and opened his eyes to a sky that was glowing faintly to the east. The sun had not yet risen. Turning his head slightly, he raised a brow at his travelling companion.

"Did you really have to pinch me twice?"

The raven-haired woman bending over the fire gave him a flat look. "You did not wake the first time. Get up. Eat something."

River Falls was a handsome woman, if anyone were ever able to get Caleb to admit it. He'd never do that in her earshot, though, because she was just as likely to geld him as not. Her ebony braids, so very like Falcon Woman's, held faint hints of silver, and there were tiny lines at the corners of her dark eyes, but Caleb knew that guessing her age would prove futile. The native peoples seemed to have a gift for amazing longevity, and she could be forty, or a hundred and forty and he wouldn't know the difference.

As Caleb sat up to stretch the stiffness out of his muscles, the Cheyenne woman passed a small bowl to the third of their trio. Caleb could smell the aroma of whiskey on the chilly morning air. "Already, Ernst?"

The small furry creature raised his head, droplets of the gold liquid quivering on his whiskers. "Breakfast is an important part of every day, Caleb." A tiny pink tongue darted out, quickly saving those drips of alcohol from being wasted, and the rabbit-like creature burped daintily, sparks flickering at the tips of his antlers.

"Mmf. Give me biscuits and butter before whiskey any day." At that request, he found a tin plate shoved abruptly into his hands. "Thank you, ma'am." She only snorted in return, settling in to her own meal.

"And how did you sleep?"

"Well, I'd have slept better, but someone kept pinching me."

River Falls rolled her eyes at him. "And how is the dreamwalker woman?"

"She's fine." Caleb tried to ignore the heat creeping into his face, hoping the morning's darkness was enough still to hide it. "She sends her greetings to you both."

The older woman made some noncommittal noise. "And the medicine man? Is he fine as well?"

"I, uh…didn't see him tonight. Just Falcon Woman." River Falls arched one dark brow at him, and he devoted more of his attention to his biscuits. He and Falcon Woman weren't doing anything *wrong*, per se, traipsing about in the dream world without a chaperone, but he still wasn't sure how it would be regarded by Cheyenne standards. And more than anything, he didn't want to offend Crying Elk, who he'd come to respect greatly. "I'll see him again in two nights. Do you want me to pass a message? I can ask if they're ready for you to come home."

"No. I will travel with you."

It was no more than he'd expected. For three months, he'd been trying to get the Cheyenne woman to go back to her people, back to her son, but she doggedly refused. Whether she still felt obligated to him for saving her child, or she was still trying to atone for her own sins, he was never sure, and it wasn't something she seemed willing to talk about.

They finished their breakfast in relative silence, if one ignored the slurping noises the tiny jackalope made as he finished his whiskey, and Caleb passed his empty plate back to River Falls when she gestured impatiently. "I'll get the horses ready."

The brown and white paint gelding raised his head as Caleb approached, whuffing a soft hello. "Hey, Moe. Good morning." The horse butted his head against Caleb's chest, and the pair just stood there for a moment, the man resting his forehead against the animal's.

While riding actual horses had changed their travelling patterns – they couldn't go as far or as fast in a day, and they always had to have food and water for the animals – there was something pleasant about having the living creatures with them. The warm, musky horse scent had become comforting, Caleb realized, and the tiny sounds the animals made even when standing still had become the sounds of safety and serenity. The horses were the first to raise an alarm if something was wrong, and could be depended on to lead them to the nearest source of water if they ever ran short. No arcane powered transport could do that.

Another imperious nudge took him from behind, and Caleb turned to chuckle at the other horse, a sorrel gelding, reaching to scratch him between his eyes where he liked it. "All right, all right. Good morning to you, too." The two animals fidgeted between themselves, vying for Caleb's attention, and he indulged them for a few moments before shooing the bigger gelding off with a fond thump to his flank. "Wait your turn. I have to saddle Moe first."

While he worked with their mounts, River Falls and Ernst went about packing up their small camp. They didn't have much, to be sure, but things like Caleb's Peacemaker trunk had to be moved carefully. The sorrel stood patiently while River Falls hooked the travois to his harness, but Moe was ever the prankster, and repeatedly nipped at Caleb's pockets as the man tried to get the saddle on. "Dangit, Moe. You could at least pretend like you think I'm the boss."

There was a small pop of displaced air as Ernst appeared atop the saddle, tilting his antlered head to look down at his partner. "He thinks I'm the boss, actually. He's really very intelligent." Moe gave an agreeing whicker, and Caleb sighed.

"I knew I was in trouble, letting the furry and four-footed outnumber the two-legs."

Once they had their belongings stowed for the next leg of their journey, River Falls approached their tiny fire and knelt beside the coals. Speaking softly in her own language, she selected one glowing ember and placed it into a container carved of buffalo horn, sealing it up.

Though his lessons in the Cheyenne language were going slowly, Caleb knew the words by heart. "Thank you, tiny spirit of flame, for your warmth and light. Please feel welcome to travel with us as long as you wish."

"Why do you do that? I could just as easily put it out and start a new one at the next camp." Snuffing a fire was simply a matter of siphoning off the energy that fed it.

"Because then we would have to start each night with a new spirit, and they cannot all be trusted. This way, it will grow to know us, and we will know that it will not leave us in the cold of night, or escape its bonds and light the prairie on fire."

River Falls had educated him very quickly on the practice of carrying their flame with them from one night to the next, and all throughout the drought-plagued summer, they hadn't had a single problem with their campfire getting out of hand, nor had their campfire ever burned out during the night, not even when they were plagued with the first rains of autumn.

While Caleb couldn't feel the Indian magic, he could see it working. There were times, still, when he was certain he could see a tiny being curled up in the carefully guarded ember, an infant elemental slumbering away. Then, the image would fade. Whatever special type of vision Falcon Woman had given him, months ago, it was wearing thin.

"How long until we reach this Silver City?" River Falls swung astride of her gelding with the ease of long practice, continuing to ride bareback even after they'd found someone who was willing to make a saddle for an actual horse.

"Hm. Mid-morning, I'd guess? Barring anything unexpected." Caleb knelt beside the dying remnants of the fire and used it to light the end of one of a cigarillo, inhaling the sweet smoke and watching it curl in lazy blue circles around his head. With so long between stops, he was back to rationing them again, but surely a town the size of Silver City would have some in stock.

He gave one last glance around their campsite to be certain they weren't leaving anything behind, then clambered aboard Moe. With the aid of stirrups, mounting the horse was certainly easier now than when they'd started, but Caleb still felt awkward and conspicuous until he was settled firmly in the saddle with the reins in his hands.

The two horses had earned them more than a few strange looks on his circuit. More, really, than River Falls herself. That he travelled with an Indian squaw got him a few raised brows and shocked whispers, most people making incorrect assumptions about his relationship with the proud Cheyenne woman.

But the citizenry seemed to accept it more readily than the fact that he'd given up on all civilized modes of transportation and instead chose to traipse about the wilds on an unpredictable beast. An Indian woman was one thing, a hairy four-footed death dealer was quite another. It just wasn't done! Caleb knew that there had been telegrams back to Kansas City from more than one concerned mayor, but he'd never received any word on it from Graeme, so he had to assume it was a non-issue.

"Ernst?" Turning in the saddle, he made sure that the small jackalope was seated comfortably on the horse's rump. A position that far back should have caused the paint gelding to go into a kicking and bucking fit, but like always, the horse seemed unaware of Ernst's light weight.

"Ready, Caleb."

"All right. Move out." With the barest touch of his heels to Moe's flanks, they set out at a ground eating trot, the other gelding following obediently behind.

As with most days, the strange little group rode in relative silence, each keeping their thoughts to themselves. The sun rose slowly in front of them, and Caleb pulled the brim of his hat down to shield his eyes. The morning light chased away the last of the chilly dew, but Caleb knew it was a matter of weeks before the dew would become frost, autumn's promise of colder weather to come.

Soon, sleeping on the ground out in the rough was going to become distinctly uncomfortable, especially as his route took him back north. After the summer's unprecedented heat, no one could seem to agree on what the winter would hold in store for them. Even Crying Elk had remarked that the spirits seemed undecided, and the ancient shaman had looked unsettled at that. Change was coming, that much seemed certain.

About the Author

K.A. Stewart has a BA in English with an emphasis in Literature from William Jewell College. She lives in Missouri with her husband, daughter, two cats, and one small furry demon that thinks it's a cat.

www.ingramcontent.com/pod-product-compliance
Lightning Source LLC
Chambersburg PA
CBHW072258130726
47910CB00012B/2158